Save the Last Dance for Me

Under Open Skies

Save the Last Dance for Me

Daris Howard

Publishing Inspiration - St. Anthony, Idaho

Publishing Inspiration
St. Anthony, Idaho
Copyright © 2017 by Daris Howard

ISBN-10: 1-62986-020-4
ISBN-13: 978-1-62986-020-6

Manufactured in the United States Of America

www.publishinginspiration.com

Table Of Contents

Dedication

I dedicate this book to my daughter Clarissa. She enjoyed a couple of years of ballroom dancing, and I am proud of her. As I watched her, the good and challenging memories of almost forty years earlier when I accidentally signed into a dance class and ended up competing in the International Ballroom Championship filled my mind.

1

Dance Class

✦

The gray-haired teacher started the class. "As you can see," he said, "we have an inordinate number of girls who have signed up for the class. When I looked at my roll this last week in preparation for today, I had forty-eight girls and two boys. For girls who asked to sign in late, I required them to recruit a boy as well. That put us up to fifty-four girls and eight boys. Do any of you know other boys who might like to join?"

No one raised their hand. I thought about my roommates. If Sherry asked them, they might, but I wasn't going to ask them. That would seem too weird.

"Well, then," the teacher continued, "that could make preparation for competition much harder. We'll have the boys rotate partners on each dance."

Sherry leaned over and whispered to me. "I'm not staying in a dance class that's mostly girls. Let's drop it at the end of the hour."

I nodded my agreement, but I was still wondering what he meant about the competition as he continued the class introduction.

"As you all know, this is Social Dance 202, fourth-semester dance," he said.

I leaned over to Sherry. "Fourth? You said it was first-semester dance."

She shrugged. "We'll be dropping it anyway."

The instructor continued. "Since this is the last of our four-semester dancing sequence, you will all be expected to know the twelve major ballroom dance forms and to compete in them. For your final this semester, you will participate in the on-campus competition. It just so happens that, for the first time, our college has been chosen to host the International Ballroom Dance Competition held this spring. The couples who win our on-campus competition will represent us in their winning dances. Though each of the twelve dance forms will have its own competition, the most coveted prize is that of the overall dance championship, which judges in all twelve forms. With that said, your grade will be based on how well you progress and compete at the end of the semester."

I could feel my heart pounding at the thought of competition. I was glad we were dropping.

When the instructor finished talking, it was time to dance. "Let's start with something lively," he said. "Cha-cha, everyone."

"Sherry," I whispered, "I don't have a clue what the cha-cha is."

"Just follow me and do what I do," she whispered back.

I tried to follow, but she was stepping fast. She turned in, so I turned in, but by the time I did, she was turning out. At one point, my foot caught her ankle, and she started to fall. I tried to catch her, but instead, we both went down. Two other couples tripped over us and fell, too. Everyone else stopped dancing and laughed. I wished I could disappear.

As I helped Sherry to her feet, she said, "Maybe we shouldn't wait until the end of the class to drop."

The college felt instructors knew what was best for students more than students did. For that reason, outside of the normal registration process, a student had to have an instructor's permission to sign in or out of a class. An instructor could also waive prerequisites. I normally wouldn't be able to sign into an advanced class like this without the teacher's permission. But his signature on the card Sherry had given me must have overridden the prerequisite requirements.

While the other students returned to dancing, Sherry and I went to the instructor. "Being in this class isn't going to work for us," Sherry told him. "We'd like to sign out."

We always carried extra add/drop cards the first few days of class for just such a purpose. Sherry handed hers to him, and he signed it. I held mine out, but he didn't even pretend he would take it. Instead, he said, "I'm sorry, but I don't sign boys out of the class. You're in for the semester."

"But I'm only a second-semester freshman, and I've never taken first-semester dance," I said, "let alone second or third. Sherry told me this was first-semester dance when we signed up."

"I'll try to remember that when I do grades," he answered.

"But I'm a horrible dancer," I said.

"I can see that," he replied. "That's all the more reason you need this class."

"It's not fair that . . ." I started to complain, but he interrupted me.

"I would suggest you find a girl to dance with and get started. You've got a lot to learn."

I looked at Sherry. "I'm sorry, Tom," she said, and she quickly left.

As I stood there, unsure of what to do, I felt discouraged and helpless. I never thought this day could go so wrong.

*****

The day started out like most of my college days. The sun was not yet even showing any glow over the ridge of the mountain as I turned the corner and sprinted the last fifty yards to my apartment. I looked at my watch. It wasn't yet six o'clock. I had run five miles in just under thirty minutes. It wasn't my best time, but considering I had changed my route to take in some fairly steep hills, and I was bundled up for the January cold, I didn't feel too bad about it.

I quietly entered my apartment. There was no sign of life from any of my roommates as I quietly showered and dressed. I hurried with breakfast, hoping I could get a few minutes to review my math before I headed off to my first class of the new semester.

I had barely set my food on the table when I heard a knock on our apartment door. I hurried to answer it, knowing my roommates were still asleep. When I opened the door, Sherry was standing there.

"Hi, Tom," she said, smiling her beautiful smile. "You're just the one I was looking for."

"Me?" I said in surprise.

Sherry went to the same church as my roommates and me. I knew her mostly through my roommates. They all thought she was pretty, and some of them had even asked her out during the previous semester. But I was much shier and more reserved than my roommates, so I was surprised she even knew my name.

"You don't have a class during the eight o'clock hour, do you?" Sherry asked.

"No," I replied.

"Good. I'm trying to get into social dance, but because there are so few men, the instructor won't let a girl in unless she brings a guy with her."

I thought of all my disastrous dancing experiences in junior high and high school, and the thought of taking a dance class that would actually count as credit made my heart pound.

"I'm sorry," I said, "but I'm not a dancer. I bet David, Bryce, or any of the others would be happy to join you. They should be waking up any minute, so you can ask them."

"Actually, I was hoping you'd join me," she replied. "You're so strong and athletic."

3

"Athletic and graceful are very different. Almost all of my previous dance experiences have been disasters."

"That's exactly why you should go," she replied. "It's first-semester social dance, so you'll learn everything, starting from the beginning. You wouldn't have to feel awkward about it anymore."

I stood there, thinking. I really wanted to feel less klutzy when it came to dancing, but I doubted there was anything to be done about my awkwardness. My dancing inadequacy was one of the big reasons I hardly dated.

"I don't know," I slowly said. "A normal load is fourteen to sixteen credits, and I'm already taking sixteen and a half. The half credit is wrestling, and that takes three to four hours per day."

"Oh, come on," Sherry replied. "It wouldn't be that much more. I know you can do it. It will be fun. And I'll be there to help you every step of the way. Besides, with all those tough classes, you really need something fun."

In my opinion, dancing and fun didn't belong in the same sentence. I hesitated another minute, but I finally nodded. Maybe it would be good for me.

"Good," she said, holding out the registration card. "I already had the teacher sign this for you. All you need to do is sign it yourself."

Late registration was time-consuming. Normally, I would have to get the card, get it signed by the teacher, and take it registrar's office. But Sherry showed me the card with my name on it, all signed by the teacher—I only had to fill in my student number and add my signature. I thought it was very kind of her to go to all that work so I didn't have to. I learned later that she thought I would back out if she didn't.

But then something else crossed my mind. "But, Sherry, I thought you said he wouldn't sign our cards unless there was a girl and a boy?"

"What I said," Sherry replied, "is that he wouldn't sign in a girl *without* a boy. He'll sign in all the boys he can because his class has lots of girls. He won't sign my card until I bring this back with your signature on it."

I hesitated one more time, so she continued. "Since you're so strong and athletic, I thought you'd be the perfect dance partner. I'll be able to teach you and make sure you ace the class."

Her compliment and words of assurance did the trick. I later learned from her roommates that it wasn't me she necessarily wanted, but any boy. She'd had the teacher sign a card for each of my roommates so if one of us turned her down, she could try another. It just happened that I was the one she saw first, so it was my card she pulled out.

I signed my name to the card and handed it back to her. She took it, smiling, and headed on her way, saying, "I'll meet you at the student center east ballroom just before eight o'clock."

I stood there, wondering if I had gotten myself into more than I could handle. I was determined to do well in my classes, and now I would have eighteen and a half credits. I didn't know anyone else who was taking that many. I also worked between twenty and thirty hours per week at different jobs trying to pay for my schooling.

Oh well, I thought. If it was too much, I could always drop it.

I shut the door, turned back to eat my breakfast, and saw my roommate, Bryce. His bathrobe was wrapped around him, and his hair looked like he had combed it with an egg beater.

I had eight roommates in my apartment. All of them but Allen were a few years older than me. Bryce was one of the oldest. He was big and jolly for the most part, but he was also one of the most outspoken of our group. If he set his mind to something, it was hard to change it, and he tended to be one of the leaders. Bryce was also the one I least expected to see this time of day. He usually slept until noon.

Bryce looked at me quizzically. "So, who stopped by so early in the morning?"

"It was Sherry," I replied. "She wanted me to sign up for social dance with her."

"You? Mr. 'I-don't-dance?'"

"Well, maybe it's time I learned," I said defensively. "She said she'd coach me every step of the way."

Bryce grinned. "Why did she ask you when she could have had a macho man like me?"

"Maybe because it's an eight o'clock class, and you don't get up until the crack of noon," I replied.

Bryce laughed. "You mean there's an eight o'clock in the morning, too?"

It was my turn to laugh. Before coming to college the previous semester, I hadn't met a single one of my eight roommates. For the most part, we all quickly became friends. And we just as quickly learned each other's idiosyncrasies.

When we signed up for classes, we filled out a little bubble sheet with preferred hours, but the computer still chose the sections for us. After Bryce had picked up his schedule the first semester, he had marched into the apartment and slammed it on the table. "That stupid computer gave me a ten o'clock class. Ten o'clock is too early to even be awake, let alone be able to think."

5

"Why don't you just go the first day and drop it?" I asked.

"That's crazy," Bryce replied. "Why should I get up at ten o'clock to drop it? The computer added the class, the computer can drop it."

Bryce was adamant that he would rather get an F in the class than get up to drop it, so I had volunteered to take the drop card to his teacher to get it signed. He finally agreed to that, and that was the only thing that saved him from an F in that class fall semester.

It was especially strange to see Bryce up this early on a Monday morning because he always got in so late on Sunday nights. Every weekend, for all of fall semester, Bryce had been driving five hours away to another university to see a girl named Shannon. When Bryce came back on Sunday nights, we could expect Bryce to sit down and tell us all about his weekend. Sam and I shared the bedroom with Bryce, and we knew there was no use turning off the light and going to bed before he arrived because he would turn the light on, and we would get the whole rundown anyway. The previous night had been no different.

"So, what got you up so early today?" I asked.

"Oh, I just had to use the restroom, and I heard you talking to Sherry."

David wandered in, stretching and yawning. "Talking to Sherry? Who was talking to Sherry?"

Bryce pointed at me. "Tom was. She stopped by to see if he would sign up for social dance with her."

David was one of the shortest of my roommates. He worked harder on homework than Bryce and wasn't against playing a few pranks on people. He was also the one who organized the big Uno games we had each week. He worked hard, but he played harder.

At the mention of my name in connection with Sherry's, David was suddenly wide awake and turned to stare at me. "She asked you? Why did she ask you? You haven't asked her out like most of us have. You've never even asked her to dance at any of the dances. And you seldom go to the dances."

"Maybe she thought he needed it most," Bryce said.

By this time, a few more of my roommates were up, and everyone seemed to think that Sherry's visit with me was a great topic of conversation. I was happy to finish my breakfast and leave for class.

My seven o'clock class was second-semester calculus. Professor Hastings had also taught my first-semester calculus class the semester before. He was tall and thin, with dark hair sporting tiny flecks of gray. He was probably in his mid to late forties and was a no-nonsense type of teacher. Though he was strict, he was friendly and willing to help students learn in any way he could.

As I looked around before class started, there was one thing that I found to be interesting. My first-semester calculus class had consisted of all guys, and most of them were in my class this semester, too. But this semester there was one girl. Though I knew I hadn't had a class with her, I was sure I had seen her before.

Professor Hastings had us introduce ourselves. As the girl stood, every boy turned to stare with rapt attention, and all seemed smitten with her beauty. She had big brown eyes, and her long brown hair, tied with a red ribbon, hung loosely down past her waist. She was dressed in blue jeans and a flower-covered blouse.

"My name is Bonnie," she said. "I am from Utah and majoring in mathematics."

When Bonnie finished her introduction and sat down, Professor Hastings added, "Bonnie is also our department's student secretary."

Instantly, I remembered how I knew her. I had visited with Bonnie once about what hours second-semester calculus was offered so I could arrange my schedule.

When we all finished introducing ourselves, Professor Hastings said, "I don't plan to assign seating, but make sure you're sitting where you want to be next class period, since I will send around a seating chart to help me learn your names. Once you've signed it, I will expect you to stay in that seat unless you talk to me and get permission to move."

I was sitting in the second row. I liked being close to the front because it was easier to participate in class, and I found I did better. Bonnie was also in the second row, but across the room. I thought about how I would love to sit by her since she was the only girl and was pretty. I knew that most people always sit in the same seat, and for an instant, I considered arriving early the next day to claim the seat next to Bonnie's. But I decided that would be too obvious, and she would probably choose a different seat to be away from me. I decided I would just sit in the same seat the next day.

After Professor Hastings finished with all the preliminaries, he lectured about the material for the first assignment. I hadn't gotten a chance to do any math review in preparation, but luckily, the material we covered was familiar. He finished the class by giving us our first homework—a review of first-semester calculus that was to be completed by the next day. When class ended, I headed to the student center for the dance class, my heart pounding faster with each step.

True to her word, Sherry was waiting outside the east ballroom.

We walked into class together and sat in chairs along the side of the hall. As others arrived, it soon became apparent why the teacher had insisted any girls signing up late had to bring a boy. The class pretty much resembled a nunnery. As the number of girls continued to increase, Sherry bit her lip as her eyes darted around the room.

That was when the instructor stepped up to the microphone and started class.

*****

My mind came back to the present. I was in a class I couldn't get out of, and Sherry had left me alone. I stared at the floor, scared, embarrassed, and apprehensive. At that point, I felt a tap on my shoulder. I turned and saw a pretty young lady with long blond hair that swept past her shoulders. Her hair was curled back from her face, and her beautiful blue eyes sparkled. But what I noticed most about her was her pleasant smile.

"Hi, I'm Ginny," she said. "I heard your dilemma. I'd be happy to dance with you if you want."

"Even with how bad I am?" I asked.

"Sure. Come on."

She took my hand, and together we went to a corner of the dance floor where we wouldn't interfere with any of the other couples. Ginny started to teach me some dance steps with little success. My heart sank further and further with every clumsy step. This was bound to be the longest semester of my life.

And probably my first failing grade.

2
Remembering Disaster

✦

By the end of class, Ginny had patiently taught me a lot of the basic steps. But as I headed back to my apartment, I couldn't help but feel overwhelmed.

Dancing had been a disaster for me from the minute it was forced on us in seventh-grade gym class. It wasn't that I didn't want to associate with the girls; it was just that when I did, I always said something stupid, did something stupid, or was something stupid. I stumbled a lot. Stumbling made me nervous, which made me stumble more.

To make matters worse, in junior high, the girls had developed more than we boys had. They were, on average, about four inches taller than we were, and they were about six years more mature. At least, they thought they were. The last thing they wanted to do was to dance with the "immature" boys their own age.

To be honest, with their attitudes about us, we weren't all that fond of dancing with them, either. Of course, in seventh grade, we boys weren't too fond of dancing, period.

To force us to choose partners, boys were lined up on one side of the gym, girls on the other. We were then marched forward, and whoever we met in the middle was our partner for the day.

But just because we had partners didn't mean we would dance. Most of us just stood there wishing we were somewhere else. As the girls' female gym teacher and our male gym teacher failed to get us dancing, they conspired on ways to make it worth it to us. They declared that everyone who had not passed a certain proficiency of dance would not be going to the amusement park in the spring. The day at the amusement park was the one thing everyone looked forward to, and most of us grudgingly attempted to dance.

We watched the gym teachers demonstrate a dance, and then we gave a half-hearted attempt to imitate what we'd seen without causing permanent damage to each other's feet. We started out okay with a simple box step, just four easy moves: forward, side, together, back, side, together. But then the teachers wanted us to move around the floor. They should have left well enough alone. Instead, the dance floor started looking like dozens of slow-moving bumper cars, all trying unsuccessfully to avoid each other.

The girls complained that the boys couldn't lead, and the boys complained that the girls couldn't follow, but in reality, neither could move in unison. The forced practice continued, and once we were practiced enough to minimize collisions, our teachers increased the music tempo. At once, the class devolved from a gentle game of bumper cars to an all-out crash-up derby, with each couple trying to hospitalize everyone else without killing themselves in the process.

We would repeat this bizarre human ritual each time with a different partner. After a month of training, we had all mastered the great art of taking four steps in a square, on a permanent position on the gym floor, with a member of the opposite gender locked nervously in our grasp. To say anything else had been accomplished would be stretching the truth.

But then came the worst part. We were to choose our partners instead of having them randomly assigned. Before long, we found ourselves socially grouped into one of three classifications: acceptable, tolerable, and avoid-at-all-costs.

To keep everything fair, the boys and girls took turns choosing partners. I had hoped that my athletic ability would earn me a spot in at least the tolerable group. In the mile-and-a-half, I could outrun everyone, and I had never been beaten in wrestling. But I learned over the weeks of dancing that being athletic and being graceful were not always measured on the same social scale. Also, the fact that I was a country boy, more at home on a horse than on a dance floor, didn't help me. Thus, when we made our way across the room to choose a partner, I quickly learned how many reasons girls had for not dancing with me. One had sprained her ankle, but it instantly healed when another guy asked her. One girl had something in her eye but was able to clear it away when another boy came along. One girl told me she was sick and didn't want to give me her cold, though she was obviously willing for the next boy that asked her to catch it.

Eventually, every boy had a partner except Rand and me, and he was the only boy even half as awkward as I was. Shanae was the only girl left who didn't have a partner. I liked Shanae well enough. She was a nice girl. Also, she wore thick glasses and was nearly blind, and I thought that might help her not mind dancing with me. But as both Rand and I approached her, she moved quickly to avoid me and accept Rand's invitation.

As the dance started, I was the only boy left, which meant I had to dance with the girls' teacher. I felt my face redden. The only thing worse than that could have been death, and even that was debatable. And to make matters worse, the two teachers had noticed my dilemma trying to get a dance partner, so after that dance, they announced that everyone had to dance with the first person who asked them. At that point, all the other students turned and looked at me.

The next dance was girls' choice, so we boys sat on the first row of the bleachers, and the girls came to ask us. I watched as each boy went to the floor with a dance partner until only Rand and I were left. Again, the last girl asked Rand. Once more, I was the only boy with no partner and had to dance with the girls' teacher.

It was at that point that I decided I didn't really like going to the amusement park, anyway.

By the time P.E. class had ended for the day, I was sure it would be better for me to stay home for the rest of the week and help load hay into the feeding barns. When I told my dad that I would be happy to help at home for the week, he looked at me curiously. He knew I usually liked school.

"Is everything okay?" he asked.

"Sure," I responded. "I'm pulling straight A's in all my classes. I can afford the time to help."

My mom called the school and got me excused, and I spent the rest of the week loading hay and stacking it in the barn. But on Friday, my dad couldn't be on the farm to work, so he felt I might as well go back to school. I tried to think of some other excuse for staying home, but I couldn't come up with one.

Not only was that to be the last day of dance practice, but it was the day of the big Valentine's school dance in the afternoon. Though we seventh graders had not experienced it yet, we'd heard about the tradition from the eighth graders. Shortly after lunch, the teachers would march us down to the gymnasium. They would be careful to make sure no one bolted for the exit. Once in the gym, they would station a teacher at every doorway and provide escorts for anyone desiring to use the restroom, in case that person got lost and forgot to return. Then they would turn on music from our grandparent's era while boys sat on one side of the gym, and the girls sat on the other, all of us playing a game of "stare down."

Things went just as the eighth graders said. The music played for about an hour without anyone moving onto the dance floor. Finally, the gym teachers danced to encourage us. After they had danced a few solos with no results, they resorted to more extreme measures. Boys were ordered into a line on their side of the gym, and girls were ordered into a line facing them, just like on the first day in class. We were marched forward as if moving in battle formation until the two lines met uncomfortably at the center. Whatever girl was across from us was our partner for the next dance. As soon as the song ended, everyone scurried back to the bleachers to continue the game of stare down.

Next came bribery. Heart-shaped sugar cookies and plastic cups full of red punch were loaded onto tables at one end of the gym. But students could only enjoy the refreshment if they finished a dance first. So, the tables full of food sat without the slightest nibble being taken as we all sat glued to our positions on the bleachers. Even threats of retribution by our principal, in the form of a decrease in the length of the lunch hour, could not dislodge us from our seats.

Eventually, an "anyone's choice" dance was announced. A few brave eighth-grade girls asked some boys, and a few boys even asked girls. Things started loosening up a bit, and a few couples danced. As for me, I knew I wouldn't get asked, and I wasn't about to ask someone just to get turned down.

That school day finally ended, and the seventh-grade year passed. But during the summer between my seventh and eighth-grade years, something happened. Summer was only three months long, but I grew almost six inches.

I hadn't realized I had been growing, but I knew no matter how much I ate, I was always hungry. Granted, we worked hard on the farm, hauling hay and changing pipe, but even though I drank a gallon or two of milk per day and ate mounds of meat and potatoes, my appetite was never satisfied. I assumed it was all caused by work. But by the end of summer, I felt strange, and I was so awkward I could trip over my own shadow.

I had also noticed that my pants were beginning to look like knickers, and my ankles would always have cuts and bleed from the hay stubble when we hauled hay. I hadn't thought about the fact that I was growing because I was too absorbed in trying to understand why I was so awkward.

Oh, I was awkward before—that's why girls didn't want to dance with me—but it increased about tenfold. Even my brothers noticed and teased me. But the reason for my awkwardness became apparent on the first day of gym class when our teacher filled out our statistics.

"My heavens, Johnson," the teacher said. "You've gained almost fifty pounds." When he measured my height, he gasped. "That can't be true! Not in three months." He measured me a half dozen times before he finally realized it was true. "You've grown almost six inches!" he exclaimed. "I've never seen anyone do that in three months."

I had been one of the tallest boys my age before, but now I was the tallest. I was also at least as tall as most of the girls. I hoped this would increase my social standing with them, but any gains I made by increased height were quickly offset by additional awkwardness. A day didn't go by that I didn't trip and fall, knock over something, or make a mess somewhere. Usually, it was in the cafeteria with everyone watching.

I may have grown taller, but not all of me had increased at the same rate. My self-confidence had been left far behind and would take years to catch up. My shoe size had increased three sizes, and my feet never seemed to cooperate with the rest of me, always having their own agenda instead. More than once in gym class, I would come down the court with a basketball, only to tumble over my own feet, sprawling onto the floor to the laughter of the other students. Or I might go for a loose ball that was heading out of bounds, only to pummel myself headlong into the bleachers.

I started hearing whispers of "klutz" and "clumsy" as I walked the school halls, always when people thought I couldn't hear. Because of all of this, I dreaded the dance practice leading up to Valentine's Day. I already felt inept in my social skills when it came to members of the female gender, and the thought that my klutziness would soon push my popularity rating off the bottom end of the social scale gripped my heart with great trepidation. By this time, I had also grown a couple more inches.

When the dreaded day arrived, I thought of staying home from school. But the dancing was going to carry on for a whole month. There was little option but to tough it out.

We were only four songs into the first class period, and my fourth dance partner was limping away from me, when the girls' teacher announced we would be dancing the rest of the period in our stocking feet. I noticed she was looking directly at my big work boots when she made the announcement.

Though the girls fared much better without my big shoes to crush their toes, it also made me much more aware of my mistakes. I could feel every misstep and trodden foot.

After a month of practice, it was time for what I was sure would be the worst day of my entire life: the day of the Valentine's dance. During practice, the teachers had skipped both girls' and boys' choice, always doing forced partners. I think the teachers had kindly wanted to avoid the humiliation of the year before. Or maybe the girls' teacher didn't want to dance with me, either.

But at the Valentine's Day dance, we were expected to choose partners instead of being assigned, especially the eighth graders. The girls' teacher announced that anyone who didn't choose a partner would have one chosen for them, and then she announced that the girls would get first choice.

As the girls made a mad dash to ask someone they would prefer rather than be assigned someone they didn't want, I was sure I would soon be the only boy left sitting on the bleachers. And very quickly, that was the case. Soon every other boy had been chosen, and I was sitting alone on the boys' side of the gym. I was looking down so I wouldn't have to face the events unfolding around me. Then I thought I heard someone say my name.

I looked up into the eyes of a beautiful young lady named Dawn, who went to the same church I did. She was new to the area and was one of the most beautiful, graceful, and kindest girls in the school. We had become friends since she had moved there. I was so sure she couldn't possibly be talking to me that she had to ask me a second time before I responded. As I timidly took her hand to escort her to the dance floor, I quietly said, "I don't dance very well."

She smiled her beautiful smile and replied, "That doesn't matter. You're nice, and I like you. I would rather dance with you than any other boy."

****

As this last memory came back to me, I thought of Ginny. I had never overcome the feeling of being an ugly duckling when it came to dancing. Ginny had seen me dancing with Sherry and had seen how bad I was, and yet she was willing to dance with me anyway. I smiled. Maybe the semester might not be so bad after all.

3
Bonnie

✦

I spent the next couple of hours studying, and then went to my next class: Scientific Programming in FORTRAN. To my surprise, Bonnie was in there, the only girl once again. That fact didn't seem to intimidate her at all, and she was not shy about participating in class.

Afterward, I hurried to my apartment to get some lunch and then went to the library to study. At three-o'clock, I headed to wrestling practice.

Our wrestling coach had told us to keep in shape over Christmas, and I had worked hard. I had been running five miles every morning and doing conditioning in the evening. So, when he announced that we were all going to run a mile and a half, I felt up to the challenge. Most of the others groaned and complained.

"Stop your whining," Coach said, "and get your Christmas flab down to the fieldhouse."

I preferred to run the outdoor track, but it was three feet deep in snow, so the fieldhouse was our only option. The indoor track was one-sixth of a mile, so we had to complete nine laps.

Coach had us line up at the starting line. He pulled out his stopwatch. "The first one done gets one free penalty without going through spats."

I thought that would be a good prize. I had already been through spats a couple of times for being late for practice, crawling through the guys' legs, and having them take a whack at me. Larry, the heavyweight, had caught me hard enough to roll me twice.

I was determined to win, and the minute Coach said, "Go!" I was off to a quick lead. I held it, and by the middle of my second lap, I had already lapped one person.

"Johnson," Coach yelled, "are you sure you can hold that pace?"

I just nodded, unable to give any breath away to speak.

By the time I finished, I had lapped everyone else more than once. A crowd had gathered to cheer me on, and as Coach yelled out my time, "Six minutes, thirty seconds!" The crowd erupted into a loud cheer.

Most of those gathered were from the track team, which was there working out, too. As I tried to catch my breath, their coach came to visit.

"You aren't built much like a runner," he said, "but that was an incredible time. You just ran an equivalent of a four-twenty mile, and you kept it up for over a mile and a half."

"Is that good?" I asked.

"Well, it's no college record, but it's still good. If you have time, consider coming out for track. You might not be our best miler or anything, but you could do an incredible leg of a relay."

Once the others finished, Coach came over to me. "Johnson, when you ran that speed at the beginning of fall practice, I thought I must have recorded it wrong. But I was careful to make sure this time. That's the best time by far that I have ever had a wrestler run. Good job."

"Thanks, Coach," I replied.

Coach was not one to pass out compliments easily, and he quickly added, "Now let's see if you can translate that into wrestling wins."

My fall start in collegiate wrestling had only been mediocre, and I knew what he meant. His words took a little of the wind out of my sails.

When everyone was finished running, we went to the wrestling room. The rest of wrestling practice was much as usual: work until you can hardly stand, and then run a mile on the stairs. Most of the team snuck away after only doing a little bit on the stairs because Coach didn't come to monitor it.

The two other wrestlers that I mostly worked out with were Larry, the heavyweight, and Jack, who wrestled at 170 pounds. I wrestled at 160 pounds, so I was the smallest. I liked working out with them because it forced me to become stronger to deal with their additional size. I also had to increase my speed and reflexes to outmaneuver them, especially Larry. If he ever did get hold of me, his weight was hard to overcome.

The three of us were also good friends outside of the wrestling room. When we traveled for matches, we often roomed together. Larry was a big Tongan and funny. When I say he was funny, it was in the way of silly jokes that made you roll your eyes and still smile. Jack was blond, lanky, and much more serious, but he liked to do fun things. Like most of the team, they didn't take their grades too seriously and teased me when I studied on wrestling trips.

There were two other wrestlers in the upper weights, both at 185 pounds. The better of the two was named Kevin. He was tall and handsome, and the girls seemed to really like him. Since none of the few girls that came to cheer for us paid any attention to me, I seldom noticed them. But I noticed one mainly came to cheer for Kevin during the previous semester.

Kevin was a good wrestler, but I didn't like him too much. I didn't like the crass way he talked about girls. And it seemed that he would maneuver all discussions in that direction, and it made me feel uncomfortable. I only worked out with him when I absolutely had to, and I didn't hang out around him any more than necessary on our wrestling trips.

After practice, Coach told us to go run a mile on the stairs.

"But Coach," Larry said, "you already made us run a mile and a half before practice."

"Yeah," Coach said, "and as slow as all of you ran, except for Johnson, I should make you run a couple of miles."

Everyone knew better than to say any more, so we all headed to the running area. However, after we turned the corner, all but Allen peeled off to go to their lockers. Allen was the other wrestler at 185 pounds. He was a little bit slow mentally, but a very kind person. He only wrestled if the other team had more than one 185-pound wrestler, but he did quite well when he did wrestle.

I finished the run long before Allen, and then slowed my pace to run the last of it with him. When he finished, I gave him a high-five as we headed to the locker room.

"Good job, Allen," I said.

He smiled. "Thanks."

By the time I got home, I was dead tired, but I didn't have time to rest. I had to study, get a little sleep, and then hurry to McDonald's for my night cleaning shift.

That was the hardest part of my day. I started at ten o'clock, just as the evening shift was finishing up. By midnight, all the customers and most of the crew were gone, and by one o'clock, I was the only one left. I had to keep moving to stay awake. I was allowed a fifteen-minute break every few hours, but I seldom took it for fear I'd fall asleep.

Around three o'clock, I finally finished up. I hurried home and tried to get a little more sleep before getting up at five o'clock to run.

When my alarm went off, I could hardly drag myself out of bed, but as soon as I stepped outside into the freezing air, I was instantly wide awake. As I ran, I could think of nothing but my dread of dance class. Yet the thought of Ginny tempered it.

I made my run, ate breakfast, and was heading off to calculus before I saw signs of anyone else stirring. I arrived at class early, hoping to find someone who would check answers with me on my homework. Professor Hastings allowed us to do that and make corrections before we turned it in for a grade.

When I arrived, there were only a few guys there, and they were all seated around the desk Bonnie had occupied the previous day. Apparently, I was not the only one who realized that people usually sit in the same seat each time.

No one was sitting on the side of the room I had occupied, and this created a dilemma for me. If I went and sat by them, I would feel uncomfortable knowing they would think I was there for the same reason they were. On the other hand, if I sat in the same seat I had the day before, I would have to speak clear across the room to check my answers.

I only stood there for a moment, considering my options, when someone passed by me. It was Bonnie. I thought she would go up and sit in her original seat, amid all of the guys, but she didn't. Instead, she went to the second row and sat in the aisle seat, right next to where I had sat the previous day.

Then she did something else unexpected. As some of the young men moved to switch seats to be by her, she turned to me and said, "Tom, would it be okay if I check my homework answers against yours?"

I was so surprised I didn't know what to say, so I just nodded. I slipped past her and sat down in my seat from the day before. The other guys stayed where they were, a couple of them glaring in my direction.

When I finally found a voice to speak, I asked, "You know my name?"

Bonnie nodded. "You introduced yourself yesterday. Your last name is Johnson, right?"

"How do you know that?" I asked.

"I saw you running with the wrestling team yesterday. Everyone was calling you Johnson."

"Are you on the track team?" I asked.

She smiled but shook her head. "No. I just like wrestling and had come to watch practice."

"You came to watch the wrestling team practice?"

She nodded. "I've been to every home match this year. I know a couple of girls whose boyfriends are on the team. They invited me to join them to watch the practices this semester. Didn't you see me on the spectator benches in the wrestling room?"

I shook my head. "I don't usually look to see who's there. Coach said it distracts us."

"Well, you did an incredible run yesterday," Bonnie said.

"Thanks," I said, feeling my face growing warm.

By this time, the calculus room was filling up, and everyone seemed to be listening to our conversation, so we decided we should check our homework answers. We had all the same answers except on two problems, and in both, I could see mine were in error, and Bonnie's were correct.

As we signed the seating chart, Bonnie smiled at me and whispered. "If you come early every day, we can always compare our answers."

"I would like that," I replied.

4
Three Advantages

✦

hen I arrived at dance class on the second day, Ginny was waiting for me. She started showing me some dance steps before the class even started. When the teacher, Dr. Carlson, started the class, he began by saying, "I expect each of you to trade partners every dance. I will grant an exception for Ginny to teach Mr. Johnson because he hasn't had any dance classes before."

When Dr. Carlson mentioned that I had never had a dance class before, I could hear snickers throughout the room. I knew they were remembering the previous class and my disaster that caused the pile-up.

I also felt awkward having him refer to me as Mr. Johnson when he referred to everyone else by their first name. It made me feel old. I mentioned it to Ginny, and she laughed.

"Don't feel bad. Everyone here, except for you and me, is on his Performance Ballroom Dance Team. And I used to be."

Dr. Carlson continued, addressing me specifically. "Mr. Johnson, I expect you to learn the dances quickly so you can participate in the class. In two weeks, you must be able to switch off partners, so you have no more time than that to learn the dances."

One of the girls near us laughed, "That will be a miracle."

I could feel my face grow warm.

Ginny was very patient and kind, and I gradually started to learn. As class ended, she suggested that besides class twice a week, I should come to the four weekly evening dances.

"But, Ginny, can't I learn enough to pass by just practicing in class?" I asked.

"Maybe," she answered. "But what about the competition? Don't you want to win?"

I shook my head. "I just want to pass the class."

Ginny's eyes filled with tears, and she quickly left. I felt horrible.

I stopped to visit with Dr. Carlson. I waited patiently until all the other students were gone. Finally, he turned to me. "Mr. Johnson, I saw that Ginny was crying when she left. What happened?"

"That's what I wanted to talk to you about," I replied. "Ginny is so kind to me, and I appreciate her training, but she apparently wants to win the ballroom competition."

"What about you?" he asked.

"What about me?"

"What do you want to do?'

I felt that was a stupid question. "I want to pass the class," I replied.

"But what about winning the ballroom competition?" he asked.

I laughed. "Right. Me, win? You've already seen how bad I am. Like the one girl said today, it will take a miracle just for me to learn anything."

"If that's the case, why are you talking to me?" he asked.

"Because as much as I appreciate Ginny helping me, I don't think it's fair to her. I think she needs the opportunity to practice with someone she can win with."

"And you don't think that's you?" I shook my head. "Has Ginny told you her story?" he asked.

"No."

"Well, let me tell you this much. She and Alexander, her dance partner, were two of the best dancers I've ever had. They were on my Performance Ballroom Dance Team. I really thought they might have a chance to win the championship this spring. With what has happened, Ginny is no longer on the team. But I know she still has dreams of winning."

"What happened?" I asked.

"That's not my place to tell. You'll have to ask Ginny. But let me just address your feeling that you can't win with one word: ridiculous."

"What?" I asked in surprise.

"You could win," he said. "You truly could if you wanted to."

"Me? You've seen how I dance."

"Yes. But I see in you three huge advantages."

"What advantages?"

He looked me over momentarily then spoke. "I understand you're an athlete?"

"Yes," I replied. "I'm a wrestler."

"I heard as much. One of the greatest things athletics teaches a person is discipline. You know and understand the dedication, training, and discipline needed to win."

"Okay," I said. "I do know those things. But what other advantages could I have?"

"You're strong. I can see muscles ripple under your shirt as you dance."

I was embarrassed by that.

"But what does that have to do with dancing?" I replied.

"Though we don't do full lifts since they're not allowed in this type of competition, if a man has the strength to effortlessly lift his partner, he can do slight ones and make the dance look more fluid and graceful."

"That is where the problem arises," I replied. "I am not the slightest bit graceful."

Suddenly his voice grew stern, almost angry. "That's where you're wrong, and that's an attitude you need to lose. You could be if you would believe in yourself. But in a sense, that's what gives you the third advantage."

"What is?"

"The fact that you don't come in here feeling that you own the dance world. Too many young people come in thinking they're prima donnas and they know everything. They're impossible to teach. Often, I have to work with them to unlearn what they do wrong, if I can convince them to listen to me at all. With you, I would be working from point one."

"Point one?" I asked.

"Yes, from scratch." He looked at me a second, and then chuckled slightly. "Actually, with how you danced yesterday, maybe it would be point zero, unless, of course, there is a negative number on the scale." Then, more seriously, he said, "But I do see great potential in you."

I left the ballroom, thinking about what he said. I still didn't think there was a chance in the world that I could win a dance competition—it was probably best for Ginny to find another partner. But I knew I needed to find out why she wasn't dancing with this Alexander that Dr. Carlson talked about.

I arrived back at my apartment just after nine o'clock, and only a few of my roommates were up. I was surprised to see that Bryce was one of them.

"Bryce, it's not noon yet," I said.

"How is someone supposed to sleep when you come prancing in from work at three o'clock in the morning and then get up at five?" he growled.

I laughed. "You were sound asleep when I got up."

"Yeah, but my bladder wasn't."

I sat down and started to do calculus problems. It wasn't too long until Joe came out. Joe had strong religious convictions, much like me. He was engaged, and he and his fiancée, Rochelle, spent a lot of time together. Both of them were nice to me, and Joe and I often put our food together for meals, and Rochelle joined us. Of all my roommates, Joe seemed the most like me, except he was not into sports.

David wandered out shortly, stretched, and yawned. I went back to my calculus homework as my roommates visited and made breakfast. Soon the apartment was noisy, so I packed up my books and went to the library to study. On Tuesdays and Thursdays, I didn't have any other classes besides calculus, dance, and wrestling, so I spent a lot of those days studying.

Throughout the rest of the day, as I studied, I was distracted. Ginny and Alexander were on my mind. Why weren't they continuing as partners? Didn't he come back to college? Had they dated and had a nasty breakup and decided not to dance together? Lots of questions and guesses ran through my mind.

When I got to wrestling practice in the afternoon, things weren't much better. When Jack easily took me down, Coach yelled, "Johnson, what's your problem? You have the fastest reflexes I have ever seen, and yet you acted like you didn't even see him coming. It's like you're not even mentally here. Use your speed to grab and control his hands."

That embarrassed me, especially when I glanced toward the bleachers and saw Bonnie sitting there. I tried harder to concentrate and did better, but I still had a hard time keeping my mind on what I was doing.

After practice, when we went running, I was in the lead as usual. Because of the cold and snow, we ran the hallways of the athletic building. Down the long hallway on the lower level, up the big flight of stairs at the end, then through the top hall in the opposite direction and down the small flight of stairs at that end.

The small flight of stairs was right next to the girls' dressing room, both with identical doorways. In my mental state, thinking only about dance class, I turned one doorway too early. Those behind were following me, and we all crashed into the wall just inside the girls' dressing room.

We quickly unpiled and scrambled out, but as my teammates started to tease me, I knew I would never hear the end of it.

"Hey, Johnson," Tim yelled through his panting, "When we're done running, remember that the men's athletic dressing room is downstairs."

When we finally finished running, and practice was over, I was happy to put that experience behind me.

I went back to my apartment, exhausted from practice and little sleep, and hoped to get a short nap before going to work at McDonald's. It wasn't good sleep, with Bryce playing music at ear-splitting levels, but as tired as I was, I still slept.

*****

The next day in calculus, when Bonnie and I checked our answers, hers were all correct, and this time I only had one wrong.

The next hour I could hardly wait to hear about Alexander.

Ginny was very quiet and didn't seem to want to talk. But I had to know.

"Ginny," I said, "I talked to Dr. Carlson yesterday. I told him you deserved someone else as a partner—someone you had a chance to win with. He told me you'd had a partner named Alexander that was really good, but he wouldn't tell me any more. Where's Alexander, and why aren't you dancing with him?"

Ginny took a deep breath and spoke quietly. "I'll tell you after practice."

She was quiet as she kindly taught me. Though she was patient, she wasn't happy, and I wondered if it was because of my attitude about the competition.

When the class ended, I said, "So, Ginny, why does winning mean so much to you? And why aren't you practicing with Alexander?"

Her voice quivered as she answered. "Alex was my best friend. He and I were dance partners from the time we were in first grade. We took the first three semesters of dance here together and hoped to win the ballroom championship someday."

"I'm sure he must be way better than I am," I said. "Why doesn't he come to class so the two of you can practice?"

Ginny couldn't hold back the tears. "He was killed in a car wreck three weeks ago, heading home for Christmas break. I had hoped to win this for him, but I can't do it alone. This will be my last chance, and there's no one else. Besides, I would prefer to try with you over anyone else."

She turned and quickly left, leaving me feeling like a jerk.

5
It's More Important to Be Kind

⟡

I knew my roommates would ask me how the dancing went, so I decided not to go to the apartment. I felt so bad about making Ginny cry two days in a row that my own feelings were very near the surface.

I went to the library and tried to study, but I could only think of Ginny. I went to my programming class early to find someone to check my homework answers against. When I arrived at the classroom, I found a few guys seated around the seat Bonnie had sat in on Monday, but none of them were fellow calculus students. It made me wonder what she would do when she came in. I took my same seat from the previous day and started checking over my work.

It wasn't long before Bonnie came in, and, as she had done the previous day in calculus, she took the seat next to me. There was an audible groan from the other boys.

As the day continued, I couldn't get the image out of my mind of Ginny running out, crying. My heart ached, and I felt miserable. She had been so kind to me, and I had made her cry. I hated myself, even though I knew it wasn't totally my fault. As I continued through the day, my mind went back to an experience I had during my sophomore year in high school.

*****

My church leader, whom we called Bishop, called me into his office. "Tom, do you remember the announcement we made in church a couple of weeks ago about the statewide dance festival, and how we wanted young people to volunteer to dance?"

I nodded. I remembered it well. They had not only announced it from the pulpit, but they had also talked about it a lot in our youth classes. The youth from congregations all over the state would learn dances in specific patterns. Then, when they came together at a big football stadium where the dance festival was to be performed, they would all look like one big synchronized group.

Our young men's leader had said to us, "This is a great chance to serve the Lord and have fun at the same time."

I remembered thinking that with the way I danced, it would be anything but fun or service to anyone. I was grateful it was voluntary.

As I thought about all of that, Bishop continued, "We would like you to accept a calling from the Lord to participate."

"But Bishop," I said, my heart pounding with trepidation, "I'm a horrible dancer."

He smiled. "I'm sure you can't be that bad."

"But I am. I'm always chosen last on girls' choice dances if I'm chosen at all. I've been a dancing disaster since junior high."

"Maybe that's why the Lord wants you to do this," he replied. "Or maybe it's because there's a girl who needs you to be her friend."

"Most of the girls in our congregation don't even know I exist," I said. "And the ones who do wouldn't be caught dead dancing with me."

He looked right at me, and in some ways, I felt he could read my heart. I could sense he understood my fear, but he was driven by something deeper.

"Tom," he said, "many girls volunteered, but not a single boy did. These girls are excited to do this, and I am sure they would be grateful to have partners. I have prayed hard about this and feel strongly that you need to do it. The boys your age and younger, as well as many older ones, really look up to you. You could be a great example to them."

"How many of the boys my age are dancing?" I asked.

"None. Most of them are not respectful to the young ladies like you are. Besides, you're at least as big as most of the seniors, and probably at least as strong. We need your size and strength for the lifts."

I wasn't experienced enough with dancing to know what a lift was, but the fear of performing, and possibly making a fool of myself in front of thousands of people, made me tremble. Still, my father had always taught me to never say no when the Lord calls. My mind went back and forth. If no other boys my age were dancing, I knew they would tease me. I wondered if my brother, Albert, had been called. I was sure he would tease me whether he was dancing or not. He was so confident with girls, and he knew how awkward I felt.

Bishop seemed to sense the internal struggle I was going through and tried to encourage me. "I'm sure if you would do it, you would do a great job, and the Lord would bless you."

"Bishop, there's one other problem. I run track, and I might have to miss some of the practices."

I hoped that would be sufficient reason to get me out of this, but the Bishop just nodded. "That's understandable. We just ask that you be there as much as you can."

I finally gave my acceptance, and Bishop stood and patted my shoulder. "I'm sure you'll do fine."

When I stepped from his office, some of my friends were waiting. "So, what did Bishop want?" Buster asked.

"He asked me to dance in the dance festival," I replied.

My friends looked at me like I had just come back from an alien space abduction.

"You?" Lenny said. "You, Mr. Crash-And-Burn? You do remember junior high dancing, don't you?"

"Only too well," I said.

"You didn't accept, did you?" Butch asked.

"I didn't want to turn down something the Lord wanted me to do," I replied.

"All I can say is that the Lord must be desperate," Lenny said.

With that, they all shook their heads and headed off, laughing. Things weren't any better when I arrived home. Albert kept asking what Bishop wanted to talk to me about, even though I wasn't inclined to discuss it. But at his continual prodding, I finally told him, knowing he would hear sooner or later.

He laughed. "You know he only asked you because they're down to the bottom of the barrel and can't get anyone else, don't you? They asked me, and I turned them down."

"Why would you do that when it was a call from Bishop?" I asked.

He smirked at me. "I don't need any stupid dance festival. I'm a better dancer than that, and I have more important things to do with my time." He looked at me and grinned. "Maybe that's why they called you. You need all the help you can get."

With all the comments I was receiving, I wasn't feeling too great about dancing by the time I went to practice on Tuesday. I quickly learned that every single boy there had reluctantly agreed only after encouragement from the Bishop. Mrs. Watson, the director, was a strong-willed woman in her late twenties. She seemed ancient compared to us.

She started to assign us partners according to size, but the older boys and some of the girls complained, so she finally let everyone choose, starting with the oldest. By the time it got to me, there was only one girl left—Yolanda. She was the biggest girl.

But even though I was a couple of years younger than most of the boys, just as Bishop had said, I was just as big, and even stronger, than most of them. And Mrs. Watson said that was good because I would be strong enough to do lifts with Yolanda. There was that word again—lifts.

I couldn't understand what lifting had to do with dancing. But I liked Yolanda. She was one of the few girls in our congregation who acknowledged that I existed and would talk to me.

The dance instructor soon became frustrated with us boys. We were all farm workers and danced with the grace of old plow horses. We wore big work boots, and the girls' feet were suffering. Mrs. Watson finally demanded that we all take our shoes off. Farm boys hate removing their boots, but she was a tough, determined lady, and eventually we complied.

I tried my best, and even though I felt awkward, I actually enjoyed it. I may not have been a great dancer, but I truly was strong, and as I learned what the lifts were, I found I could do them quite easily. Yolanda was pretty, and though she was big, she wasn't overweight. She just had big parents. But because she was bigger than most girls, she hadn't had a lot of dance opportunities, and she was kind and forgiving of my inadequacies and seemed happy to have me as a partner.

The dancing went fairly well until a point where the girls jumped into our arms, after which we dropped them onto their feet in front of us. Ted dropped Alice perfectly, except that the horns of the bull on his belt buckle caught her dress and ripped it from hem to waist. At that point, a frustrated Mrs. Watson ordered us boys from the room, saying that practice was over.

We practiced for a few more weeks, and then I missed a couple of practices for track meets. At the next practice, after I returned, we danced to the point that I had learned, and as everyone else continued, I turned to see what they were doing. The girls all dropped back against the boys, and the boys caught them and lifted them back to their feet. But I was facing the other way, watching the other couples, and I wasn't ready. Yolanda fell on her back at my feet. She wasn't hurt, landing against me on her way down, but I felt horrible, stammering apologies as I helped her up.

Yolanda's fall seemed to be the last straw for Mrs. Watson. The boots, the belt buckles, and awkward farm boys were just too much for her. She got right in my face, yelling at me.

"You arrogant, despicable young man! You don't know how to treat a young lady, and you will never be able to dance right! Get out, and don't ever come back!"

I turned and fled from the room. My heart was pounding, and my breath was coming in short, wrenching gasps. I felt horrible about Yolanda falling, and I was humiliated and embarrassed. I climbed onto my bicycle and sped the four miles home. When I got home, my mother asked me how it went, but I didn't even answer. I just changed into my work clothes and headed out to do chores, not even stopping for something to eat, like I usually did. Climbing onto the back of Blackie, our horse, I rounded up the cows for milking, wanting to avoid everyone. I had just started milking when Mrs. Watson showed up, coming right into the barn to speak to me.

"Tom, I'm sorry," she said. "I know it wasn't your fault. You weren't there to see what you were supposed to do. I shouldn't have said what I did. Won't you please come back?"

I didn't even look at her, keeping my eyes on my work as I answered. "I know I'm not a good dancer. I'm sure I never will be. I think it would be best if you just get someone else."

She tried to convince me, but I said nothing and just continued with my work. Eventually, she fell silent. She stood in the doorway for some time as I worked and ignored her. Finally, she turned and went away. The next week, shortly after the dance practice ended, Mrs. Watson came again, once more coming right into the milk barn. When she asked me once more to come back, I again refused. But she wasn't alone. This time, she brought Yolanda.

Yolanda stepped right into the milking parlor in her nice dancing dress. She stood in front of me, making me step backward to make sure she didn't brush against my filthy work clothes. She wouldn't let me pass so I could continue my work. She looked at me with her big, brown eyes and pleaded with me.

"Tom, please come back. If you don't, I won't get to dance. None of the other boys will dance with me."

I hesitated. There was nothing in the world that I wanted to do less than go to dance practice, but I finally nodded. I came the next week, but much of the fun was gone out of it for me. It seemed like I would never catch up, especially after missing so much practice.

Mrs. Watson tried to be friendly, but I still only spoke to her if I had to. Feelings of inadequacy plagued me, but I worked hard, and Yolanda patiently taught me. I still had to miss some more practices, but I would come early or stay late to try to make up for it.

When the performance came, and we joined the thousands of other dancers on the football field, I felt I did okay. I know I was far from the best dancer there, but I didn't make any big mistakes.

As our final number ended, and our group was exiting the field, the other girls hurried off together, but Yolanda hung back by me. When we were completely off the field, and somewhat alone, she grabbed my arm and pulled me to face her.

"Tom, thank you for coming back to dance with me."

"Thank you for being patient with me," I said. "I'm sorry I'm not a better dancer."

"You're something far more important," she said. "You're kind."

She hugged me and then ran to catch up to the other girls, leaving me to think about what truly was most important.

*****

As I thought about that experience, I thought about Ginny. I hadn't been very kind, but not because I meant to be mean—I just didn't understand. I knew I would rather be kind than be a good dancer. I was still sure I could never win a championship, but I was determined to at least try—not for me, but for Ginny.

6
Dedication and Work
✦

It seemed like forever until the next dance class. The next day, I was there early, which surprised Dr. Carlson. On the first few days, I had slipped in reluctantly at the last minute

Ginny was almost always there when I arrived, but I was so early that she hadn't come yet. When she finally did come, she seemed surprised to see me waiting for her.

I hurried to meet her. "I was afraid you might not come back," I said.

"Even if we don't compete to win," she replied, "I thought you might still need me."

"Ginny, I may never be as good as Alexander, but that shouldn't stop me from trying. If you'll help me, I promise to do my best."

She smiled. "Then let the training begin."

I laughed. "Speaking of training, I will think of it like athletic training, since that's all I know. You will be my coach, albeit a lot better looking than the others I've had."

This time she laughed. "I'm grateful you think so."

"Ginny," I said, "I know what kind of discipline and dedication it takes to win in athletics, but I don't know what it's going to take to win in dance. You do, so you guide me."

"Okay, first, we can't do it in four class periods per week."

"How much more will it take?"

"Every minute you can give it."

I told her my schedule, and she shook her head. "Eighteen and a half credits. Are you crazy?"

I smiled. "Pretty much. But I only had sixteen and a half before Sherry talked me into this class. I also work twenty to thirty hours a week to pay my way through college."

"Our best chance to practice dance is in the evening," she said. "Can you work some time in then?"

"I've been working nights at McDonald's," I replied, "but the farmhand that worked for my father on our dairy farm has quit, and my father has asked me to come home to work for him on Saturdays. Maybe I can work long hours then and quit my McDonald's job."

"I hate to have you give up what you need to go to school," she replied.

"I've been thinking of switching anyway. I could use more sleep. I'll go ahead and give McDonald's my two-week notice tonight."

"Are you free at this hour on Friday?" she asked.

"Yes."

"Come here, then," she said. "It's open practice, and we can get some specialized help from Dr. Carlson."

"I'll do that."

"Also, are you free at one o'clock every day?"

"Yes," I replied.

"Let's meet at one o'clock at the dance studio. The Performance Ballroom Dance Team practices there from one to three. I'll talk to Dr. Carlson and get permission for us to practice in a small room off the studio. We'll have their music to dance to, and we can watch them through the window, but we won't be a distraction to them."

"I'll have to leave in time to be at wrestling practice before three o'clock," I said. "If I'm late, I have to go through spats."

"What's that?"

"The other wrestlers spread their legs, and you crawl through. They whack you on the backside as hard as they can when you pass."

She shuddered. "That sounds painful."

"It is," I replied. "I was the first to go through this year, too. At the first of last semester, I forgot my lock combination, and by the time I got it from the secretary and got dressed, I was late. Larry, our heavyweight, hit me so hard he rolled me end over end twice, and some of the other guys were mad that they didn't get a good whack at me."

"I'm glad they don't do that if we're late to dance class," Ginny said. "We'll make sure you're out on time."

"Is there anything else?" I asked.

"Yes. The evening dances that I mentioned. They're Wednesday through Saturday. Eight to eleven on Wednesday and Thursday, and nine to midnight on Friday and Saturday. I'd like you to come to those whenever you can. They're probably the most important."

"Why?'

"Because they play a variety of music and there are a lot of people there. You'll need to recognize the kind of song and know what kind of dance it is just by the rhythm. You'll also need to dance with lots of different girls so you don't get familiar with just a few."

"Why?" I asked.

"Because it will broaden your skills and sharpen them."

"But I'm not very good at asking girls to dance," I replied. "That's why I usually don't go to dances."

"We'll work on that," she said. "But there's one thing I insist on."

"What?"

She smiled and squeezed my hand. "No matter what other girls you dance with, if we're both there, I want you to always save the last dance for me."

"It's a deal."

By then the class was beginning, so we couldn't talk more. Ginny continued to teach me, and I concentrated hard, my new goal strongly in mind.

At one o'clock, I met Ginny at the dance studio as I promised. We went into a small room off one side of the studio where we could practice the same dances the ballroom team was working on. The music from the sound system went in there, and there was a window between the room and the studio.

Before practice started, the other dancers came over. I recognized many of the girls and a few of the boys from dance class, though I didn't know any of their names.

"Hi, Ginny," one girl said. "It's good to see you."

"Yeah," a boy said. "We miss having you on our team."

"We were sad to hear about Alex," a girl from our dance class said.

Ginny mostly just nodded and said nothing until one boy asked, pointing to me, "So is this your new partner? Are you coming back to the team?"

"No," Ginny said. "This is Tom. We're practicing to compete in the International Ballroom Competition, and we can use the extra practice."

A girl laughed. "From what I've seen in dance class, he'll need more than that. He'll need a miracle." I realized she was the same girl who had made a similar comment in dance class.

I stared at the floor, shifting my feet as she talked about me like I wasn't even there. Ginny glared at the girl and started to say something, but just then, Dr. Carlson started the class, and everyone else went back into the studio.

Ginny and I practiced what the others were doing, but when I glanced through the window at these superb dancers, I felt like I would never be that good. Ginny must have understood. She guided me away from the window and suggested I concentrate more on what she was teaching me and not watch them.

"The perfection will come, and maybe you can learn from watching them later," she said.

We practiced nearly the whole two hours, with Ginny carefully and patiently correcting my mistakes. Just before three o'clock, I left for wrestling practice.

That night, I gave my two-week notice at McDonald's, and my boss said he would hire someone else and start working me out of the schedule. I also talked to my father about coming home to work on Saturdays, and he was happy for the help. I obviously wouldn't be able to make up the full twenty to thirty hours I usually worked each week at McDonald's, but I could start by six o'clock in the morning, work a fifteen to sixteen-hour day, and have enough money to get by. There just wouldn't be any left for other activities, like movies. Also, if I hurried after work, I could even make it back to the campus for most of the Saturday evening dance.

The next day, I met Ginny at eight o'clock in the same ballroom where our class was held. We were one of only three couples there. As Ginny had said, Dr. Carlson was there to teach anyone who wanted some personal help.

He started the music and then walked from couple to couple, giving suggestions. The other couples appeared annoyed by his advice, but Ginny seemed to eat it up. As for me, I knew I could use any help I could get.

Dr. Carlson also must have sensed the other couples' lack of enthusiasm for his advice, and soon he worked almost solely with us.

"Mr. Johnson, bring your elbow up more . . . Mr. Johnson, hold her closer—she's not going to bite . . . Mr. Johnson, don't act like you're going to break her . . . Mr. Johnson, remember that it's you who gives her direction on where you plan to take her. . . Mr. Johnson, use your strength in the turn to lift her so it's like she's floating to you . . . Mr. Johnson . . ."

With as much correction as he was giving me, I felt I would never be a good dancer. But Ginny said he wouldn't do it if he didn't think I had the ability.

We met again at one o'clock at the dance studio, and the dance practice went much like the previous day. I had to work that night, so I still couldn't go to the evening dance.

On Saturday, I went to work for my father. I left for home by five o'clock in the morning, even though I hadn't gotten in from my

McDonald's shift until two. I worked at home from six in the morning until six that night before heading to work at McDonald's again.

My boss had someone there for me to train and said I would only work Monday and Tuesday, training the new person those days as well, and then I would be done. I was happy about that. I was so tired I found myself making mistakes and having to repeat my work. I didn't want to train the new person incorrectly.

The next day I was tired, and I fell asleep in church. Then, after church, I went back to my apartment and decided to take an afternoon nap. I didn't wake up until almost midnight when Bryce came in from his trip to see Shannon. He, of course, had to wake me to tell me about it. I was glad he did so I could set my alarm. Then, when he finished, I just went back to bed.

On Monday, when I told Ginny I would be free in the evenings after Tuesday, she was excited and told me she would meet me at the dance on Wednesday.

Because of my credit load and all that I was doing, I had to use every minute I could for study. This included any time spent standing in lines, something we seemed to do a lot in college. The worst line was while waiting for access to the punch card machines for my programming class.

All programming was done on punch cards with a machine that looked like a giant typewriter. Each card carried one line of code. We would stick the card in and type out the code. The machine would punch holes through the card according to the letters typed.

Once we had typed all the cards for our program, we would wrap a rubber band around them and put them into the inbox to be run through the

computer. Then the next day we could come to the outbox and pick them up, along with the printed output.

There were only two punch card machines on campus that students could use, and there were multiple programming classes. The line was always long. I spent lots of time in that line and did much of my homework sitting on the floor waiting for my turn. Bonnie was often there, and we stood by each other when we could. She also did her homework there, so even though we didn't talk much, it was nice to be together, and we became better friends. We also always evaluated each other's programs before we punched them onto the cards. Professor Hastings suggested we do this so we could take less time debugging them, and that meant we had to stand in the line less often.

*****

As the second week progressed, I began to dance better and better with Ginny. On Wednesday, Dr. Carlson informed me that he felt Ginny had taught me enough for me to trade partners like the other boys did.

I felt timid asking other girls. They had all seen how bad I was at dancing, and they were all in fourth-semester dance because they were good. Ginny encouraged me. Without expounding, I told her a little bit about being turned down in junior high.

"Don't worry," she said. "I'm sure college girls won't act like junior high girls."

I started asking girls as I was directed to do, but most of them had ready excuses. One girl said she had a homework assignment to work on that was due the next hour, but she put it aside when another boy asked her. One girl said she hurt her back. One girl said she had a sprained ankle, but when another boy asked, she danced just fine. I began to feel just like I had back in junior high.

Pretty soon there were only five girls besides Ginny who had accepted my invitation to dance. Every one of them had been at the Performance Ballroom Dance Team practice. Their names were Sally, Linda, Brenda, Danielle, and Jill.

I learned a lot about them as we danced. But what I noticed most about them was always their eyes, probably because I spent so much time looking into their eyes when we danced.

Sally was a first-semester freshman, but she was such a good dancer that she made the Performance Dance Team. She had sparkling green eyes, reddish hair, and a slight fiery streak to match it. Sally was also the biggest tease of the girls, and the most spontaneous, saying whatever she thought for good or for bad.

Danielle was also a freshman, but this was her second semester. She was also a slight tease but much more reserved than Sally. She had brown hair and beautiful blue eyes.

Linda had blonde hair and blue eyes. She was the quietest of the girls and seemed to think more about what she said before speaking like

Ginny did.

Brenda was engaged to Brett. He was a nice man. He sometimes came and met Brenda at the end of class. Brenda was, in many ways, very mature, though Ginny still seemed more so. Brenda had dark black hair and brown eyes. When we danced, she often shared the goals she and Brett had for their lives, and I enjoyed that.

Jill was a different story from the others. She was also the girl who had made the comments about me needing a miracle. I had been reluctant to ask her to dance after the comments she had made, but Ginny said Jill was nice and was surely just teasing. Ginny said Jill was one of the best dancers and felt I could use Jill's expertise.

Jill seldom talked to me, even when we danced together. She also would turn her head slightly away from me, so we seldom looked at each other. Even though she accepted my invitations to dance, I felt she would rather not be with me.

All these girls were good friends with Ginny. But I think anyone who knew Ginny felt she was their friend.

I tried to give the girls who turned me down a second chance if I thought their reason was valid, but the results were the same, and I soon gave up on them. Ginny had noticed all the girls turning me down, and it made her mad. Dr. Carlson also noticed, and he was even angrier.

I had just made the decision not to ask anyone except the six girls who had accepted when Dr. Carlson spoke angrily into his microphone.

"I've noticed that some of you girls think you have better things to do than to accept when asked to dance. Well, this is a dance class, and you are supposed to be practicing dance. You young ladies are to be dancing. If you aren't dancing with a young man at least every third dance, you find another girl to practice with, or you'll not pass this class."

The girls groaned, and many of them glared at me as if it was my fault. Dr. Carlson motioned me over. "Mr. Johnson, I've seen a lot of girls turn you down. I'm sorry. I've never had that happen like this before. I didn't expect it, and I won't expect you to ask any girl that has turned you down previously unless you want to."

"Thanks," I replied. "I don't want to."

From then on, I only asked those six girls who had accepted. They were all kind, and I began to feel more sure about asking them, except for Jill. She was always a question to me.

I still felt awkward. Dancing with them felt different than dancing with Ginny, and I started making the same old mistakes again.

Ginny gently scolded me. "What's the matter? You know the dance."

"It feels awkward and different with someone else," I replied.

"Well, if you want to be a champion, you better get so you can dance with any girl."

Over time, and with Ginny's encouragement, I became friends with four of the girls. Jill never seemed to warm to me, but Ginny kept encouraging me to ask her.

"Besides," Ginny said, "Jill is nice, so I don't think she's actually reluctant to dance with you. It's probably just a difference in your personalities."

I continued to work, and Ginny continued to coach me, and soon I was dancing well with each partner. Ginny was a perfectionist and had an eye for detail. She insisted that I do everything right, even in being more graceful escorting the girls to the dance floor.

"You walk like a bowlegged cowboy," she said.

"I *am* a bowlegged cowboy," I replied.

"That doesn't mean you have to walk like one."

With Ginny coaching me, I started gaining dancing skills I never thought I could have. But more importantly, I found a change of heart. I became less concerned about my grade and more concerned about doing well with them in competition. Ginny and the other girls were becoming my friends, and friends matter more than grades do.

7

The Special Girl

+

My roommates seemed so much surer of themselves when it came to dating than I did. Bryce would travel hours away to date Shannon. A person had to have great confidence in a relationship to do that.

I had never met Shannon, but I felt well acquainted with her. At least I was acquainted with her picture—it was posted prominently in our bedroom. We had told Bryce we wanted to meet her for real, and he wanted to work it out so we could. Obviously, any girl that was worth a weekly ten-hour drive had to be incredible. But she always had something that kept the meeting from happening.

Over Christmas break, Bryce had had such a wonderful time with Shannon that he had no sooner returned for winter semester before he was planning a way we could meet her. In the second week of the semester, he burst into our apartment with such jubilation that he didn't even have to speak to let us know something was up.

He waved two tickets in the air. "Guys, this weekend, when I go to see Shannon, I'm asking her to come up for the basketball game so you can all meet her, and then maybe I can invite her up for the Winter Formal!"

When Bryce returned Sunday night from his usual trip to visit Shannon, he slowly entered the apartment. He wasn't his exuberant self. He flopped dejectedly into a chair.

"Guys, Shannon can't come. And I already bought the tickets."

To cheer him up, we suggested he invite someone else. He was so hooked on Shannon it was hard for him to think about going with someone else, but we thought it might cheer him up. However, Bryce didn't have a lot of courage in asking girls out. Besides me, he was the worst. So he agreed to let Joe and David set him up. Because he was tall, they chose Lori, a girl who attended church with us who lived in a nearby complex. She was pretty, extremely shy, and tall like Bryce.

Because of Lori's shyness, her roommates had strongly hinted that it would be nice if someone in our apartment would ask her out. When Joe made the call, the girls' excited squeals could be heard on the phone from across the room where I was sitting. As for Lori, she hadn't had a single date in college and readily accepted the invitation.

All week we talked about his date with Lori. But on Friday, the day of the basketball game, we were eating dinner when Bryce came charging into the apartment. "Guys! Guys! Guess what?! I got up the courage and asked a girl in my chemistry class to the basketball game!"

We all looked at him, dumbfounded. "But what about your date?" I asked.

"Oh, don't you remember?" Bryce replied. "Shannon couldn't come."

"Not Shannon!" Joe blurted out. "Lori!"

Bryce's gasped. "Oh, no! I forgot about Lori!"

We knew that if he didn't go out with Lori, she and all her roommates, and probably every other girl in our church congregation, would hate us as well as him. So we humorously attempted to be supportive roommates and help him determine his options, such as drinking poison, having us put him in the hospital, etc. While we were considering all of this, a knock came at our door. We were in the back kitchen, so I got up and walked to the front door to answer it. There stood a girl I had never met.

She smiled. "Is Bryce here?"

At the mention of his name, along with the smile on her face, the picture in our room suddenly flashed into my mind.

"Your name wouldn't happen to be Shannon, would it?" I asked.

Again, she smiled. "Yes."

I invited her in and told her I would get Bryce.

I hurried to where he was still debating his options and grabbed him by the arm. "Bryce, if the girl that just came is who I think she is, you're really in big trouble!"

Bryce peeked around the corner, and when he turned back to us, his expression told the whole story even before he gasped, "Oh no!"

To make a long story short, a girl that Bryce would travel five hours away to see was the most important, so he obviously went with Shannon. He called the other two and gave them some lame excuse, like his aunt's sister's cousin's best friend's mother died, and he needed to go to the funeral. Then he took Shannon to the game.

But the story didn't end there because God has a seemingly wry sense of humor. A person couldn't write a worse scenario than what happened to Bryce that evening if he tried for a year. He and Shannon arrived at the game, and who do you think they ran into? Of course, it was Lori and the girl from Bryce's chemistry class, and the two of them were together. They happened to be best friends from the same hometown, and when, for some strange reason, their dates canceled at the same time, they decided to go together.

From then on, Bryce's name was mud around campus. But he informed us it didn't matter. The whole episode of considering dating someone else had solidified how important Shannon was to him. He was going to ask Shannon to marry him. That was Friday.

On Wednesday evening, I came in exhausted from wrestling practice and dropped into a chair. From the back kitchen, I realized something strange was going on. I could hear most of my roommates chattering, then they would all hush each other. Suddenly, they would cheer or boo. As tired as I was, I had to find out what was going on.

I got up and walked to the back and found a strange sight. Bryce had a poster-sized picture of Shannon tacked to the wall with a target drawn on it. Everyone was throwing darts at it.

I gasped. "Bryce, what are you doing?!"

He didn't even answer but handed me an envelope and some darts. Inside the envelope I found a wedding announcement. Shannon had been engaged the whole time he had been dating her.

Maybe my lack of dating wasn't the worst social problem to have after all.

8
The Winter Formal

✦

The Saturday after Bryce received the wedding announcement from Shannon, I had to work all day on my dad's farm. When I got back in the evening, the whole discussion in our apartment was about the formal coming up next week. Most of the guys had already asked someone. The only exceptions were Bryce and me. Bryce, because of Shannon, thought he would stay out of the dating scene for a while.

"Are you going to ask someone, Tom?" Joe asked.

"I would like to," I said, "but I'm not sure who I would ask."

"What about Sherry?" David asked. "Didn't she ask you to be in the dance class with her?"

"Haven't I told you what happened when we went?"

They shook their heads.

"As busy as you have been, we've hardly even seen you," Sam replied.

Sam was probably the quietest of my roommates. He was stocky, quite studious, and kept to himself most of the time. He also shared the bedroom with Bryce and me. I knew if I hadn't told him, I probably hadn't told anyone. So they all gathered around, and I told them the story.

"Basically, I don't think Sherry really wanted to dance with me. I was just a ticket into the class. And now I'm stuck in a class I'm not even sure I can pass."

"Isn't there anybody you would like to ask?" Joe asked.

I nodded. "There are a few girls I like. I'm just sure they could find someone better—better dancer, better social skills, better everything."

"I think you sell yourself short," David said.

"Why?"

"You're a varsity wrestler," David replied. "You're strong and athletic."

"And you're smart," Joe added. "Even with your work and athletic training, you're taking harder classes than any of us."

"I may be a good student, but I'm a lousy dancer."

Bryce, who had overheard our conversation from another room, came walking in. "But isn't that dance class you're taking helping?"

I nodded. "I'm getting better. But considering where I started, that may not be saying much. Everyone else in the class could dance circles around me."

"You still ought to ask," Joe said. "You'll never know unless you do."

"That's the problem," I replied. "Right now, I imagine there's a chance someone might go out with me, but if I ask them, and they turn me down, then I'll know for sure they won't. And that's worse."

"I suppose you and I will just stay single the rest of our lives," Bryce said.

I thought about what he said for the rest of the weekend. I didn't want to be single my whole life. I finally decided I would ask Bonnie on Monday.

I played the scenario over and over in my mind. In every case I imagined, she ended up turning me down. I kept talking myself out of it, only to renew my resolve and determination to ask her.

Eventually, Monday came. I went early to calculus. Bonnie also came in early, as usual. She sat down and smiled at me. I just about asked her, but my courage failed me. We checked our homework, and we both had the same answers.

There were only a few minutes before class started, and Professor Hastings was coming in. I decided it was now or never. I took a deep breath.

"Bonnie."

She looked at me and smiled.

I swallowed hard and continued.

"I was wondering if you were free Saturday and would like to . . ."

I didn't get a chance to finish my question. Professor Hastings had reached the front of the room, and he slammed his books on the desk and turned to glare at us.

"I mentioned the first day of class that Bonnie is our student department secretary," he said sharply. "She has let me know that certain young men have asked her out for the sole purpose of trying to get advance copies of my exams. First, let me tell you that Bonnie is extremely honest and would never attempt to look at my tests for herself, let alone for anyone else.

"I want to make one thing extremely clear. The college has policies against fraternizing between employees and students who could benefit on grades from the relationship. I suggest that while you are a student in my class, and perhaps even while you are taking any class from any math teacher, you refrain from any such solicitation of our employees."

He paused for a moment and looked around the room. Then he asked, "Do I make myself clear?"

Everyone nodded.

"Good," he said. "Now, everyone pass in your homework."

As we passed in our papers, Bonnie leaned over and whispered. "Was there something you wanted to ask me?"

I just shrugged and looked away from her. I knew I couldn't ask her now. Because she and I worked together, I was sure most of the class probably thought Professor Hastings was talking about me already. I appreciated having someone as good as she was to check answers with, but I would never ask her to do anything dishonest.

I'm sure Bonnie had to know what I had planned to ask her, but she never said anything. I wondered if she was glad that she didn't have to respond.

The only other girl I felt I could ask was Ginny. In dance class, I tried to get up enough courage to ask her, but after what had happened in calculus, I couldn't. Tuesday came and then Wednesday, and I still couldn't bring myself to ask her.

The dance was only a few days away, and every one of my roommates had a date for the big dance. Even Bryce had changed his mind at the last minute and had asked a girl from his English class. Some of my roommates started teasing me about being the only one not going.

When Thursday came, I knew it was my last chance to ask Ginny, so I arrived at dance class early. My heart was pounding, and when she walked in, I felt so dizzy I thought I might pass out. I knew I had to just ask her before I changed my mind.

When she sat down by me, she smiled, and that gave me courage. "Ginny, are you free on Saturday night?'

She pursed her lips together and asked, "Were you wanting to ask me out?"

I nodded, and she smiled kindly, but differently from her usual smile. "Tom, I'd love to go with you, but I can't."

"Oh," I said, trying to mask my disappointment. "You already have a date?"

She shook her head. "No. And I love spending time with you, but I just feel it's better if we don't date."

"Why?" I asked.

"I'd rather not talk about it," she replied. "Maybe sometime I can explain why, but not now."

I just nodded. In my mind, I could think of a million reasons why she probably didn't want to go out with me. I also considered that maybe Alexander's death was still weighing on her, and she wasn't ready to start dating again.

I tried not to think about it and focus on dancing, but I was making a lot of mistakes. Apparently, Ginny noticed.

"Tom, it's not that I don't want to go out with you," she said, "because I do. I just can't. Please believe that I would if I could."

When I didn't answer, she continued, "I can't believe a great guy like you doesn't already have a date."

I shrugged. "I'm not very good at that kind of thing."

Suddenly, her face lit up. "Hey, I know. Yesterday, after you left the dance studio, Jill was saying how she wished some guy would ask her out. Why don't you ask her?"

"Jill?"

She nodded. "I'm sure she would love to go out with you."

"I'm not sure Jill does more than tolerate me."

"Oh, Jill is just a big tease. Seriously, she's really nice."

Maybe I was just reading Jill wrong, like Ginny thought. I considered asking her, but I held back. By the time class finished, I still hadn't asked her, even though I had danced with her a couple of times.

As we were gathering our backpacks, Ginny grabbed my arm. "Did you ask her?"

I shook my head.

"Ask her. She's not going to bite."

"I don't want to offend her," I said.

"How can asking a girl out be offensive?" Ginny asked. "Promise me you'll ask her at practice this afternoon?"

I nodded. "Okay. I'll try."

"Good," Ginny said. "Be there early, since you have to leave afterward for wrestling practice."

My stomach was so tight I felt sick through study time. Still, I had made a promise, so I went. Ginny was waiting for me.

"Jill is already here," Ginny said. "This is the perfect time to ask her."

I nodded and walked over to where Jill was standing. I paused briefly, looking back at Ginny, and she motioned for me to go on. So I turned back to Jill.

"Uh, Jill," I said, "I was wondering if you were free on Saturday and would like to go with me to the Winter Formal."

The look she gave me was similar in many ways to how she looked at me when I asked her to dance. But the intensity of it was far greater. Her look of disgust, anger, or whatever it was, was so deep it was impossible to miss. Even I was surprised by it.

"I did my charity dating in high school, and I wouldn't go out with you if you were the last man on earth."

I could see that I wasn't the only one shocked by her response. The other few dancers who were near enough to hear her stood with their mouths open

I nodded. "I'm sorry. I promise I won't bother you again."

I turned and walked back to where Ginny was waiting expectantly. "Well, how did it go?"

I didn't want to talk about it or think about it, so I forced a smile and said, "It went."

"Good," Ginny said. "I think you two will have fun together."

I hadn't lied, but I hadn't told Ginny the truth either. I felt bad about misleading Ginny, but I didn't want to hurt her feelings. Really, I just wanted to leave and be away from there, but if I walked out, Ginny would know something was wrong.

Dr. Carlson arrived soon after, and the dance class started. Ginny and I started practicing, and I wasn't doing well. Finally, she stopped and looked at me.

"Is something wrong?"

I forced another smile. "I guess I just have a lot on my mind."

She nodded. "I understand. With a big date coming up on Saturday, you probably have a lot to think about and a lot of planning to do. Maybe we should call it quits for today."

"That might be good," I replied.

I was glad to head over to wrestling practice, even though I would be well over an hour early. I hoped it would get my mind off the hurt and discouragement I felt. But that didn't go well, either. I found that my emotions were in such turmoil that it affected me physically, and more than once Coach scolded me for "not being on planet Earth."

When practice was over, I ran extra, knowing that sometimes physical pain can replace emotional pain. It did help, but it didn't take care of all of it. I just wanted to find a way to be away from life.

I went back to my apartment. Bryce had his music blaring, and everyone was talking excitedly about their dates for Saturday.

Joe saw me and asked, "Did you ask the girl you wanted to ask?"

"Yes," I replied.

"And?" Bruce said, putting down the comic page he was reading.

"And she said no."

David turned from the stew he was stirring. "Did she say why?"

"She said she felt we shouldn't date, and said she'd like to, but she can't."

"Does she already have a date?" Bryce asked.

"No."

"Sounds fishy to me," Joe said.

"Are you going to ask any other girls?" Bryce asked.

I shook my head. "Ginny suggested I ask another girl in our dance class, and I did."

"So, she accepted?" Joe asked.

I shook my head. "She said she did all of her charity dating in high school and that she wouldn't go out with me if I was the last man on earth."

Suddenly, everyone went quiet, and it was very uncomfortable.

"You know, guys," I said, "I ought to get over to the library and study because . . ."

Joe interrupted me. "We know some girls that I'm sure you could ask."

I shook my head. "That's nice of you guys, but I think my dad needs some extra work done Saturday, anyway. I think I'll just skip this dance."

I knew I wasn't going to find the solitary time I wanted in our apartment, so I took my books and headed to the library. I sat in the most remote corner I could find and concentrated on calculus so I wouldn't have to think about anything else. I studied until late, and when I went to my apartment, I hurried to bed so I wouldn't have to spend a lot of time talking to anyone.

At open dance practice the next day, Ginny happily talked about Jill and how they had become friends when they both ended up on the performance team. I didn't say any more than I had to, and I only talked to keep Ginny from thinking something was wrong. I messed up a lot more than usual.

Ginny laughed and said, "It's hard to think about anything but the winter formal, huh?"

I forced a smile and nodded.

I told Ginny that I wouldn't make it to practice at the studio. She said she understood, but I knew she really didn't. I made it through the rest of the day, and I was happy when it was time for bed so I could sleep and not think about life.

On Saturday morning, I got up at five o'clock and headed home. I worked hard all day, hauling hay and working with the cattle. I worked until way after dark. I didn't want to get back to my apartment until after my roommates had already gone to the dance.

When I finally did head back, the moon was up, and the sky was clear. Despite how I felt, I considered what a beautiful evening it was. I was in no hurry, so I pulled off for a little while and just enjoyed watching the moon rise over the eastern mountains.

When I got back to my apartment, it was quiet. I thought about what studies I should work on, and I realized that with everyone at the dance, the lines for the punch card machines would likely be empty.

As I walked to the tech center, I could hear the music from the dance wafting across the breeze. It was really quite beautiful and added to the crisp winter evening. Just as I suspected, there was no one in the tech center, so I had the punch card machines to myself.

I sat down at one of the machines and started punching the cards for my program. I always tried to have the code written out for three programs ahead, hoping to get them punched up whenever I could get a turn on the machines, so I had plenty to keep me busy all night.

The only sound was the *pat pat pat* of the keys punching the holes in the cards. I was concentrating so hard that I didn't hear anyone come in. I nearly jumped out of my skin when a voice said, "Tom, I didn't expect to find you here."

I turned, and there was Bonnie. I wondered why she wasn't at the dance. She was so nice and pretty.

"I didn't expect to see you here, either," I said.

She laughed. "I guess we don't have great expectations."

"How could we when you scared the Dickens out of me?" I said.

She laughed again. "You're pretty sharp. I haven't read that book in years."

"So, why are you here?" I asked. "I thought you would have had dozens of invites to the dance."

"Why?"

"Because you're pretty. You're smart. And you're fun to be with."

She blushed slightly. "Thank you. But boys seem to be afraid of a girl who's smart, especially in math. And Professor Hasting's talk to the class didn't help."

Bonnie slid into the seat at the other punch card machine. The two machines were back to back, so as we sat at them, we were facing each other.

"So, I wasn't asked," Bonnie said. "What about you? Surely there was some girl you wanted to go with."

I just shrugged. "I'm not really good at that kind of thing. Whenever I ask someone, something always goes wrong."

She sighed and was quiet for a moment, and I thought she was probably remembering when I started to ask her in Professor Hasting's class. Sometimes I felt like all the powers of the universe combined against me when I tried to ask girls out. It seemed like they were saying, "Let's see what we can do to wreak havoc on Tom's social life this time."

As we punched up our programs, we talked. We talked all night, and it made much of the hurt from the last week fade away. Just before eleven, a security officer came and told us he was locking up the tech center.

"Bonnie, would you like some company back to your apartment?" I asked.

She smiled. "Sure."

As we walked, we could hear the music from the dance, and I could feel just a tinge of regret that I wasn't there. I wondered if Bonnie felt it, too. But having someone to talk to made it better. The night was beautiful, but cold. The stars were out, and the moon was full. Even with the cold, we didn't hurry. I felt warmer just having a friend.

When we got to Bonnie's apartment, we stopped. She turned to me and smiled.

"I'm glad you came to the tech center tonight," I said, shuffling my feet as I realized how that might sound. "I mean, I'm not saying I'm glad you weren't at the dance because a wonderful girl like you should have been asked, but I'm glad we could talk."

I felt the more I said, the stupider it sounded, so I thought I should just stop talking.

Bonnie reached out and squeezed my hand. "I'm glad we were able to spend the evening together, too."

She smiled again and then went into her apartment. I headed back to mine. I looked at my watch and realized it was almost midnight. The dance would be over soon. I wanted to be in bed before my roommates got home. I knew they would all want to tell me about their evening and, even though mine had turned out better than I had anticipated, I was still melancholy over not going to the dance.

I ran all the way to my apartment and hurriedly prepared for bed. I hadn't been in bed for more than ten minutes when the first of my roommates came into the apartment. I listened to them talking and laughing. The sound of voices increased as more joined them. I could hear female voices in the mix and knew some of my roommates must have brought their dates over before walking the girls back to their apartments.

Occasionally, Bryce or Sam would slip in to get something. I would pretend I was asleep. I started to doze a little, but the noise kept me from sleeping deeply. Finally, around two o'clock, the apartment grew quiet.

When Bryce and Sam came into the bedroom, they were trying to be quiet, but in their exuberance from the fun evening, they couldn't contain themselves.

I sat up. "So, how was the dance?"

"I'm sorry," Sam said. "Did we wake you?"

"It's okay," I replied. "I was already awake from all of the noise."

"I can imagine," Bryce said.

"So, did you have fun?" I asked.

They both nodded. "Most of us went to the restaurant together before the dance, and it was just a great evening."

"It's too bad you missed it," Sam said.

"What did you end up doing?" Bryce asked.

"Oh, I worked late for my dad," I replied. "Then I realized that the lines for the punch card machines would likely not be too bad, so I went over and punched up three complete programs for my computing class."

"So, how were the lines?" Sam asked.

"Not a soul there when I arrived."

"Sounds pretty lonely," he replied.

"Yeah. But a girl from my class showed up, and since there are two machines, we were able to both work, and we talked while we did. So, it wasn't so bad."

"Well, maybe you'll get asked to the girls' preference formal in a couple of weeks," Bryce said as he slipped into bed.

"Yeah, maybe," I replied.

But I doubted it was likely.

9

Hitting Rock Bottom

✛

Bonnie and I had a nice visit before calculus class started on Monday, but I dreaded going to dance class. I knew Ginny would think I had gone to the dance with Jill. But I obviously couldn't dance with Jill after what happened. Ginny was sure to notice. I hoped I could avoid telling Ginny—I knew she would feel bad since she was the one who suggested I ask Jill.

Throughout the class, Ginny kept dropping hints for me to share how it all turned out, but I pretended I was clueless about what she was saying.

The class was finally ending, and I was thinking I might be able to avoid having to say anything. Dr. Carlson told us we were excused, and I headed to get my pack. But Ginny wasn't about to let me get away that easily, especially since she'd seen that I hadn't asked Jill to dance at all during the class.

She beat me to my pack and put her hand on it to stop me from picking it up. "You haven't told me how the dance turned out."

I paused, and she must have sensed all was not right.

"You did go, didn't you?" she asked.

I shook my head.

"Why not?"

"She said no."

Ginny bristled. "She said no? But she announced in class she would love to have some guy ask her out. Why would she say no?"

"She obviously didn't want to go with me."

"What did she say to you?"

I shook my head. "I'd rather not talk about it."

"I'd really like to know."

"It's not a big deal."

"I want to know," Ginny said, so strongly it surprised me. "I'm the one that suggested you ask her, and I think I should know what she said."

I took a deep breath and said, "She told me she had done her charity dating in high school, and she wouldn't go out with me if I were the last man on earth."

Suddenly, Ginny's face flushed red, and fire burned in her eyes. She turned and stormed toward Jill. I intercepted her just before she got there. "Ginny, it's okay. Really. I don't want to make a big deal of it."

Ginny pushed past me and glared at Jill. "Who the devil do you think you are? You said you wanted somebody to ask you out, so I asked Tom to, and you treat him like dirt?"

"If you think he's so great, why didn't you go with him?" Jill retorted. Then she answered her own question, her voice in a snarl. "Oh, I know, you were just like the rest of us, embarrassed to be seen with him in public. Afraid he would humiliate you if someone outside of dance class, who doesn't know how bad he is, saw you dancing with him."

"He's getting to be a good dancer, and I've never been embarrassed to be with him," Ginny said, almost yelling. "I just have personal reasons I couldn't go out with him."

"Yeah, right," Jill said sarcastically. "And all of us girls have the same personal reasons. We personally don't want to be seen with him."

I was finally able to push my way between them and face Ginny. "Ginny, please. I can't blame Jill for not wanting to go to the dance with me. I'm not a very good dancer. I hardly know how to dance, and she's on the performance team. She's in this class because she's good and hopes to win in the competition, and I'm not good enough to win anything. Besides, I'm used to girls turning me down because they don't want to dance with me, so it's okay."

Ginny glared past me for a moment, eyes glued on Jill. She finally turned and stormed back to where our packs were, and I followed her. She was still fuming. She picked up her pack.

"What do you mean you're used to it?'

"Do you remember when I told you about learning to dance in junior high?"

She nodded, so I continued.

"I was so awkward that the girls didn't want to dance with me. If I asked them, they had every excuse in the world why they couldn't dance with me."

I went on to tell her more about that experience and finished by saying, "The names stuck with me, and girls quite often turned me down, even in high school. I pretty much just quit asking." I paused a moment and looked away. Finally, very quietly, I said, "So, you see, I'm used to it."

"That doesn't make it right," Ginny said softly. "Nor does it make it easier. No one really gets used to it." She reached out and took my hand. "Tom, I want you to know that I value your friendship more than any dance championship." She paused, and then added sternly said, "And it's never right to treat someone that way."

She looked past me as she said the last part. I turned around, and most of the class was there with Jill at the front. Even Dr. Carlson was there. I thought they had all left, not gathered near Ginny and me. I was mortified that they had heard everything.

"I think I better get to my studies," I said. I pulled my pack to my shoulder and walked from the room. I didn't want to go back to my apartment. Many of my roommates would be up, and I didn't feel like talking to anyone. I found a quiet corner of the library and tried to work on my calculus homework.

I looked at it for a long time, but my mind was far away, thinking about the things Jill and Ginny had said. My feelings were in such a quandary. I enjoyed dancing with Ginny and the other four girls who would dance with me, but with what had happened, I was so embarrassed I could hardly think about going back.

For the first time in my life, I considered not attending class and just failing it. But then I thought of Ginny. I couldn't do that to her. Things had turned out worse than I even imagined they would, but it was because she had defended me. I thought about how my dad had always said, "If you are at the bottom, things can only go up." But every time I thought I was at the bottom, things just seemed to get worse.

When it was time to go practice at the dance studio, I reluctantly gathered up my books, put them into my pack, and headed on my way. When I got there, I could see Jill hanging around the door of the studio. I had never seen her there before–she usually joined her classmates. But there she was by the door, alone. I wondered why.

I was glad they were glass doors so I saw her before I entered. She was the last person I wanted to run into. I was also glad I had seen her before she had seen me so I could slip out of sight until she moved away. I waited outside around the corner until the music started and I knew Dr. Carlson had started the class. Once I was sure Jill had joined her dance team, I slipped in and went directly to the side room where Ginny and I practiced. Ginny was waiting for me.

"I was afraid you might not come after what happened in class today," she said.

"I was just waiting outside," I replied. "Jill was by the door, and, to be honest, I really didn't want to run into her."

"I noticed her there, too," Ginny said. "I can't blame you for avoiding her. I'm sorry I ever suggested you ask her out. I had no idea she could be so mean."

As the performance team practiced, Dr. Carlson did something I had never seen him do before. He set the music on continuous play and told the dancers to just keep practicing; then he came over to the room where Ginny and I were.

"Mr. Johnson," he said, "may I have a word with you?" I nodded, and then he said, "Alone?" He pointed to his office and said, "I hope you'll excuse us a minute, Ginny."

Ginny glanced at me, and I could see she felt as puzzled about this as I did. I walked with Dr. Carlson to his office. As soon as we entered it, he shut the door. He pointed to a chair and said, "Please have a seat."

I sat down, still unsure about what he wanted. He went and sat behind his desk, facing me. "Mr. Johnson, would you mind explaining what happened in my classroom this morning?"

"It's a long story," I said.

"I'll take the time," he replied, sounding annoyed.

"Well, it started last Thursday. I asked Ginny if she would go with me to the winter formal, but she said she couldn't. I suppose with what happened to Alexander and all, it was just too much."

Dr. Carlson nodded. "Perhaps."

"Anyway, she said that Jill had mentioned here in the studio that she wanted someone to ask her to the dance, so Ginny suggested I ask Jill. I told Ginny that I didn't think Jill really liked me. But Ginny said she was sure Jill was just teasing because she was nice. Ginny convinced me to ask Jill. So just before you started the Performance Dance class, I asked her, and she said no."

"Why would that be enough to make Ginny mad?" Dr. Carlson asked.

"I don't think it was so much that she said no as how she said it. I didn't want to hurt Ginny's feelings because she was so kind, so when I went back over, and Ginny asked me how it went, I tried to act like it went well."

"And let me guess," Dr. Carlson said, "on Monday, Ginny couldn't miss that you weren't dancing with Jill." I nodded, and he continued. "I also wondered what was going on."

"Ginny finally asked me outright how the dance went, and I had to admit that Jill had turned me down. Ginny wanted to know what Jill had said when I had asked her. I told her I'd rather not say, but Ginny felt she needed to know since she was the one who had convinced me to ask Jill."

"What did Jill say?" Dr. Carlson asked.

"I'd rather not say. It's not important."

He looked sternly at me. "I think I should be the judge of that, considering the commotion it caused in my class."

I repeated what Jill said, and a look of disgust came over Dr. Carlson's face. He leaned back in his chair. I looked down, unable to face him, wishing I wasn't there.

"No wonder Ginny was so mad," Dr. Carlson said. "I've never seen her like that before. And I never imagined Jill could be so mean."

"It's okay," I said. "I can't blame Jill. She's on the performance team and is really good. I'm sure it would have been humiliating for her to go to the dance with me."

"That does not excuse that kind of behavior," Dr. Carlson said. He was quiet for a moment, and then he looked up at me and spoke kindly, calling me by my first name for the first time.

"Tom," he said, "I'm sorry. I feel that I am at least as much to blame as anyone. You wanted to drop the class that first day, and I wouldn't let you. I needed boys in the class, and I thought it would be good for you to get any practice you could. I never imagined the girls would treat you the way they have. The days right after I told you that you had to dance with other girls besides Ginny, I watched as girl after girl refused your invitation to dance. How many ended up accepting?"

"Six," I replied. "Well, five now. You won't expect me to dance with Jill, will you?"

"Of course not," he replied. "I would never force you to dance with someone who has treated you like she has. It wasn't even fair for me to force you to stay in the class when you didn't want to."

"I'm actually glad you did," I replied. "Otherwise, I wouldn't have met Ginny."

"She is a marvelous young lady," Dr. Carlson said.

"The other four are really nice, too," I replied.

"I'm glad you've had them to help you. But, Tom, to be fair about this, if you want to drop, I will sign your card. I can't justly put you through any more of this."

"Do you want me to drop?" I asked. "I didn't mean to be the cause of the commotion that happened this morning."

He shook his head. "Actually, I don't want you to drop. What happened today wasn't your fault. Ginny is one of the best dancers I have ever had, and she sees the diamond you are within. I, too, see your untapped ability, even if you don't see it yourself."

"What would happen to Ginny if I dropped? Would she have a

dance partner?"

Dr. Carlson shrugged. "Without you, there would be about eight girls for every boy in the class. I suppose that would mean she would have a one in eight chance of having a partner for any given dance."

"Today, after class, I didn't want to come back," I said. "But Ginny has been so kind to me, and no one has ever believed in me like she does. The other four girls seem to believe in me, too."

"You don't have to make a decision right now," Dr. Carlson said. "But the semester drop deadline is in two days, so you'll have to decide before then."

I nodded, and he stood. "You're a good man, Tom, and I think you have it in you to be an incredible dancer. I've already seen a great change in you. I hope you'll decide to stay with us."

"I'd like to talk to Ginny before I make any decisions," I replied. "I'm also concerned that I came between her friendship with Jill. I don't want to do that to them nor to any of her other friends."

He nodded and extended his hand. I shook it, left his office, and went to the room where Ginny was waiting.

"So, what did he want?" she asked.

"He wanted to know what caused all the commotion in class today."

"What did you tell him?"

I told her what I had shared with Dr. Carlson, and then she asked, "So what did he say to that?"

I told her Dr. Carlson had been surprised so many girls have turned me down for dancing and felt it was unfair that he forced me to stay in the class. "He said he would sign my drop card if I wanted."

Ginny lowered her eyes and spoke quietly. "So, are you going to drop? I can't blame you if you do after what happened."

"I told him that I wanted to talk to you first," I said. She looked up at me as I continued. "I'm not sure I can help you win that championship, Ginny, but I enjoy learning with you. If you're okay with me staying in the class, I'd like to stay."

She threw her arms around me and hugged me. "Yes! I want you to stay!"

Her sudden exuberance caught me off guard, but I felt a happy surge run through me. She held me close for quite a while, and that felt good, too. When she finally let go, I looked right into her eyes, and she was crying.

"Ginny," I said, "I want to stay and dance with you, but I also don't want to come between you and your friends. I want you to promise me one thing."

"What?"

"If you ever want to dance or compete with someone else, I want you to promise that you won't let any concerns for me hold you back."

She frowned. "Why would I want to dance with someone else?"

"Because you would likely have a better chance of winning with someone else."

"If there's one thing I've learned today, it's that winning isn't the most important thing."

"I still want you to promise."

She rolled her eyes. "All right. It's never going to happen, so I'll promise."

I hugged her. A new song was starting, so I said, "I guess we ought to get practicing. We've already lost half the time."

I glanced through the window that separated our small room and the dance studio. I saw Jill staring at us. She wasn't the only one. Most of the other girls from the team who were in our dance class were also watching us, including the four who would dance with me. But Jill caught my attention the most because she seemed to be the most interested in Ginny and me. When I looked in her direction, she looked away.

Ginny and I visited as we danced. By the time I headed for wrestling practice, I felt a lot better.

10
How Not to Pick Up Girls
✦

When I arrived back at my apartment after wrestling practice and was hauling in all of my books, my roommate, Paul, laughed. "Don't you think you study too much?"

Paul was just shorter than me and had brown hair that hung in a slight curl over his forehead. He was one roommate I didn't see too much. He almost always slept late and was off on dates most of the time he was awake. He also received lots of money from his parents, so he didn't have to worry about his finances. His biggest characteristic was he was the salesman of all salesmen.

"I doubt I can ever study too much," I replied. "I need to keep good grades so I can retain my scholarships, or I won't have enough money to pay for college."

"I'm glad my parents are paying for my college so I don't have to worry about that," Paul said.

"You know, it really wouldn't hurt for you to put a little more time into your schooling and make better use of your parents' money."

"Actually, I was waiting to talk to you for that very reason. I've got something to show you."

He sounded serious, which was unusual for him.

Paul was probably the most charismatic of all my roommates. He was new to campus and new to our apartment this semester, but I think half the girls on campus already thought they were in love with him. He went on a date almost every night and had sometimes been on more than one in a day with different girls. But academically, he was horrible. He was failing all six credits and complained he was overworked. And the classes he was taking were first-semester social dance, bowling, and tennis. I wasn't even sure how a person could fail bowling.

I, on the other hand, was trying to maximize my education for the cost of the tuition, so I took all of the credits I felt I could handle.

Paul grinned as he handed me a letter, and I knew something was up. The letter was from a prominent church leader from the church we both attended. He was not a local leader, but one high up at the central office. Paul had made friends with this man some years previous. Paul pointed to a section of the letter, and I started reading.

. . . Paul, you have more potential and talent than almost anyone your age. You can go far in life. But the problem is that you don't apply yourself. You need to learn to study and work harder, and you could be anything you want to be.

If you don't learn to work, you will never reach the potential for which God put you on earth. You have the ability to influence and shape important events in the world and be a great asset to mankind.

I feel that part of your problem is that you have never learned to work. For that reason, I am going to give you an assignment. I want you to choose one of your roommates, one strong in his religious conviction, a hard worker, and good at studying. Tell him that I am making a calling to him, one from God, to teach you to study.

Paul, it will be your responsibility to learn from him. Keep in touch with me and let me know how it goes.

"Paul," I said. "I know what you're thinking, but . . ."

Paul cut me off. "You just need to teach me to study, nothing big."

"But it is big. In order to really study, you must want to. You don't seem to feel a need. Your parents pay for everything, and you enjoy playing too much."

"But you are going to try to teach me, aren't you?" he asked. "I'm failing my classes and need help." I didn't say anything, so he added, "It's a call from God."

I felt quite skeptical. Paul was charismatic, but he wasn't a worker. Bryce said Paul could sell freezers to penguins at the South Pole but was allergic to sweat.

"Paul," I said, "I'm not sure there's a person on earth who can teach you to study."

"Hey," he replied. "I have an idea. You teach me to study, and I'll teach you how to pick up girls. That way you might get a date to the Valentine's formal."

I laughed. "Paul, similarly, I don't think there's a person on earth who can teach me to pick up girls."

"But you do want a date to the Valentine's Formal, don't you?"

The Valentine's formal was a week from the coming Saturday, and it was all my roommates could talk about. It was girls' choice. Every boy, of course, hoped that there was some girl that liked him enough to ask him.

Only Paul and John had already been asked, and each of them had been asked multiple times. None of the rest of us had yet received an invitation, but most of my roommates already had word of girls who planned to ask them.

In this, I was pretty much the only one who didn't have any indication of a girl that might ask me. And with what had happened with the Winter Formal, I felt the probability of me getting an invite was close to zero.

I had my doubts about the feasibility of this venture for either of us.

"Paul, I don't think I can teach you to study, or that you can help me get a date, but I suppose we can try it as an experiment. I don't have time to teach you formally, so let's do it this way. Just go to the library with me, and you simply sit by me and do like I do."

He agreed, so we went to the library and found a round table in a quiet area. I pulled out my computer programming assignment and tried to write out the flowchart we were required to do before we started writing the code. Paul pulled out his book on social dance and ignored it.

I worked for quite a while, with only a limited awareness that Paul wasn't really studying, just staring around. I finished the flowchart and started writing the lines of code. I hadn't noticed that a pretty girl had come and seated herself at the table next to us, but Paul hadn't missed it. She couldn't have been there more than a minute before he walked over to her.

"Aren't you in my chemistry class?" he asked.

She shook her head. "No, I'm not taking chemistry."

"Really? I could have sworn you were in my class."

He continued to visit, and I turned to watch him. I didn't think I could get myself to go up uninvited to a girl I didn't know. I would be too afraid she would be annoyed. A short time later, he came back with the girl's phone number.

When he sat down, I said, "I didn't know you were taking chemistry."

Paul shrugged. "I'm not. Haven't you ever heard of pickup lines? It would sound stupid to ask a girl if she was in my bowling class."

I went back to studying, and Paul and the girl kept flirting from a distance. After a while, she looked at her watch, gathered up her books, and left. It wasn't too long before another girl came in and took a seat at the table the other girl had vacated. Paul didn't miss a beat.

He elbowed me and grinned. "You think the last line was good, just listen to this one and watch the master at work."

Paul approached the girl and smiled. "So, hey, is it hot in here, or is it just you?"

I tried not to roll my eyes as the girl giggled. If I had to say stupid things like that to get a date, I was probably going to be single forever. Paul didn't even pretend he was going to come back and attempt to study as long as that girl was there. He just stayed and visited with her the whole time. Meanwhile, I finished writing out the first draft of my computer program and started working on my English paper.

After Paul had visited with the girl for a while, she left, and Paul returned with her phone number.

"Did I tell you I was the master or what?" he said. "You know, I'm really good at this. Maybe I should try to collect a few hundred girls' phone numbers and see if I could make a profit selling them to guys like you."

"What would I do with the phone number of a girl I don't know and haven't been introduced to?" I asked.

"What?" he said as if it were a dumb question. "The same thing you would do with the phone number of a girl you know, of course."

"I'm not going to call a girl I don't know," I said.

"That's your problem. There's nothing wrong with calling a girl you don't know. Why do you have a problem with that?"

"Why? Because she probably wouldn't want to have anything to do with me. How can you just assume she does?"

"I've never had a girl that doesn't want anything to do with me," Paul replied. "They're grateful a guy like me would be interested in them."

"Well, I'm not that confident about them feeling the same way about me."

"I still think selling girls' phone numbers could be lucrative," Paul said. "Not all guys that don't get dates could be as pathetic as you."

"What about having the girls' permission to sell the phone numbers?" I asked.

"Why would I need their permission?"

"You can't just go around collecting girls' phone numbers and sell them to other guys. The girl gave it to you, just for your use."

"That's true," Paul replied with an arrogant grin, "but I can't date every girl whose number I get, so I should be able to make a profit from them. After all, you plan to make a profit from what you do, like programming."

"That's a whole lot different than selling someone's personal information without their permission."

Paul just shrugged. He looked at his book for about thirty seconds and then at his watch. "Shouldn't we take a break? We've studied for a long time. It's been, like, two hours."

"Fifty minutes," I replied, "and you haven't studied at all, at least not social dance." I pointed to his book and asked, "Can you name the twelve main forms for ballroom dance? That's the page you have your book open to."

"That's dumb," he replied. "Who cares what they're called?"

"I can name them," I said, "because we go over them in class."

"From what our other roommates say, that's because you think you're a bad enough dancer that you need to go to class. I already know how to dance, so attending class is a waste of time."

I sat there quietly, thinking about his last comment.

He must have realized it because he said, "I'm sorry. I didn't mean to say that."

"So, the others talk about me that way?"

He nodded. "They were talking about that being the reason you didn't get a date to the Winter Formal. But to be honest, they feel a lot of it is probably more the lack of confidence in yourself than your actual dancing."

My roommates and I had gone as a group to some of the evening dances the previous semester, and they knew I struggled to even ask a girl to dance. Now that I met Ginny on dance nights, I went separately and seldom saw them. But I hadn't known that my roommates talked about it.

"I probably ought to get back to my homework," I said.

"I'm sorry," Paul said. "I didn't realize you didn't know they said those things."

I started studying, and Paul concentrated on his book for almost a whole minute. But when another pretty girl walked in, his studying, at least book studying, was over. He was too busy studying her.

When I realized he wasn't studying, I looked up, and to my surprise, I realized the girl sitting at the table next to us was Bonnie. Paul obviously wouldn't know I knew her, nor would he likely care. Bonnie, with her big brown eyes and beautiful brown hair down to her waist, could have been a model. That was all that mattered to Paul.

Bonnie had no sooner started studying than Paul stood up. She looked up, saw me, and smiled. At least I think she was smiling at me. Paul was standing between us, so she could have been smiling at him. No matter who she was smiling at, Paul assumed it was him.

He elbowed me once more. "Watch the master again and learn."

And indeed, I did plan to watch. I was sure Bonnie was unlike any girl Paul had ever approached before, other than the fact that she was pretty. She was the only girl I knew that was a math and computer science major. I was curious to see how this was going to go.

As Paul drew near to her, he smiled his most charming smile. "Is it hot in here, or is it just you?"

Bonnie fixed her big brown eyes on him and spoke with disgust. "Did you break your leg, or are you always this lame?"

I almost choked trying to hold back my laughter. Bonnie looked up at me and smiled again, and this time I knew she was smiling at me. Paul came back, utterly shocked at his failure. He looked like he had been run over by a freight train.

"I've never had a girl respond like that before," he whispered. "She must be one strange chick."

This time it was me who grinned. "Well, Paul," I said. "I think I could really fall for that girl."

11
Wrestling

As I went to dance class the next day, I wondered what would happen. I hoped to keep a low profile, but I had hoped to do that before, and it didn't work. With what happened between Ginny and Jill, it put me more in the limelight than I wanted to be.

However, other than a few girls seeming to stare at me more, nothing much changed. Ginny was nice, as always, and the four girls that danced with me seemed even nicer and more patient than usual when I danced with them. As we danced, Sally even asked me to tell her more about my struggles with dance in junior high.

After I told her about it, she said, "You're doing really well. I like dancing with you."

Other than Ginny, Sally was the angriest of all the girls about how Jill treated me.

The other three girls asked similar questions and gave similar encouragement. They also seemed upset about what Jill had said. All five of the girls were positive and encouraging. By the time the class ended, I felt somewhat less self-conscious.

Then something else happened. Ginny brought the other four girls into a group with me in the center.

"The girls and I have talked, and they would like to join us for practice on Fridays in the open time. Would that be okay?"

I nodded. "Sure."

"Ginny thought it would be good if we all prepared to compete with you, if that's okay," Danielle said.

"I would like that. I still don't understand much of what this competition is like, but I'm happy to have all the help I can get."

We talked another minute before heading to our other classes. As I turned to leave, I thought I saw Jill smile at me. She puzzled me. Why would she smile at me when I knew she didn't like me? I wondered if she was just laughing at me and how I danced. A few times during the class I felt like she was walking toward me, so I quickly moved away, not wanting any embarrassing scene like the previous day. Each time I did, she retreated back the other direction.

Later in the day, when I got to the dance studio where the Performance Dance Team practiced, Jill was once again hanging around the door. Once more, I didn't enter until Dr. Carlson called the class to order, and Jill moved away.

By Wednesday, things had settled back to a normal routine. On Thursday, our wrestling team was leaving at seven o'clock in the morning. I let all my teachers know I'd be gone for the rest of the week. Bonnie said she'd help me when I got back with any math I didn't understand. Ginny hugged me and said she'd be glad when I got back.

Ricks College, where we went to school, was in southern Idaho. It was only a two-year college, but it was so far from other two-year colleges that we mostly competed against universities. We were heading to a match against the University of Montana in Missoula, then to a match against Montana State University in Billings, and finally to a full-day tournament, Saturday, at Northwest University in Powell, Wyoming. We would travel back to Ricks on Sunday.

While we traveled in the van, I studied. Most of the other wrestlers teased me.

"Hey, Johnson," Larry said. "You're on vacation from school. You can put the books aside for a while."

"Yeah," Jack said. "Take a break and prepare yourself for the wrestling matches."

Jack, Larry, and I made an interesting trio. Larry, the big, handsome, Tongan with brown skin, had bear-like paws for hands. He was jovial and amicable. Everyone liked him. Jack was mild-mannered, quiet, and had also been a national champion the year before. I was the runt of the three. We were part of the four varsity wrestlers in the upper weights that were considered a formidable force. Part of the reason for our success was because we pushed each other to excel.

Larry was the strongest, and I was the fastest. Jack was in between on both qualities. My speed forced Larry and Jack to react faster, and, likewise, their strength forced me to be cautious and alert. Because of our training together and our traveling as part of the team across the Western U.S., we developed a strong bond of friendship.

The other wrestler in the upper weights, Kevin, was a gifted wrestler. But he seldom palled around with us. I understood that he was engaged, but he was usually off talking to girls on these trips, so we seldom saw him at the meets except when we were actually wrestling. Being engaged didn't stop him from flirting with the cheerleaders and every other pretty girl he met. He seemed to view girls and their attention as a trophy to be won. Frankly, he disgusted me with the way he treated

65

and talked about women.

Even though Paul, my roommate, annoyed me with his mindset about girls, at least he wasn't engaged and acting like he wasn't. Kevin, on the other hand, would flirt with any girl he thought was pretty. But what bothered me more was that I had seen him do it right in front of the girl I'm sure was his fiancée. Sometimes, with the way he acted, it was hard to tell which one was his fiancée. I think it was probably my disgust with the way he acted that made him dislike me.

As we traveled, I still stuck to my studying as much as possible despite the teasing. I was busy concentrating when Larry reached out and popped me in the forehead.

"What did you do that for?" I asked.

Larry grinned. "The sign said, 'Stop Ahead,' so I was just stopping your head."

I rolled my eyes, but that just made him and Jack laugh. Both were always on the lookout for anything they could do to annoy me.

We got to Missoula in the late afternoon and did our weigh-in. We then went to get a little bit to eat before the match. When we returned to the university, we sat in the bleachers. Most of the team watched the women's basketball team practice, and I did homework.

"Johnson," Jack said, "you ought to watch this team. They've got some good-looking ladies."

Larry laughed. "They're all too tall for him."

"Why do you always study so much?" Jack asked.

"I'm taking eighteen and a half credits, and I have to keep my grades up to maintain my scholarship, or I can't afford to go to school," I replied.

Larry gasped. "Man, are you crazy? That many credits is like taking two semesters worth of work in one. I only have ten and a half."

"Yeah," Jack added, "and that half credit for wrestling is like ten itself."

The match that night went well. Since we weren't a university and they were, no team score was recorded, but the two teams were quite even. Jack, Larry, and I all won. The next night was almost a repeat of the first night, with almost exactly the same people winning.

The tournament on Saturday was a fairly big one, starting at eight o'clock in the morning and going all day. The championship round was at eight o'clock at night. Jack, Larry, and I all made it to the championship matches. They both won, and I lost in a close contest.

Most of the varsity squad were sophomores. I was one of only two freshmen, so Coach felt I did well. As for me, a loss was a loss.

As we headed home on Sunday, I had a second-place medal, but I still felt bad I couldn't pull out the first-place win.

"You know why you lost, don't you?" Jack asked me.

"Why?"

"Because you couldn't do math on your opponent."

Jack and Larry laughed, and I smiled. Just like most of the wrestling team, their whole worlds revolved around athletics, and so did most of their classes. Most members of the team planned to be high school wrestling coaches, and it was strange for them to think about one of us liking math and science.

"Hey, Johnson," Stephen, our 112-pound wrestler, said. "Maybe you can become famous for figuring out the best calculations for winning matches."

"Leave him alone, guys," Coach said. "At least there's one wrestler on this team that I never have to worry about being academically eligible. This next week before the conference tournament, the secretary has to check everyone's grades before you can compete."

An audible groan came from almost everyone in the van, but I smiled. I was glad that wasn't a concern for me.

Our return trip took us through Yellowstone Park. Most of the park was closed, but the road straight through was a thoroughfare for traffic between Wyoming and Idaho and was plowed in the winter.

Snow stood ten to fifteen feet high along the sides where we traveled. The mountains were beautiful covered in snow. There was a peaceful atmosphere watching the beauty of nature out the van windows. I took a break from studying on Sundays, so I just sat back and enjoyed the majesty of the mountains and forests. The radio was playing a tribute to America sung by the Mormon Tabernacle Choir, and that just increased the effect of that stunning trip.

When I arrived back at our apartment on Sunday evening, all talk was about the girls' preference dance coming up the next Saturday. It was not considered appropriate for girls to ask guys out except for that one time each semester, so it was a big event. Each girl went all out to make the invite and the evening memorable, her only chance to show that certain guy that she liked him.

I learned that while I was gone, my other six roommates had been asked. Since John and Paul had been asked previously, that meant I was the only one without an invite.

After the winter formal, my roommates had wanted to create two apartment pools, one for who would be asked first, and one for who would be asked last. I hadn't been too excited about it, sure I would be last, but I went along with it for fun.

We had all put in one dollar—fifty cents for each pool, and we had written on papers who we thought each would be. Once Paul was the first one asked, we had pulled out those papers, and they were quite evenly split, four for John, five for Paul. I won on that one.

When everyone had been asked except me, that meant I was obviously last if I would be asked at all. So, Sunday night we pulled out those papers. I wasn't sure I wanted to know what everyone put. Sure enough, everyone put they thought I would be last.

"You put yourself?" Paul asked in surprise. "You need to get more confidence."

Despite the embarrassment I felt, I joked, "What are you talking about? I was confident I would be last."

The others all laughed.

"Hey, guys," Bryce said. "I think we ought to give the money to Tom so he can buy some ice cream or something."

Bryce liked ice cream.

"That's okay, Bryce," I replied. "I would have to wait until after wrestling season to eat it anyway."

"I know a girl that could ask you," Paul volunteered.

I shook my head. "It'd be weird having someone ask a girl to ask me. She should ask whatever guy she's interested in. It's better I don't have a date anyway. We have the conference wrestling tournament here Friday and Saturday, and it doesn't get over until mid-Saturday afternoon. I just thought I might use that evening to catch up on my computer programs while the punch card machines are empty."

I knew that I wasn't fooling most of my roommates about my disappointment in not having an invitation to the dance, but pretending that I didn't plan to go made it easier for all of us.

To change the subject, I showed them my wrestling medal.

John said, "Big deal. Anybody can wrestle."

John was tall, blonde, and handsome—at least all the girls must have thought so. They hung around him like flies around rotted roadkill.

He was probably as much of a ladies' man as Paul. Like Paul, John was new to our apartment this semester. His family had been quite wealthy, but something happened, and they lost much of their money. Still, they provided John with enough money that he didn't need to have a job while going to school. When John had first come, he had seemed lost. I had helped him with his schedule and even helped him with his apartment chores. But it seemed no matter what I did, there was something about me he didn't like. I tried hard to be his friend, but he always seemed to avoid me unless he needed my help.

After John's comment, Bryce turned to him. "What do you mean? Wrestling takes a lot of skill and practice."

"I could beat Tom in wrestling if I wanted," John replied.

"You can definitely beat me in getting girlfriends," I said.

"Wrestling is a different matter," Joe said. "Tom is on the varsity team."

Joe was often the most thoughtful and articulate in what he said. He studied engineering, and sometimes he asked me for math help. If there was ever a disagreement in our apartment, he was usually the one who could diffuse it.

"I'm bigger and stronger than he is," John said. "I also wrestled in junior high, so I know I could beat him."

I could see where this was going, and I wanted to avoid wrestling John. He had hinted at a wrestling challenge since he joined our apartment in January. I'm not sure why he felt the great need to prove that he was better than I was in this area. But it seemed that if I was doing something athletically, he had to try it, too.

I would get up at five o'clock in the morning to run the five miles my coach expected, then I'd lift weights. On my way back to our apartment, I would often pass John as he trotted across campus to the field house. He would wear adult footie jammies with a bathrobe over them, his bathrobe flying behind him like a peacock with loose tail feathers. He would act like he didn't know me, and with the way he was dressed, I was glad. It would have been embarrassing for anyone to know we were roommates. They might have thought we shared a room in an insane asylum.

I had been able to avoid John's strange obsession to beat me at sports. At least, I had until now, but this time it wasn't looking promising.

"Come on, John!" Bryce said. "Tom is a varsity wrestler. What makes you think you can beat him?"

"Yeah," Joe said. "You might be taller, but Tom has more muscle in one finger than you have in your whole body."

That made John mad. "Well, if he's scared, I understand."

I hadn't said anything to that point. I had hoped to avoid this because John had a big ego, and I knew if I beat him, he would likely hold a grudge for a long time.

"I'm not scared, John," I said. "But I don't think this kind of competition is good for roommate relationships."

"Just admit you're afraid you'll get beat," John replied. "It's understandable."

As much as I wanted to take his challenge, I thought it was better not to. However, our other seven roommates felt it was time John learned a lesson.

"You're not going to let him talk that way to you, are you?" David asked me.

Before I could even answer, Bryce jumped in again. "Of course Tom is going to take the challenge. I'll reserve the wrestling room for tomorrow night."

"You'd better make it for late in the evening so Tom has time to recover from wrestling practice," David said.

"Yeah," John laughed. "We don't want him to have any excuses for his loss."

"What about your excuses when you lose?" David asked.

"I won't need any," John said, "because I won't lose."

I reluctantly nodded. "All right, John. I'll take the challenge, but only if there are no girls there."

"Afraid you'll be embarrassed, huh?" John said with a laugh.

"Just promise," I said.

"Okay," John said with a smirky grin. "I wouldn't want you to be embarrassed."

"I won't be embarrassed," I replied

Bruce excitedly raised his hand. "I wrestled in high school. I get to be the ref."

Joe raised his hand, too. "And I get to be the scorekeeper."

"And I'll keep the time," David said.

John shrugged. "Sure. Whatever. But it probably won't matter because I don't plan to hold back and will probably pin Tom within the first minute."

Most of my roommates laughed. That made John mad, and he stormed out the door.

After he left, Bryce asked, "Tom, why did you insist that he not bring any girls?"

"If John brought his harem to watch the wrestling match, then he would never forgive me if he loses in front of them," I answered.

"If?" Bryce replied. "You mean when. He just doesn't get the fact that you're more experienced and stronger."

"I think you should let him bring girls," David said. "I think the humbling would do him good."

12
The Challenge

✦

onday morning came, and Bonnie helped me with the math problems I hadn't been able to understand on my own. She was not only good at math, but she was also a good teacher.

Ginny welcomed me back with a hug, and dance practice continued. I had brought back six little key rings with a picture of a buffalo on each one. I gave one each to Bonnie, Ginny, Sally, Linda, Brenda, and Danielle.

"We have a conference tournament this weekend," I told Ginny. "Next week we travel to Coeur d'Alene for the Regional Tournament. Hopefully, I'll win there and go to nationals the following week. After that, wrestling will be over, and I can put all the time I've put into wrestling into practicing dance."

"You don't have to do that," she replied. "You already put in a lot of time."

I shrugged. "Once wrestling is over, I won't know what to do with myself. I'll need something to take its place."

"What about track? A friend of mine is on the track team, and she said her coach asked you to join their team."

I was surprised she knew about that.

"I considered it," I replied, "but I think I will just put the time into practicing dance. I thought we could see if Sally, Linda, Danielle, and Brenda might have time to practice on some evenings after they finish with the Performance Dance Team practice. Since they want to compete with me, maybe it will help me do better. And that time after the Performance Dance Team practices is the time I usually practice for wrestling, so I'll be available."

Ginny nodded. "I'm sure Dr. Carlson will let us. But just remember one thing."

"What?"

"You always have to save the last dance for me when I'm there."

I smiled. "Absolutely."

When I went back to my apartment, I learned that Bryce had been able to schedule the wrestling room for eight o'clock. It had cost ten dollars for a one-hour reservation, and all of my roommates, except John, had chipped in. All the talk in the apartment was of the wrestling match. It had even replaced talk of the girls' preference dance.

I didn't stay there long. I needed every minute I could get to catch up on missed homework. I also didn't want to think about wrestling John. Keeping busy also helped me to forget about the fact that no girl had invited me to the dance.

Practice finished not too long after five o'clock. Coach had a rule that if you didn't outscore your opponent in the final two rounds, you had to run an extra mile. But even on the match I lost, I outscored my opponent on the last rounds because I was in good shape.

I didn't go back to my apartment after practice. I just went to the library to study. About twenty minutes before eight, I made my way to the athletic building. I dressed and went to the wrestling room. All my roommates except John were there.

"Do you think John will show up?" Joe asked.

"Of course he will," Bryce replied. "He's arrogant enough to think he's going to win."

And sure enough, just a few minutes before eight, John marched into the room. Behind him were a couple dozen girls.

I was not happy. "John, you promised no girls."

He smirked. "You said you weren't afraid, so I knew you wouldn't mind. But if you're afraid, you could forfeit."

"He's not afraid of you," Bryce retorted. "He just doesn't want you to bawl when he kicks your butt."

"It's him that'll bawl," John said with a sneer.

"You've got to do it," Bryce whispered in my ear. "We all put up the money to rent this room, and I'm not going to live with his arrogance. You need to teach him a lesson."

John continued to mock me, and I realized all my roommates agreed with Bryce, so I agreed to continue.

David held up a stopwatch. "How long are the rounds going to be?"

"In high school, they were two minutes, two minutes, and two minutes," I replied. "In college, we go two, three, and three."

"Let's do it like college," John said, winking at the girls. "I run every morning, and I'm in good shape."

"Okay," I replied.

Bryce had us come to the center across from each other. "Do we want any extra ground rules before we start?"

"Like what?" I asked.

"We don't want someone to get pinned quickly and then say it was all a fluke, and the other person got lucky, do we?" he replied.

"That's true," John said. "I wouldn't want Tom going around saying I was just lucky pinning him right off."

"How about we set a point difference a person has to reach before I'm allowed to call a pin?" Bryce asked. "Meaning, the score of the person who is ahead has to be at least that many points more than the score of one who is behind."

"I like that idea," John replied.

"What should we set it at?" Bryce asked.

"How about thirty-five points," John said.

Bryce's eyes twinkled with mischief, and he was barely able to hold back his grin. I knew what he was doing. He wanted John to truly be humbled. So Bryce was feeding John's ego, making him feel like he was doing it for John's benefit. He was also making it so John was the one who set the requirement.

"Are you okay with that, Tom?"

"Thirty-five points is a lot of points in a wrestling match," I replied. "No one usually scores that many."

"If you're afraid of getting tired, don't worry," John said. "I should be able to score that many in the first round."

I sighed, entirely taken aback by his arrogance. "Alright. Thirty-five it is."

John turned to the crowd of girls that were seated in the bleachers at the end of the room. "I'm afraid this might take a little while. I said we ought to make it so a pin can't be called to end the match until the person is ahead by thirty-five points. So it might take me most of the first round to get that many points."

One of the girls yelled, "Go, John!" and he smiled and waved.

While John was distracted, Bryce said, "Don't let him off easy. Score the thirty-five and then pin him."

"I thought I would just put him on his back and hold him there," I replied.

"No way," Bryce replied. "Score the thirty-five. He's the one who set the number."

I nodded, but I didn't like it. However, Coach had taught us to never hold back. If he ever thought we were, he made us run extra.

John finally turned his attention back to the match. Bryce had us shake hands, and then he blew the whistle.

I immediately shot in, hooked my leg behind his leg, and dropped him on his back and held him there as he struggled.

"Two points— takedown," Bryce called out to Joe. Bryce then counted briefly and said, "Three points—near fall."

John was already in a pinned position, but I knew Bryce wouldn't call it. I had still considered just holding him there and not running up the score, but I could feel the adrenaline and my competitive spirit kicking in. My mind and body went into autopilot from years of training. Knowing Bryce wouldn't let me pin John, I let him loose just enough he could roll to his stomach. I put him in a half nelson and an armbar and turned him over again.

Bryce counted then said, "Three points near fall."

The girls, who had started out cheering, went quiet. I let John roll back to his stomach and then locked him into a cradle and threw him on his back again.

Bryce counted again and announced, "Three points near fall."

Three more times I let John roll to his stomach only to flip him on his back again and hold him for the count. By the last one, he was struggling very little. He was gasping for air, and his lips were blue.

Barely audible, he said, "Hasn't it been two minutes yet?"

"Still twenty seconds to go," David said.

I let John roll to his stomach and just let him lie there. If he acted like he was going to try to get up, I would throw him back to the mat. I actually did think he would be more competition than he was. He was bigger than me. But it had hardly been any effort on my part.

Finally, David called, "Time."

"Twenty to nothing," Joe said. "And I'm sure I don't need to say who's ahead."

I thought John might call it quits, but his pride wouldn't let him. And amazingly, he still thought he could win. He struggled to his feet, still gasping for air.

"You jumped the whistle, so I didn't have a chance," he fumed.

"He did not," Bryce replied.

"He did too," John yelled, turning to Bryce. "That way he could take me by surprise and keep me down so I couldn't do anything." John then turned to me. "You let me have top position, and I'll show you something! Once I get hold of you, you're dead!"

I doubted his speech was as much for me as it was for the girls. The same girl as before said, "Go, John," but this time it sounded weak.

"You can have the top position, John," I replied.

"Before you get down," Bryce said to me, "I want to say something. Tom did not jump the whistle, but I want to make sure that no one can use that as an excuse. After I blow the whistle, John, you go for it.

But, Tom, I want you to wait a few seconds until I tell you to go, so John has no excuse. In fact, why don't you tell John what you plan to do, so he won't be surprised."

John just stood there scowling and didn't say no, so I said, "I thought I'd just stand, escape, then take him down."

"Did you hear that, John?" Bryce said. "We don't want you to be surprised."

"Just shut up and start the match," John growled.

I got in the down position, and John got on top. Bryce blew the whistle, and I didn't move. John slammed my arm with his, but I didn't even give. Instead, I redirected the force, twisted my arm free, and got back into the same position. He tried two or three times to knock me to my stomach, and I was surprised at his lack of strength and skill. I wasn't used to it, and it almost confused me.

I don't know how long Bryce waited—I'm guessing five to ten seconds—but he finally said, "Okay, Tom, wrestle."

Instantly I stood, grabbed John's hands, twisted, and pulled free. I turned to face him as Bryce pointed at me and called out, "One point, escape."

John shot in, and I blocked him and sprawled. I didn't take him down, but just let him back up. He stood to face me, and I dipped down on one knee and picked him up in a fireman's carry, lifting him as high as my shoulders. I set him gently on the mat on his back, then held him there.

Bryce counted, then called out, "Two points takedown, three points near fall."

And then it all started over. I let John roll to his stomach and then turned him to his back again. But Bryce knew the points were adding quickly to the thirty-five-point mark, and he was in no hurry to end the match. If he didn't think it was a hold that made John suffer enough, he would say loud enough so all could hear, "I don't like that one. It's not fancy enough, so I'm not going to call any points."

By the time David announced we were in the last minute, John was exhausted and hardly struggling at all. Bryce decided to let the points rack up, and soon Joe called out that the score had reached the thirty-five-point mark.

The next time I turned John, Bryce didn't immediately call the pin. Instead, he asked in a voice loud enough that all could hear, "John, are you ready for me to call the pin?"

"Yes," John gasped.

"I can't hear you," Bryce said even louder.

"Yes!" John yelled.

Bryce slapped the mat.

I let John go and stood up. John just lay there, his sides heaving from exhaustion. After he had been there for nearly a minute, I reached my hand out to him to help him up. He slapped my hand away and turned to his stomach. He started to stand, and then stopped, resting on his knees for most of another minute.

Finally, he stood and, trembling, he wobbled his way out the door. The girls immediately flocked around him, supporting him with their arms. I sighed as I watched them leave. I felt sorry for John. I knew he was humiliated, and I had wanted to avoid that, but his arrogant attitude had precluded the outcome that occurred.

All of our other roommates gathered around, slapping me on the back and laughing. But I didn't feel much like celebrating. I had done something I hadn't wanted to do, and frankly, I didn't feel like a hero.

"Hey, guys," Bryce said, "what say we treat Tom to some ice cream?"

They were all shouting their agreement, but I shook my head.

"Sorry. I'm going to have to decline."

They looked at me in surprise.

I knew I just couldn't celebrate, but I couldn't tell them I was upset about the whole thing. Then I thought of a good excuse.

"Coach's training rules, you know. No ice cream during wrestling season."

"You bet, buddy," Bryce said. "We understand."

"It will take me a while to get showered and dressed, and then I need to finish my homework from the days I was gone," I said.

"We'll buy some extra ice cream and put it in the freezer for when wrestling season is over," Joe said.

I nodded. "Sounds good."

They headed off to celebrate with lots of jubilation and laughter, while I walked slowly to the locker room. I showered and dressed. I went to the library to study, but I struggled to concentrate. My thoughts were all about John.

I was hungry. I hadn't had anything to eat since breakfast, but I didn't go home until I was forced to when the library closed at eleven. When I did go home, I quietly entered our apartment, not that I thought anyone would be asleep. I was trying not to draw any attention to myself. I sat in a chair in the dark in the small foyer near the front of the apartment. I could hear the voices of my roommates coming from the kitchen in the back.

I heard John's voice. "I'm sure Tom really thinks he's great, beating me like that."

"The thing you don't seem to understand is that he was holding back," Bryce replied. "He could have decimated you. To keep from finishing off the match in the first round, he simply kept forcing you to the mat."

"And from the side, we could tell he wasn't using all of his strength," David added. "That's probably why you're here and not in the hospital."

"I don't think he held back," John answered. "And I feel like I ought to be in the hospital. I'm sure it makes him feel good beating me like that."

"What are you talking about?" Joe said. "You're the one who challenged him, not the other way around. And all you could talk about was humiliating him."

"I just thought he needed to be humbled a little bit," John replied.

"That makes a lot of sense," Bryce said sarcastically. "You're the one doing all the bragging about how great you are, and it's him that needs humbling?"

I didn't feel it was right for me to stay there just listening, so I got up and walked back to the kitchen. John saw me and walked right up to me, sticking his finger in my face.

"You think you're really great, don't you? Well, I could outrun you."

I could feel anger swelling in me, and I took some deep breaths to calm myself.

Joe laughed at John's comment. "John, you know how you come over to run in the field house while I'm there? You know how, in the whole mile you run, you might pass me once, if at all?"

John turned to him. "Yeah. What of it?"

"You and I each run a mile. I once started a mile at the same time Tom started a mile and a half. He lapped me every lap, and by the time he finished, I still had a half mile to go."

"I have an idea," Bryce chimed in. "Let's invite all of your girlfriends and let Tom show you."

"I don't know," David said. "Wouldn't Tom have to wear footie jammies to run in to make it fair?"

Everyone except John and I laughed. John stood there breathing hard.

He then turned back to me and said, "I hate you."

That was the last straw for me. I got right back in his face.

"You are so arrogant. I didn't challenge you. You challenged me. You told everyone how you were going to humiliate me when you beat me. I did everything I could to avoid what happened tonight. I tried to talk you out of it. I made you promise me you wouldn't bring any girls. But you couldn't even keep that simple promise. Do you think I like beating a roommate? Do you think I feel good about what you forced me to do? But what did you expect from me, that I just roll over and play dead so that you could humiliate me more than you already try to?"

Everyone was suddenly quiet. They weren't used to me getting angry. I paused for a moment, and then I had to say more.

"John, I've tried to be your friend, but you have always disliked me. I have helped you with your chores when you were busy. I helped you figure out your schedule when you were new here. I've shared food with you when you were too busy to make your own. No matter what I do, you think of me as selfish and prideful. What is your problem?"

The room was silent for quite some time, broken only by the sound of my heavy breathing. John finally spoke, and when he did, he spoke quietly.

"I've never considered it before, but I guess I'm jealous of you."

I don't think he could have said anything that could have stunned me more. I just stared at him. When I finally did speak, I couldn't keep the shock from my voice.

"Jealous of me? Why in heaven's name would you be jealous of me?"

"Why?" John's voice sounded so incredulous. "I'll tell you why. All I've heard since I came here was how strong you are. What a good athlete you are. How you're taking, like, fifty million credits, including calculus, computer programming, and every other hard thing imaginable, and you're acing them all."

I stood there just staring at him for a moment. When my shock subsided, I said, "Have you ever considered that I might be jealous of you, too?"

This time, his voice betrayed his amazement. "What could I have for you be jealous of?"

"How about the fact that even though your parents lost quite a bit of their money, they still have enough to help you. They paid your tuition, paid your housing, provide money for your food and other things. If I don't keep my grades up, and if I didn't have my wrestling scholarship, I wouldn't be able to stay in school. I also must work a job every chance I can to have money for food and other things I need. Did you stop to consider that your clothes and everything you have are much nicer than mine? But do you want to know what I'm most jealous of?"

"What?" he asked quietly.

"How many invites have you had for the preference dance?"

John shrugged. "I don't know. Eight or so, I guess."

"And when did your first one come?"

"I can't remember," John replied. "A few weeks ago."

"Well, the dance is only five days away now, and I haven't had one. And I doubt I ever will."

"But I thought you were planning to do computer programming," John said.

"It's easier to pretend that's what I plan on doing than it is to admit to myself that even though there are hundreds more girls than boys on this campus, there's not a single one that likes me enough to ask me."

"But what about all of the wrestling fans?"

"Have you ever been to a wrestling match?" I asked.

John shook his head, so I continued. "The number of fans there is about fifty. Of those, maybe fifteen are under forty. The five or six that are girls are almost all girlfriends of the other wrestlers. Occasionally, we might have a cheerleader there if she has nothing else to do and is assigned by the cheer squad to come. But none come voluntarily."

"What about your math classes and stuff?"

"Do you know how many girls take math?" I asked. "Almost none. Most of my major classes don't have any girls. Two of my classes only have one girl, the same one in both classes, and we aren't allowed to date her because she's the department student secretary. And the few girls I asked out to the winter formal all turned me down. And do you know why? Because I grew up in the middle of nowhere and have the social skills of a porcupine when it comes to dating."

"I never thought about any of that," John replied.

"And do you know what else, John? I'm sure that all of those girls you invited tonight are probably saying, 'Poor John. Tom is so mean.' But if it were you who had won and done the same thing, they would all be saying, 'John is so cool. John is so strong. John is our hero.' But I'm not a hero. I'm just a big jerk for doing what I didn't want to do in the first place—something you forced me to do. And the reason for that difference is because I'm just a big social zero, and you're not."

When I stopped, the whole room was quiet. No one said anything. I felt exhausted.

My roommates had never seen me that angry before, and they all seemed stunned. They just stared at me until I said, "I think I should go to bed." Then I turned and walked into my bedroom.

I prepared for bed and climbed in. I lay there for a long time, still hungry and mentally exhausted. It was a long time before I slept. My roommates talked quietly, and I wondered what they were saying and what they thought of me.

13

Computer Code and Wrestling Tournaments

✦

Tuesday, I avoided our apartment and my roommates as much as possible. I was embarrassed about my outburst and wanted to forget about the whole thing. Then on Tuesday, as programming class ended, Bonnie asked, "Are you excited about the dance on Saturday?"

I just shrugged.

She looked at me with surprise. "Aren't you going?"

I shook my head.

"Haven't you been asked?"

Again, I shook my head.

"I'm sure the punch card machines will be empty again," I said. "I figure after our wrestling tournament ends Saturday afternoon, I'll just go punch up some more of my computer programs."

She just nodded and didn't say anything more.

*****

Wednesday morning, when I came in from running, John came wandering out of his bedroom.

"You're not out jogging?" I asked.

To my surprise, he laughed and was friendly.

"The main reason I went jogging was to beat you. Since I know that isn't going to happen anymore, I decided it wasn't worth getting up to go jogging."

I was taken aback by his friendliness and didn't know what to say.

"Tom," he said, "I want to apologize for what I did Monday. Your comment about how if I'd won, I would have been a hero, but when you won the girls would think you were a jerk, really struck home to me. After the girls and I left, that's exactly what they all said about you. And I realized how right you were and how wrong I was in what I did. You've tried to be kind, and all I've ever done is antagonize and mock you. I'm sorry, Tom."

"It's okay," I replied. "Maybe besides being roommates, now we can be friends."

He nodded. "I hope so." He paused for a moment and then smiled again. "Hey! I know I can't undo everything I've done. But I spent a lot of time yesterday talking to the girls that were at the match and explaining that it was my fault. If you still don't have a date to preference, I'm sure there is more than one of them that would love to go with you."

"I think I would feel really awkward. They should invite someone they know and want to go with."

"Okay," he said. "But let me know if you change your mind."

In calculus, Bonnie handed me some computer code. "Tom, would you check this for me to see if my work is correct? I want to make sure the output is right."

"I'd be happy to," I replied. "What's the output supposed to be?"

"I don't want to tell you so I don't prejudice you. I know you have a tournament that starts on Friday, so I was hoping you could get it back to me by tomorrow."

"Sure," I said. "You've helped me more than I can ever repay."

She smiled. "Thanks, Tom."

*****

After wrestling practice, I went to my apartment, but all my roommates were talking about their fun plans for Saturday, so I went to the library to study so I wouldn't have to listen. I did all my homework, and then I pulled out Bonnie's program. Bonnie was better than I was at math, but in programming, I shined. It wasn't uncommon for her to ask for my help in that.

I took the page with the data file and laid it beside the program so I could trace the inputs at each point where the program read them, and then I started through the logic.

The first number the program read was fifty-four. It took the number, added one hundred and thirty-seven, then subtracted fifty. It continued adding and subtracting until it ended with fifty-four. It then called the ASCII function and transformed the number to its equivalent alphabetic letter. I pulled out my ASCII table and looked it up. It was the letter *T*.

The next number read in spelled the letter *o*. The third number transformed to *m*.

Obviously, it was spelling something. The program seemed to always come back to the input number before transforming to a letter. I wondered if that would always be the case. I analyzed it and realized it would as long as the input was a positive number. I checked the data file, and every number was positive.

I took the next number, forty-four, and ran it through as a final check, and it came back to forty-four. When I changed it to its alpha equivalent, it was a comma. Suddenly, it dawned on me that the program had spelled, *Tom,* and there was a lot more to go. My heart started to pound. I started taking the input and merely changing the numbers to their ASCII alphabetic equivalent. When I put it all together, it said, "Tom, will you go with me to preference?"

I could hardly believe it. I was so excited I could scarcely breathe. Bonnie had asked me to the dance. I didn't have much time to think of anything creative to do in return, so I just created an input file for her program. It simply said, "Yes! I would love to!" I knew Bonnie would just check it against the ASCII table.

The next morning in calculus, I gave Bonnie the program. I had written her output on it and put my data numbers underneath it.

She didn't even wait to figure it out. She grabbed an ASCII table from her pack, working on it while Professor Hastings talked. When she finished, she whispered, "Cool!"

After class, we talked all about what we would do. She planned to come to the conference wrestling tournament on Friday and Saturday, and then Saturday afternoon, we would each go home and get dressed for the dance. I was supposed to come to her apartment at seven, and we would have dinner with her roommates and their dates before going to the dance. It all sounded fun.

By the time we finished talking, I was already late to dance class. It was in full swing when I came in—in fact, the dance was a swing. I quickly joined Ginny and the other four girls I danced with.

"Tom," Ginny asked. "Did you ever get a date to preference?"

I nodded and smiled. "I got asked just yesterday."

Ginny smiled. "Good!"

*****

The week seemed long after that. I told my roommates about my date to the dance, and they were all excited for me. But none seemed happier than John. I ordered a corsage, and Bryce said he'd pick up for me since I'd be at the tournament.

I could hardly wait for both the conference tournament and the dance. Friday finally came, and the tournament went well. Jack, Larry, and I, along with a few others from our team, all survived the first rounds and would be vying for the championships in our individual weight classes on Saturday afternoon.

There was a break at lunchtime before the championship round. When I went to the locker room to dress for it, Jack was already there. Soon the room filled with the others from our team who were competing. Larry was the only one who wasn't there yet. That was fairly typical. Larry was always late.

Coach came in with a big smile on his face. He looked around until he saw Jack and me. "Hey, guys. Larry's family is going to be here for the championship round. Don't tell him. Just let it be a surprise."

After Coach left, Jack and I began to talk. Coach had tried to get Larry to invite his family all year. Since Larry had been a national champion the previous year, Coach was justifiably proud of the job Larry had done. Whenever we were wrestling at a university close to where Larry's family lived, Coach told Larry that he should invite his family to come. But Larry never did pass the word on to them. We knew Larry was the youngest in his family of eight kids, but he never told us much more than that.

Larry's reluctance to invite his family made Jack and me curious. We were talking about that when Larry entered the dressing room, and we quickly changed the subject. As soon as we were all dressed, we went to the gym. The other competitors were trickling in, so we all congregated on the mat and started warming up.

Jack and I scanned the crowd but could see no one there that looked like Larry. Larry looked at us quizzically and asked who we were looking for, but we managed to evade his question.

Jack, Larry, and I were all unbeaten in our weights in the conference and were expected to win. The two of them, as previous national champions, dominated their weight classes. I, on the other hand, had some competitors that I had barely beaten in our past meetings. The one who had given me my toughest challenge had worked his way through the other side of the bracket and was to be my opponent in this championship round.

Jack, Larry, and I knew each others' opponents, and as we warmed up, we suggested strategies to each other. Larry and Jack, being more experienced, were especially busy giving me suggestions. Larry was the main one coaching me. Jack was mostly watching all the entrances into the gymnasium.

At one point, as Larry was showing me some weaknesses in my take-down defense, Jack reached over and smacked me. I turned to him, and he pointed toward a doorway on the upper level. There, entering the gym, was the biggest Tongan woman I had ever seen. With her were two men, the spitting images of Larry, but much bigger. I immediately knew they were Larry's mother and brothers.

Larry turned to look at what had grabbed our interest, and he gasped. "Oh, no!"

Jack and I both looked at each other quizzically.

When it was time for the matches to start, we lined up across from our opponents and shook hands with them. As we moved through the weights, our team did well, winning most of the matches in which we had a wrestler.

Finally, it was my turn. I dominated the first round and was a few points ahead going into the second. But in the second round, I made a bad mistake, and my opponent took advantage of it. I fought hard, but it was all I could do to keep from getting pinned. By the time that round ended, I was exhausted. Still, in the third round, as tired as I was, I fought my way back. I pulled within two points by the time there were about twenty seconds left.

"Johnson," Coach yelled, "escape and take him down!"

I fought myself free of his grasp, narrowing the point difference by one. I turned, faked, and shot in. He fought hard not to be taken down, but finally, I was able to pull him up. The buzzer sounded just before I dropped him to the mat. The ref gave the signal, no points. I had lost.

We untangled, and I was exhausted. My opponent, Glen Hamilton, was excited. We had met twice before, and I had beaten him by one point each time. This time it was his turn. Even though he and I were keen competitors, we had also become good friends.

I shook his hand. "Good job, Hamilton. See you at regionals."

As I walked from the mat, I looked up at the crowd. I saw Bonnie there. She smiled at me. In all the excitement of wrestling, her being there had slipped my mind until then. I was embarrassed that she saw me lose, and I hoped she had seen some of my other matches when I won.

But there was another surprise. Sitting off a little way from Bonnie, I saw Ginny, Sally, Danielle, Linda, and Brenda, along with Brett. When they saw me looking their way, they all smiled and waved enthusiastically. I knew Bonnie said she'd be there, but I never expected the others to come.

Then I heard my name called out and looked in the direction of the voice. What I saw surprised me even more than the others. Some of my roommates were there with their preference dates, and John was among them. He also had his female entourage with him. They had taken a break from their prom activities to cheer for me.

Coach's voice brought me back to the team. "Johnson, that was the stupidest move ever! What were you thinking?"

"Yeah," Larry chimed in, his voice full of humor. "What were you thinking? Math?"

"I can handle it, Larry," Coach said sternly. Coach then proceeded to express his displeasure with my performance while Jack prepared for his match. "You've beaten that guy every time before, Johnson. Make sure you do it again at regionals."

Jack's match was next, and I was glad when Coach could turn his attention to that instead of my loss. It ended up not being much of a contest. Jack pinned his opponent in the second round.

Kevin's match was between Jack's and Larry's. Kevin had placed third at nationals the previous year and was very good. He won, but not by much. When he stood at the end of the match, he waved to the crowd. A pretty, blond girl waved back. I had seen her before and was sure she was his fiancée.

Finally, the last match of the afternoon was the heavyweight. Coach gave Larry a last-minute pep talk, and then Larry turned and headed out to the mat. Just as he approached the mat, one female voice boomed out, "Go Shooga Beahr!" That was followed by two male Tongan voices in unison, yelling, "Go, Sugar Bear!"

Larry stopped and shook his head, though he did not turn around. I could see him almost wilt as the crowd roared with laughter. Jack and I turned to each other with incredulous grins.

"Sugar Bear?!" we both said at the same time.

I looked at Larry as he lined up across from his grinning opponent. Larry had beautiful brown skin, dark black hair, and usually had a big ear-to-ear grin. The grin was missing.

Jack and I both laughed. "Sugar Bear?" I said. "Of course, Sugar Bear. What else would he be?"

For the duration of the match, the crowd, led by Larry's enthusiastic mother, cheered for "Shooga Beahr!" Even the opposing side yelled it. By the end of the match, hardly anyone was following the score, and only a few paid attention to the fact that Larry won. They were all too enthralled with the fun of cheering.

But then Larry walked off the mat. Jack and I stood side by side at the edge of the mat, still grinning stupidly. Larry grabbed each of us by our warmup jackets with one of his big bear-paw-size hands. He pulled us so close that our faces were almost touching his, and he growled at us.

"If I hear one more 'Sugar Bear' out of either of you, you are *dead*!"

14

Formal Dances and Wrestling Tournaments

✦

I received a second-place trophy for the tournament, and I was quite disappointed, knowing I should have had a first. Even though I outperformed my opponent in the third round, I was sure Coach would have me run extra the next week. That didn't bother me as much as my loss.

As soon as we had our trophies, I went to see Bonnie. I visited with her for a minute before she headed off to get ready for the dance. Ginny and the girls with her were heading out of the gym, so I hurried to catch up to them.

I touched Ginny's shoulder, and she turned to me. "You're not going to leave before I get to talk to you, are you?" I asked.

She smiled. "We saw you talking to a pretty lady, and we didn't want to interrupt. Is she your date for tonight?"

I nodded. "Her name is Bonnie. Are you all going to the dance tonight?"

"Brenda is going with Brett," Linda said. "But none of the rest of us have dates."

"Why not?" I asked.

Ginny shrugged. "I'm not ready to date yet."

"How about the rest of you?"

Sally laughed. "We've decided to have a girls' night together."

"But you're all such wonderful, pretty girls; I thought your biggest problem would be deciding which guy you wanted to ask."

"We decided we couldn't all ask you," Sally teased.

"Oh, right," I replied, laughing slightly in embarrassment. "But thanks for coming. I wish you could have seen some matches where I won."

"Oh, we did," Danielle said. "We were here for the whole tournament, including yesterday."

"I'm sorry I didn't see you," I replied. "You should have come and said hello."

Sally reached out and playfully squeezed my biceps. "We were too busy looking at your big muscles. We didn't realize how strong you are."

I shrugged in embarrassment, and all the girls laughed. We talked another few minutes, and then I needed to get changed so I could go home and prepare for the dance. By the time I got to the dressing room, most of the other wrestlers were dressed and leaving. They were in a hurry to get to the dance activities.

Jack was still there, and Larry hadn't come in yet.

"Hey," Jack said. "We probably shouldn't tease Larry about his nickname in practice. But I don't see any reason we can't cheer for Sugar Bear when he's in an actual match."

I grinned and nodded my agreement. Just then, Larry walked in.

"Johnson," he said, "I hope that grin isn't about what I think it is. Because if it is, I might just have to wipe it off your face."

Jack laughed. "But you make such a cute. . ."

Larry didn't even let him finish. "Don't say it! Don't even think it!"

Jack and I both laughed.

Soon we were all dressed and heading our separate ways. When I got back to my apartment, my roommates were mostly ready to head off on their dates.

"Great job in the tournament," Bryce said.

"Thanks for coming," I said. "It's too bad you didn't come yesterday when I won."

"You did awesome anyway," David replied.

Bryce handed me the corsage he had picked up for me.

"Thanks," I said, and paid him for it.

"Sure," he replied. "Remember that someday we want to meet this girl."

Most of the girls my roommates were going with had already been to our apartment, so we knew them. But this was my first date with Bonnie, so none of them knew her.

I had already showered in the locker room, so it was just a matter of getting dressed for the dance. I put on my best suit, then tied and retied my tie four times before I felt it was just the right length. I put on the slightest bit of cologne from a bottle that Bryce loaned me. By the time I felt I was the best I could make myself, my roommates had already left, and it was almost time for me to meet Bonnie at her apartment.

As I walked up the hill, my heart pounded, and I could hardly breathe. When I arrived at Bonnie's apartment, I took a deep breath and knocked. Almost instantly, the door opened, and there stood a girl I didn't know, dressed in a beautiful red gown. She smiled and raised her eyebrows as if questioning who I was there to see.

I tried to talk, but my mouth was too dry, and nothing came out. Finally, my voice joined me for the evening, and I asked, "Is Bonnie here?"

The instant I said it, it sounded stupid to me. Of course she was there. It was her apartment.

The girl smiled. "Yes. Come in."

I was shown to a seat on the couch.

"Bonnie will be ready in just a minute."

Soon three other boys arrived and were brought in to sit near where I was. Most of us sat there nervously, saying nothing. But one boy was calm, confident, and talked a lot. I was grateful. It meant the rest of us could say nothing and not feel uncomfortable about it.

Eventually, all four girls joined us. I thought Bonnie was the most beautiful of all, but each boy seemed to feel the same way about his own date. Bonnie was dressed in a sky-blue dress, and her hair, which usually hung to her waist, was pulled slightly back and curled around her face.

The girls invited us into the kitchen, which had a table set for a candlelight dinner. The girls had all worked on the meal, and it was delicious. There was everything from roast chicken to apple pie. None of us boys knew each other, and I didn't know any of the other girls, but soon we were all friends, and it felt like we had known each other forever.

When we finished, it was time for the dance. But first, we had the corsage pinning tradition. Girls were lucky—they could just pin the boutonniere to our lapels. But we had to pin the corsage to the girls' dresses. This meant reaching inside the collar, which, itself, was embarrassing. And then we had to poke the pin through and try not to draw blood from our own finger.

A couple of the boys were more experienced and did a quick, efficient job. The other boy and I both drew blood, me by far the worst. It was humorous for everyone, and I joined in the lighthearted laughter at my expense. After putting on a Band-Aid and helping the girls with their coats, we all headed arm-in-arm with our dates to the dance.

It was a clear night, and the stars shone brightly. Bonnie's apartment was far enough up on the hill that there weren't too many street lights to interfere with the beauty of the night sky. The moon cast a silver path for us to walk. Bonnie smiled at me. She let go of my arm and reached down and took my hand in hers. My feet hardly touched the ground the whole way to the dance.

As we danced, I found myself sensing the style of the music and stepping into the form I learned in class. I suddenly realized the many hours of practice from dance class were starting to embed themselves into my mind and reflexes. Bonnie didn't know most of the dance styles, so we danced simpler dance steps. But all that mattered was that I had someone I liked who also liked me.

When the dance was over, it was hard to have the night end. I would have been happy having it go on forever. We had a pleasant walk back to Bonnie's apartment. She leaned her head against me, and the world just seemed so perfect. Before I left, I asked Bonnie if she would like to join me for Sunday dinner at my apartment the next day. She enthusiastically agreed.

When I arrived back at my apartment, a few of my roommates were there. Gradually, the kitchen grew fuller as more arrived. The room was full of excitement and energy as each told of their wonderful night.

I didn't want to say much. I just wanted to enjoy the wonderful feeling that had engulfed me. It was almost two o'clock before it was quiet enough in the apartment that we could sleep.

The next morning, we had church, then in the evening, I took a roast I had brought from home and cut it into small chunks. I put it into a stew pot and added lots of potatoes, carrots, and other vegetables.

After it had cooked for a while, I turned it to simmer and walked up to Bonnie's apartment. When I knocked, Bonnie opened the door. She stepped out, holding her coat, and I helped her put it on. We then walked hand in hand the six blocks to my apartment.

When we walked into the apartment, my roommates gathered around for introductions. When we sat down to eat, some of my roommates did, too. Some of them planned to eat at the same time as Bonnie and me, and others just wanted to be there to visit.

The one that made me smile the most was Paul. He wasn't eating dinner, but he kept finding reasons that he needed to come into the kitchen. At one point, when I got up to get some bread, Paul pulled me aside.

"Tom," he said, "why does she look so familiar?"

I grinned and whispered, "Did you break your leg, or are you always this lame?"

He stared at me for a moment with a blank stare, and then, suddenly, his eyes lit up. "Yes! That's it!"

I then turned to Bonnie. "Bonnie, you remember my roommate Paul, don't you?"

The disgusted look on her face told volumes. She nodded. "Of course."

"So," Paul said, "how did you two meet?"

"Bonnie is the only girl in my calculus and programming classes," I replied.

"That explains a lot," Paul muttered.

Bonnie and I had a fun meal together. Besides the delicious stew, I had bread from home that my mother had made, and some home-canned fruit. For dessert, I brought out some chocolate chip cookies I had made.

About halfway through our meal, Joe and David came with their dates, the same girls from the night before. The two girls, Rochelle and Shannon, were roommates. Joe and Rochelle were engaged, but the preference dance was David and Shannon's first date.

Joe and David had made some lasagna, and it smelled good. They liked the smell of the meat and vegetables I made, so they joined us, and we all shared both meals. Joe and David had purchased a cream pie, and we put that with the cookies, and it was better for all of us.

When I walked Bonnie back to her apartment, she stayed close to me, and I felt life couldn't get any better.

*****

Through the next week, Bonnie and I ate dinner together almost every night. Either she would accept the invitation to my apartment, or I would go to hers. When it was my turn to prepare the meal, I would put something together the night before since I barely finished wrestling practice in time.

When Thursday came, I went to calculus, and Bonnie brought me a poster. It wished me good luck at the Regional Wrestling Tournament. She was in a calligraphy class and had written it in her best penmanship.

Dance class was the last class I could attend for the day since our wrestling team left for the tournament right afterward. I saved the last dance for Ginny as always, and as we finished, she held on to my hand and took me over to where her backpack was. The other girls I danced with gathered around as Ginny pulled out some cookies and handed them to me with a smile. "This is from all of us for good luck. But only after you weigh in."

There was also a good luck card signed by all of them. They all hugged me goodbye. Then I hurried to my apartment, grabbed my small duffle bag, and tied on a tie. Coach insisted that since we were representing our school, we had to dress up. He also said we acted better when we did. As soon as my tie was on, I went to meet the team.

We loaded into the van and were soon on our way. Late in the evening, we got to Coeur d'Alene, Idaho, where the tournament was to be held. After weigh-ins, we went to a restaurant to eat. While we were eating, a young man came up and said hello.

Coach laughed. "Won't you look at what the dog dragged in?" The young man laughed, too, and Coach continued. "So, what are you up to now, Jones?"

"I'm wrestling for another school now," the young man replied.

"How are you doing financially and academically?" Coach asked.

"I have a job now," the young man replied. "So, I have plenty of money to stay in school here."

"That's wonderful," Coach said. "What do you do?"

"I clean the executive suite at the college when they need it done. They pay me five hundred dollars per week to be on call to do it whenever they need."

"How much time does it take to clean?" Coach asked.

The young man shrugged. "I don't know. I'm still just on call. They haven't needed me to do it yet."

"Wow!" Larry said. "Sign me up for that job."

Coach growled something at Larry and then turned back to the young man. "I'm glad you're doing well."

"Yes. And I'm pulling straight As," the young man replied.

"Really?" Coach said. "What are you majoring in?"

Jones shrugged again. "I'm not sure. I think it's some kind of science or something. I don't attend class."

"How do you pull As if you don't attend class?" Coach asked.

"My coach works it out for me."

The young man visited for another minute and then went back to his team.

After he left, Larry teasingly asked, "What school did he say he wrestled for? I need to find out if they need a heavyweight."

"Larry," Coach scolded, "you're too good a man to do that kind of thing. Jones was a good wrestler, but schools that break NCAA rules and encourage their athletes to do so as well are beneath the standards of the life you live."

We thought the rest of the meal couldn't be very eventful after that. But at one point, Larry decided to show us the best way to get ketchup from a bottle. When it didn't come out, he started pounding it, and when his hand slipped, four of us, including Jack and me, ended up covered in ketchup. We thought we would take him down and pour ketchup all over him, but Coach said the four of us, with our white shirts and ties ruined, was enough.

As we were trying to scrub our clothes in the bathroom, Jack said, "I'm for sure calling Larry 'Sugar Bear' now."

*****

The next day was probably the toughest tournament I had ever wrestled in. I won all of my matches, but none by more than three points. My second opponent was Glen Hamilton, the wrestler who beat me in the conference championship the previous week. I was careful not to make any mistakes, and I won.

When I came off the mat, Coach smacked me on the back. "That's more like it, Johnson."

By the end of the day, half of our teammates were out. Jack, Larry, Kevin, and I were still undefeated in the tournament in the upper weights. Seth, at one hundred and thirty-three pounds, had lost but was working up through the loser bracket. I had watched Jack and Larry dominate their weight classes all season, but here they both had matches they barely won. Jack especially came close to losing. He was thrown on his back for almost a full round. He ended up winning by a take-down in the final seconds.

On Saturday, my first match was in the semifinals. If I won it, I couldn't get lower than second and would go to nationals for sure. But in the middle of the second round, there was a loud pop, and I felt an explosion of pain in my knee. Even though I was ahead, my opponent seemed to sense my distress and used it against me, twisting my leg every chance he got. I ended up losing by two points.

When the match was over, I tried to stand and fell. I tried again and fell.

Coach came out on the mat. "Johnson, just stay down."

Eventually, Coach and Jack, one under each arm, helped me to the side. My knee was swelling quickly.

"We heard the pop clear over at the side of the mat," Coach said. "Are you going to be all right?"

I gritted my teeth and tried to grin. "Do I have a choice?"

My knee had swelled up like a small basketball and was still getting bigger. While the others continued wrestling, Coach Pearson, the assistant coach, took me to the nearest medical clinic.

The doctor said, "You've torn some ligaments. It should heal on its own, but we should drain some fluid out of it."

He took a long syringe with an equally long needle and stuck it into the area around my knee. He drew out multiple syringes full of slightly bloody fluid.

"Can I go back and finish wrestling?" I asked.

He looked between Coach Pearson and me and shrugged. "I wouldn't suggest it. But if you do, wrap it heavily to make sure you don't tear more. I can give you a shot of cortisone to help it heal faster, but it goes in the bone and is very painful."

I thought of wrestling through the rest of the day and considered going without. But then I thought of continuing dance practice and knew I needed to heal quickly.

"Do it," I said.

The doctor stuck the needle into my leg, and when it went into the bone, I didn't think there could be anything more painful. But when he squeezed the fluid in, the burn in the bone of my leg felt like the fire of Hades. I had to pant to deal with the pain.

We went back to the tournament, and Coach Pearson explained the diagnosis.

Coach asked, "Well, Johnson, what will it be? Continue competing or not?"

"I still want to try for third to see if I can make it to nationals."

Coach nodded, so Jack and Larry wrapped my leg. I learned that Jack and Larry had both won while I was gone, earning their spots in the championship round. Kevin and Seth had lost, so they would join me in fighting for third.

My next match came way too soon. My leg was wrapped so tight I couldn't bend it at all. It also made an obvious target for my opponent. Despite that, I was able to pull a win. When I made my way to the side of the mat, the world was spinning. Coach grabbed me, and he and Larry helped me to the bench.

Coach made me look at him and said, "Johnson, you're as white as a ghost. Are you all right?"

I nodded, but I felt nauseous. I asked Larry to help me to the locker room. He did, and I was no sooner in there then I found a toilet so I could throw up. Once I had done that, I felt better.

Kevin and Seth both won their matches. That meant the three of us would be wrestling for third in our weights.

In the next round, Seth won, taking third. There were a few more matches, and then I was up again.

Jack applied a few more wraps of tape. When I stood, I wobbled, partly because I couldn't bend my leg at all.

Coach grabbed me by the shoulders and looked into my face. "Johnson, you don't have to do this."

"If I have a chance of making it to nationals next week, I've got to try."

"Would you even be able to wrestle next week if you won?" he asked.

I shrugged. "I guess I would find out next week. But if I don't try, I won't ever know." I paused a second, and then asked, "By the way, Coach, where are we on team points?"

"Right now, we're barely holding on to second. As luck would have it, your opponent is on the team that is close behind us in third place."

I went to the middle of the mat and shook hands with my opponent. The ref had no sooner blown the whistle than the other wrestler shot in and slammed my hurt leg. The pain engulfed me. I went down, and he worked that leg hard. I was grateful it was wrapped too much for him to bend it, but the pain was still excruciating.

By the time we went to the second round, I was quite a few points behind. I took top position and was able to turn him and score a few points, bringing my score closer to his lead, but I was unable to do more, having only the strength of one leg to support me.

In the third round, he worked my leg again, and I knew I couldn't win against him with the amount of pain I felt. Instead, I turned my focus to fighting as hard as I could so that he would gain as few points as possible, thus lessening his team's point gain. He won by only five, and I felt lucky to keep it to that. It meant he only gained the minimal team points for his win.

If he had won by eight points or more, his team would have received more team points. It was the only consolation I had since I would have fourth place and not go to nationals.

Kevin won his match, and had third, so he would be going. His win also gave us a few team points.

We had a slight break before the championship matches. The wrap around my leg felt like it was cutting my leg in pieces, so Coach took some medical scissors and started snipping through it. He had only cut a little when it exploded, ripping the rest of the way.

My leg was swollen much as before. Coach Pearson took me back to the medical clinic to have the fluid drained from it, and then we went to a local drug store to get me a pair of crutches. By the time we got back, the championship round was starting. Jack won his match. Larry fought hard, but he lost by a few points to a man the size of a small pickup.

As the matches finished, they called the top three placers in that weight to the medal stand. No medal was given for fourth, so I would have nothing to show for my effort except my swollen leg.

After the individual medals had been given, it was time for the team trophies. One team had dominated the tournament. They won first in half of the weight classes and were definitely in first place. The question was who would be the second and third place teams. When our team was called out for second, and the team of my opponent in the last match for third, our scores were announced, and we had beaten them by only one point.

Coach turned to me and patted me on the back. "Johnson, if you had forfeited that match or lost by a major decision or a pin, we wouldn't have had second."

Later we learned that there was only a point difference between third and fourth place, too. If I had forfeited or lost by a major decision, we not only wouldn't have won second, we would have placed fourth and wouldn't have had any trophy at all.

That was a fair amount of consolation to me, and my teammates patted me on the back. Coach's congratulatory words also helped, but nothing could entirely take away the disappointment of not going to nationals.

We stayed in the hotel that night, and by seven o'clock Sunday morning, we were heading back home. I wasn't the only one who was disappointed. Others had worked hard, as well, and had not made it to nationals. Larry was disappointed in his second place finish, too, even though he would still be going.

It was a long drive and seemed even more so with the pain in my knee. I was given a seat on the aisle side of the van so I could stick my leg out, and that helped, but I felt every little jarring bump. Whenever we stopped to eat or get gas, I got out and tried to loosen the muscles in my leg. When we arrived back at the college, Jack offered to carry my duffle bag to my apartment.

I just slung it over my shoulders and said I'd be okay. I made my way slowly across campus on my crutches. It was nine o'clock, and all my roommates were there. When I came in, they all had to hear the story.

When I finished, David said, "Two girls called to see if you were home and ask how you did. One was named Bonnie, and one was named Ginny."

I called both of them and told them all about it, and it was fun to talk to them. That night, as I climbed into bed, it felt strange to know that for me, wrestling season was over.

15
More Dance Practice and Cancelled Dates

✛

When I came into calculus on crutches Monday, Bonnie was there to meet me. "How are you doing?" she asked.

"I'm okay," I replied. "The doctor said I should gradually put more weight on it, and by the end of the week, I shouldn't need the crutches. I just can't do anything that might stress the tendons as they heal."

She then wanted to hear about the tournament in more detail than I shared on the phone.

At dance class, Ginny and the other four girls I danced with were waiting for me. Ginny pulled me into a big hug.

"When I heard you were hurt, I was worried. Are you okay? Is there anything I can do to help?"

"And us, too?" Danielle added.

I laughed. "I'm okay. I might not be able to dance today, but I should be able to by about midweek."

"Can we carry your pack or something?" Sally asked.

Before I could answer, she took it.

"Actually, I'm plenty capable of . . ."

"Oh, don't be so macho," Sally said. "We want to help."

The other girls all nodded, and it was impossible to convince them I was okay. They kept close to me as I made my way to the row of chairs on the side. Linda held out a plastic bag full of brownies.

"We thought you could use something to cheer you up."

Since I couldn't dance, I sat on the side, ate brownies, and watched the other dancers. Ginny sat on one side of me the whole hour, and Sally, Linda, Brenda, and Danielle traded off sitting on the other side. During the dances, the girls helped me see what other dancers did that was good and what could be better.

When the hour ended, it was all I could do to get my pack back from Sally. She wanted to carry it to my next class for me. She seemed skeptical when I said I could carry it myself.

"I did carry it here," I said, and she reluctantly let me have it.

By Wednesday, I was off the crutches and able to start dancing a little. My leg was still wrapped and stiff. Dr. Carlson said it would give me a good chance to practice keeping a straight posture. He worked with me on it, and once the girls understood what he wanted, they all coached me, too. They also quit fawning over me so much. I will admit I kind of enjoyed their attention, but I was ready to have things back to normal.

As we finished class on Wednesday, Ginny gathered together the girls I danced with at my request.

"Now that I don't have wrestling practice, I can spend more hours practicing during that time," I said.

"When would that be?" Danielle asked.

"Normally, I have to leave during the last part of the Performance Dance Team practice for wrestling. But since wrestling is over, I could spend the two wrestling-practice hours in extra dance practice."

The girls thought that would be a good idea. They decided to split up which days they stayed. They would rotate two per night, with me spending extra practice time with Ginny. Ginny would be Monday and Thursday, Danielle and Sally would be on Tuesday, and Brenda and Linda would be on Wednesday. Every other Friday, Danielle and Sally would alternate with Brenda and Linda. This way I ended up with lots of practice with each of them.

On Saturday night, I always went to the dance with Bonnie. I looked forward to the evening with her. But on the other three dance nights, I danced with Ginny and the other four girls in our group. Brett would come with Brenda, and he didn't seem to mind at all when she would take turns practicing with me. He would dance with one of the other girls, and Brenda was okay with that, too.

But the thing that was most important to me was that Ginny always saved the last dance for me. I always looked forward to ending the evening with her. That Friday, after we finished, I walked her home, as I often did. When we got to Ginny's door, she paused before going in.

"Tom, when you go home and work on the weekend, what's it like?"

"Well, we own a large dairy farm with lots of cattle. I mostly spend time working with the cattle, fixing fence, hauling hay to the feeding barn, and things like that."

"Would it be okay if I tagged along with you on some weekends?"

"I'd love to have you along any weekend you want to go. But I leave between five and five-thirty in the morning."

"Would your parents be okay with me coming?"

"I'm sure they'd love to have you come. I have nine siblings, but I only have one younger brother and one younger sister left at home. I'm sure my mother would include you in like another daughter, and my sister would enjoy feeling she has a sister home again. You probably wouldn't see me much, though, since I only come in for lunch."

"Can I go tomorrow?" she asked.

"Of course," I replied. "I'll pick you up at five-thirty."

She hugged me. "Thanks. I look forward to it."

She slipped into her apartment, and I walked home, looking forward to more time with her.

The next morning, I pulled up in front of her apartment. I climbed out and was walking to the door when she came out, ready to go. Her excitement and enthusiasm were boundless. As we traveled, the moon was high in the sky. The streets were empty, and it was calm. I loved that time of day. Almost everyone was still asleep, and the world was peaceful.

As I predicted, my mother and sister were especially excited to have Ginny there. Mom had breakfast for us, and I was soon out working. I watched the sun rise as I loaded hay from the stack onto the truck. We did it all by hand, and it was backbreaking work. I had to be extra careful because of my leg, but I was still able to do it.

At noon, I stopped for lunch. The house smelled of hot bread, cookies, and pies. Mom and Ginny had made a good, hearty soup. We all ate together, and I enjoyed that short time with Ginny. I was sweaty and dirty from work, but that didn't seem to bother her at all.

As I returned to work, the wrapping around my leg reminded me that I was missing the national tournament.

By the time I finished up my work, the sun was dropping toward the western horizon.

Ginny and I ate dinner with my family. Ginny and Mom had made fried chicken and mashed potatoes with rhubarb pie for dessert.

"Have you ever had rhubarb pie before?" I asked Ginny.

She nodded. "I grew up on a ranch in Montana. It was a lot like here."

As Ginny and I drove back to the college, the sun disappeared below the horizon and shone its light on the clouds above. The orange and red hues looked like fire dancing across the sky.

Ginny and I talked all the way back. I learned more about her years growing up on a ranch. She also talked more about her time dancing and about Alex. We had an unusual friendship. Ginny didn't want anything romantic between us, but I felt she was one of the greatest friends I had ever had. I think she felt the same way about me.

Every week that I went home after that, Ginny went with me. She seemed to feel right at ease with my family, and though I didn't get a chance to see her much during the day, I especially relished our time traveling together.

*****

Ricks College tried to have a formal dance about every three weeks, so we had another one coming up soon. That Saturday night, after Ginny's trip home with me, I asked Bonnie to the formal, and she readily accepted. My roommates had different groups they planned their formal dates with. Joe and David invited me to join with them and their dates. I was excited about that.

On Sunday, I was able to find out the results for those who went to nationals. I learned that Jack won first, Larry won second, and Kevin and Seth won third. We ended up with fourth as a team in the tournament. I was happy our team brought home a trophy, but I was sad I wasn't part of it.

On Tuesday, there was going to be a big banquet for the wrestling team. We could bring a guest, so I asked Bonnie to go. She said she would be delighted.

The banquet was fun. Bonnie and I sat with Larry, Jack, and their dates. I received the award for being the top academic athlete on the team. Larry smacked me as I headed up to get it.

"Big surprise," he said.

Coach also told everyone about how I had fought to wrestle despite my injury, and that gave us second for the Regional Tournament. For that honor, he gave me a roll of gauze for my leg. There were lots of other gag gifts for different wrestlers, and it was fun.

When the banquet was over, Kevin immediately brought his fiancée over.

"Hi, Tom," he said. "Have you met Melanie?"

"Not personally," I replied, shaking her hand.

He looked at me and then at Bonnie.

"Oh," I said. "Excuse my manners. This is Bonnie."

He took her hand in his, and he held it for a long time as he chatted away. I didn't care for the way he was looking at Bonnie. Melanie kept shifting from foot to foot and looking down, and I could tell she wasn't comfortable with it, either. Kevin didn't even try to meet Jack's or Larry's dates.

The next morning in math class, Bonnie never came to check her answers with me. I looked out the door of the room, and I could see her standing there holding Kevin's hand. Then I saw him kiss her before she slipped into the room just as Dr. Hastings started class. She had turned and seen me watching her. She averted her eyes from me, and neither of us said anything.

When class ended, she grabbed my arm. "Tom, can we talk? I need to ask you something."

I nodded, and we went out into the hall and found a quiet place.

"Tom," she said, "Kevin and I . . ."

She paused and looked away.

"You like each other?" I asked.

She nodded. "A lot."

"But you don't know him very well. And what about his fiancée?"

"He said it isn't working out with him and his fiancée, and he's going to call off the engagement. I know we just met, but there was this instant thing between us, and it just seems right."

"So, what did you want to ask me?"

She took a deep breath and spoke quietly, her eyes on the floor. "Tom, Kevin asked me to go to the midwinter formal this Saturday with him. But I promised you I'd go with you, and I . . ."

She paused, and her voice wandered off.

I knew what was coming, and my heart wrenched within me.

"You'd really like to go with him, wouldn't you?" I asked.

She looked at me and nodded. "It all just seems so right, he and I."

As much as I wanted to spend time with Bonnie, I didn't want her feeling stuck with me when she wanted to be with someone else.

"Well," I replied, "if you want to go with him, you should go with him."

She smiled. "Really?"

I nodded, and she hugged me.

I still hoped that maybe she would want to spend some time with me, so I asked, "What about the other Saturday night dances?"

"We were hoping we could do those, too," she replied.

When she said that, I knew she was ending our relationship altogether.

"Of course, you should go with him, if that's what you want," I said.

"Thanks, Tom," she said. "I appreciate you being so understanding."

I just nodded, and she hugged me once more before running down the hall to meet Kevin, who was waiting for her.

I stood there for a short time, feeling like someone had just knocked the wind out of me. I slowly made my way to dance class. By the time I arrived, I was late, and the class was already in progress. I tried to act cheerful. But Ginny noticed something was wrong, as she always did. When she asked me about it, I said that I had a lot on my mind.

Later, when I came into my apartment, Joe and David were finalizing plans for the dance.

"We're planning on going to dinner at about six o'clock," Joe said to me. "Will you be back from work in time for that?"

"You guys will have to do this one without me," I replied.

"What happened?" David asked.

"Bonnie decided she'd prefer to go with someone else."

Bryce had come in during the last of that, and he shook his head. "If you didn't have bad luck in dating, you wouldn't have any luck at all."

Despite how much I hurt, I smiled slightly at his words. Then I took my books and headed to the library. I studied until it was time to practice dance. Practice with Ginny during the Performance Dance class went well. So did evening practice with Brenda and Linda. That evening, I enjoyed dancing with all the girls, and it helped me feel better. But it was impossible to forget about Bonnie.

When I arrived back at my apartment, Joe and David were waiting for me.

"Hey, we have the perfect solution to your problem," David said.

"You remember Rochelle and Shannon's roommate Carol, don't you?" Joe asked.

I nodded. I didn't know her well, but I had met her at church.

"It's the perfect solution," David said. "Three roommates dating three roommates. Carol hasn't had a date all semester. She'd love to go with you."

"Are you sure?" I asked.

Joe nodded. "We already asked her."

I agreed to go, partly because I knew Carol a little bit, and partly because I thought it would help me forget about Bonnie. We continued planning our weekend, and it was fun to think about still doing a dinner and activities with my roommates.

The next day, when I went to calculus, Bonnie didn't come early enough for me to check my answers with her. I asked some other guys if I could check with them.

One of them laughed and said, "Like we would be stupid enough to check our answers with a dumb athlete."

Math class had already started when Bonnie finally came in, and I was sure she'd been out in the hall with Kevin. There was another surprise in class that day. Dr. Hastings announced a pop quiz. Everyone groaned, even me, but I was glad I had done my homework, even if I didn't have the chance to check it with anyone else. He said that was all we would do for the day and that we could leave when we were done.

Bonnie was done in about fifteen minutes and had soon gone back to Kevin. After thirty minutes, everyone in the class was done except me. I was still only halfway through and felt I must be doing horribly compared to everyone else. I wondered if there were concepts I had missed while I was gone for wrestling. It wasn't that I didn't know the problems; it was just that they were long and hard. At the end of the hour, I turned in my paper, barely finishing the last problem on time.

"How do you think you did?" Dr. Hastings asked.

"I think I knew how to do them all," I said, "but I obviously must not have known as much as everyone else."

He didn't say anything, so I packed up and left.

The next day in class, Dr. Hastings handed our tests back and told us not to discuss the problems on them. He said the average on the test was eighty percent. I looked at my test, and I had seventy percent. My heart sank.

"How did you do?" Bonnie asked.

"Seventy. How about you?"

"One hundred," she replied.

I just nodded and tried not to think about it. When class ended, Dr. Hastings called me by name and asked me to stay.

After everyone left, he sat on the edge of his desk and looked at me. "Mr. Johnson, have you been dating Bonnie?"

"Yes," I replied.

"Did I not expressly condemn asking her out?"

"Yes, Sir," I replied. "That's why I didn't."

The look on his face changed from stern to stunned. "But if you were dating her . . ."

"She asked me," I said.

"Oh, I see," he replied. "I'm sorry. That whole quiz thing yesterday was to see if you knew the material and to make sure you weren't getting the tests dishonestly. Your quiz was much different than everyone else's, and much, much harder. I was surprised you scored as high as you did. I will add points to your score, but I would like you to keep this just between the two of us. You have proven yourself, and, especially if she asked you first, I think it's okay if you keep dating her."

"She's not dating me anymore," I replied. "She decided she likes someone else."

"When did that happen?" he asked.

"Two days ago. She ended our relationship."

"Then I'm especially sorry I put you through this," he said. "You probably didn't need it with her doing that to you."

I sighed. "It's alright. But I do wish I still had someone to check my answers with."

"What do you mean?"

"Bonnie and I used to check our homework answers before class, but the last couple of days, she hasn't come until after class has started. I tried to see if anyone else would check answers with me, but they think I'm stupid because I'm an athlete."

He laughed. "Next to Bonnie and Fred Taylor, you're the best student in the class." He paused a moment and then said, "Why don't you check your answers with Fred?"

"Who's Fred?"

"He's that small guy with big glasses that sits on the right side of the class about halfway back. No one sits by him. He said others aren't kind to him, and nobody will check answers with him, either."

"If no one wants to sit by him, would it be okay if I just took that seat?" I asked. "I don't think anybody will miss me sitting up front."

"By anybody, you mean Bonnie?"

I nodded. "Basically."

"That would be fine for you to switch seats," he said.

I was late to dance class again, and I told Dr. Carlson that my teacher held me over. He told me that he wouldn't mark me late, but that I needed to jump right in and start dancing. Dancing with the girls in our group helped me feel better.

That Friday evening, it was Sally's and Danielle's turn to stay for dance practice with me. With their fun-loving spirits, by the time the two hours were up, my spirits were much higher. That evening, I met the girls at the evening dance and practiced with all of them. I had lots of fun.

The next day, I went home to work for my father, and Ginny went with me. But I made sure we came back early enough to be ready for the dinner by six o'clock. Our other roommates were eating at restaurants, but Joe, David, and I were making dinner together at our apartment. David had put a small turkey in to cook. I was in charge of the potatoes, and the brownies for dessert. Joe had purchased a Jell-O and corn.

Since I barely knew Carol, we decided I would stay and watch over dinner while Joe and David went to get the girls. When they walked in, I thought Carol was beautiful. She was wearing a pink dress, and she had long, dark brown hair curled in ringlets down her back. She smiled at me, and much of the hurt from not being with Bonnie left me. I thought maybe the powers of the universe decided I needed a social break and provided me with someone who could help me get over my feelings for Bonnie.

We all had an excellent dinner together. We had three hours before the dance started, so I had time to get to know Carol. We played a few games of UNO after dinner before eating the dessert. Carol said I made the best brownies in the world, even though I had used a mix.

When it finally came time for the dance, we walked up to the student activity center. It was a beautiful February night, and it was just chilly enough that the girls stayed close to us. It was an excellent night of dancing.

Carol had taken social dance, and we were able to dance many of the dances from my class. She was nowhere near as polished as the girls that I danced with in class, but she and I blended together better as the night wore on. I felt more confident in my dancing, and that helped.

I did see Kevin and Bonnie once, but I quickly steered Carol across the dance floor away from them.

*****

In Monday's calculus class, I quickly realized who Fred Taylor was. He was a small, wimpy looking guy that sat alone on the side of the room. I had never really noticed him much before. When I sat down by him and asked if we could check our homework answers, his face lit up, and he nodded vehemently. I found I had one wrong. He also had one wrong, but they were different ones, so we were able to help each other.

As we were working, three boys came by. One of them knocked Fred's books to the floor. I was sure it wasn't an accident.

"Oh, sorry, Nerdboy," the boy said. He and his friends laughed and went to their seats.

I picked Fred's books up for him, and I was fuming.

The next day as Fred and I were checking our answers, I saw the boys coming. As the same boy reached for Fred's books, I grabbed his wrist. With my fast wrestling reflexes, I did it so quickly that the boy said, "Sorry, Nerdboy," before he realized the books had not even been brushed to the floor.

I held his wrist tightly and said, "If you're sorry, you won't do it."

The boy's two friends stepped up beside him as if challenging me.

105

I stood to face them. They knew I was on the wrestling team. They were the ones who had called me a dumb athlete. They acted tough for a moment, as if they would truly challenge me, but when I didn't back down, one of them faltered and said, "Come on, Will. Let's go."

After the boys went to their seats, Fred said, "Hey, thanks, man."

"No problem," I said as I sat back down.

No one ever bothered Fred again after that.

*****

Joe, David, Rochelle, Shannon, Carol, and I spent a lot of time together after that first dance. Not only did I grow to care for Carol, but I became better friends with the others. We did something together every night. We always had dinner together. Sometimes Joe, David, and I made dinner, and we ate at our apartment. Sometimes the girls made dinner, and we ate at theirs. And even when we ate at the girls' apartment, we sometimes brought food or desserts with us as they did when they came to ours.

We loved to play UNO, and when we did, it was always at our apartment. Many of our roommates joined us. We usually had ten or more playing. I went home every week on Saturdays to work, but I always made sure I was back in time to go to the dance with Carol. Ginny knew that was why I came back, and she encouraged it.

The weeks flew by. I spent every free minute between classes on homework so I could do other things in the evening. I spent lots of time practicing dance with Ginny and the other girls, and I looked forward to that time. And the better I became, the more I enjoyed it. I went to the weekday, evening dances to practice with them, but I always saved Saturday dances for Carol.

Before I knew it, we were into the first part of March. The next formal dance was coming, and Joe, David, and I decided we would ask Rochelle, Shannon, and Carol all at the same time. We took a simple song, changed the lyrics, and sang it as best we could in three-part harmony. The girls hugged us, and all said yes. It was a good time.

After we finished the evening dance on the week before the Spring Formal, we were walking the girls back to their apartment, talking about plans for the next week, when Carol pulled me aside.

"Tom," she said, "there's one thing I should tell you."

"What?" I asked.

"I've been pen pals for a couple of years with a guy named Mitch who is in the Navy. I've only met him once, but he's getting out soon and wants to come see me."

"How soon?" I asked.

"He doesn't know. It's a medical release, so it's whenever the Navy decides. But don't worry, there's nothing between us. You're the greatest guy I've ever known, and I want to stick with you."

"Thanks," I said.

And with her assurance, I put it out of my mind, and we walked on to her apartment.

16
A World Falling Apart
✦

hurch was enjoyable on Sunday. David sat by Shannon, Joe sat with Rochelle, and I sat with Carol. It felt good to have friends, especially one that was a young lady. I enjoyed the closeness I felt to Carol. After church, I held her hand as I walked her back to her apartment. I had invited her to lunch, but she said there was something important she had to do. She didn't want to elaborate, so I didn't question her further.

Afterward, I walked back to my apartment. David and Joe were there with Shannon and Rochelle, preparing tuna fish sandwiches. I pulled out some of my homemade bread.

"Trade you some tuna for some homemade bread," Joe said.

"Sounds like a deal," I replied.

We all ate together. When we finished, I offered them some chocolate chip cookies. "It's my turn for dessert tonight," I said, "and I made plenty."

Dinner was going to be at the girls' apartment, but, as we often did, we traded who made certain things. Rochelle was in charge of the main meal, and I was bringing cookies for dessert.

When lunch was over, I offered to clean up while David and Joe walked with the girls to their apartment. I finished about the time they returned. While they visited, I took a nap. After I woke, I dressed in some nice Sunday slacks and a white shirt. I visited with Joe and David before we headed to the girls' apartment for dinner.

"Tom, was Carol acting strange today?" Joe asked.

I shook my head. "No. Why do you ask?"

"When we walked the girls back to their apartment this afternoon, she acted funny. It was almost like she didn't want us there."

David nodded in agreement. "It was like, 'don't let the door hit your backside on the way out.'"

"She didn't say why she wouldn't join us for lunch, did she?" Joe asked.

"No, other than to say she had something important she had to do at her apartment."

"What could that be?" David wondered aloud, but no one had an answer.

As six o'clock rolled around, I grabbed the big plate of cookies I had saved for dinner. I made sure to save the very best ones, hoping to impress Carol. The three of us walked down to the girls' apartment, talking and laughing as we went. The conversation from earlier was forgotten.

We climbed the stairs, and Joe knocked on the door. Carol opened it, and she had a strange look on her face. She motioned Joe and David in, but as I was about to walk in, she stepped in front of me and forcefully pushed me back out on the landing.

"Tom, I need to talk to you."

I thought she meant privately, but she didn't close the door. If anything, she deliberately opened it wider.

"What is it, Carol?" I asked.

She took a deep breath and then spoke forcefully. "Tom, I don't want to see you anymore."

The shock I felt stunned me, and I couldn't speak for a moment. When I finally was able to say something, I asked, "Did I do something wrong?"

Carol looked at the open door, and a slight smile creased her lips. She shook her head.

"No. It's just that you are the dullest, most average guy I've ever met. You think you're cool because you're an athlete, but wrestling is a stupid sport. You think you're interesting because you take math classes, but math is only for nerds, and you're as nerdy as they come. But mostly, you're just dull, common, and average. I want someone who is exciting."

Carol continued to tell me how uninteresting I was, and I was so shocked I couldn't say anything. It seemed like she went on forever, though I'm sure it was probably only a few minutes, but I was so stunned I couldn't move. What paralyzed my understanding more than anything was the smug grin on her face as she talked. She seemed to enjoy saying the things she was saying.

I was confused. Only a few hours earlier, she was sitting close by me in church and then walking hand in hand with me to her apartment. But now, the more she talked, the meaner things she said.

And then, as she continued, some memories started to come to my mind. I thought of the conversation I'd had earlier with Joe and David. I thought of her having to get home for something important. I thought of what she'd said the previous night on the way home from the dance. I watched her continually glancing at the open door. Suddenly, it was as if my mind pulled everything together in the only reasonable explanation it could find, and I was sure I knew what had happened.

"And mostly," she said, as if finally concluding, "you're just a loser. You're just a common nobody, and you'll never be more than just a common nobody, dull and unexciting. I want more than that. I want to be somebody in life and not be tied to a loser that's never going to amount to anything."

She finally stopped. I struggled to lift my eyes from the floor, but I felt I had to.

I looked into her eyes and asked, "So you're saying Mitch is here, and you want me to leave?"

Instantly, the smug smile on her face disappeared and was replaced with one of shock. I could tell she didn't expect me to guess. She lowered her eyes and slowly nodded.

"I presume you're also saying you don't want to go with me to the dance this Saturday because you would prefer to go with him?"

She never even looked up, but slowly nodded.

"Well, then," I said, "if you would prefer to go with him, you should." I paused for a moment, but she never looked at me, so I continued. "And you're also saying you want me totally out of your life?"

This time she looked up at me for an instant. She paused for some time, looked at the open door, and then lowered her eyes again as she slowly nodded.

"Okay. I promise never to bother you again," I said. She looked up at me then slowly lowered her eyes as I continued. "And Carol, thank you."

She looked up at me with total bewilderment showing on her face, as if questioning what I was saying.

"Thank you for the good times we've had together, and thank you for letting me know how you feel about me," I said. "I'm sorry I have been such a disappointment to you, but I'd rather have you tell me you can't stand me than pretend you care for me when you don't. Thank you for being honest with me." I then reached out my hand. "All the best to you."

She looked at my hand, then looked into my eyes. She then lowered her eyes to look at my hand again and slowly reached out and took it. We shook hands, and I turned to leave, then I remembered the cookies and turned back to her.

I held out the plate of cookies. "I almost forgot these. It was my turn for dessert tonight."

I dropped the plate into her hands, and then I turned and walked briskly down the stairs. When I reached the bottom, she called out to me.

"Tom?"

I turned back to her, and she started to speak, but then she looked at the open door and stopped. She lowered her eyes and spoke quietly. "Goodbye, Tom."

"Goodbye," I replied.

I turned and headed up the street toward my apartment, unable to believe what had just happened. The farther I went, the faster I walked. I felt a desperate need to get away from there, and it was as if my heart was taking control of my body. Suddenly, without thinking, I broke into a run. I ran up the hill past our apartment. I ran faster and faster. The pain in my heart was pushing me harder and harder.

I ran past Bonnie's apartment and continued past the water tower on the hill. I came to the T in the road where I usually turned right to make the five-mile loop, but this time I turned left onto the road leading to the farmland on the hillside. It quickly turned to gravel.

I continued to run, pushing myself, making the breath pull hard into my lungs, and still my heart would not let me stop. The road turned from gravel to dirt, and my feet pounded along the edges of muddy ruts, and still I continued. The pain I began to feel in my body seemed to be fighting against the pain I felt in my heart, each battling for domination over the other. As I continued mile after mile, the pain in my muscles and lungs gradually overpowered the ache in my heart, and with it, my pace slowed. Still, I continued on as the pain in my body continued to draw away the pain in my heart until all that was left was numbness.

When I could run no more, I slowed to a walk. Ahead, on the side of the road, a smaller road led into a field. Beside that smaller road was a large boulder. I made my way to the rock and sat down on it, still breathing hard.

The sun was beginning to set in the west, painting the sky in different red and orange hues. It reflected on the snow in the field like a mirrored projection on a silver screen. Realizing the sun was setting was the first time I realized how long I had been running. I looked back toward town and could barely see the top of the houses on the hill. They looked like miniature toys. As I sat there, the stillness of the evening filling the air, I felt a calmness begin to settle over me.

As the evening light faded, I could hear the swish of bats flying back and forth chasing insects. In the distance, I could hear the hooting of an owl as it prepared for its night foray to find food. I don't know how long I sat there, but it must have been hours as dark as it was. My mind felt blank except for the sense of calm around myself, but I suddenly realized I was shivering.

I only had on a light jacket, and the temperature was dropping quickly. I realized that as sweaty as I was from running, and as far away as I was from town, I needed to get back to my apartment before the temperature dropped too low. When I stood, my muscles rebelled, sending thousands of needle-like pains through my body. My previously injured leg was stiff.

I started walking back, but I continued to shiver, and I knew I needed to run to get warm. I started jogging, but the path was treacherous with the ruts in the road. There was a half-moon out, and it helped me to avoid the worst of them, but I did trip on one and hit the dirt full force. I stayed more on the side of the road after that, a path that was more slanted but less pocked with holes.

I tried to keep an even jogging pace, enough to stay semi-warm, but not so fast that I couldn't recover when I tripped. I was moving along quite well when the road rose upward, catching my foot and causing me to fall. I had reached where the gravel started. I crashed hard into it, sliding and catching myself with my hands.

I could feel a sticky liquid roll down my legs and wrists, and I knew my hands and knees were bleeding, but there was nothing I could do but force myself forward. If I didn't, I knew I would freeze. The gravel road was, in some ways, rougher than the dirt had been, but the deep ruts weren't there. I jogged on, using what moonlight I had to make sure I stayed on the road.

When I finally saw a shadowy monster looming high against the moon, I knew it had to be the water tower, and the pavement had to be near. Even knowing that, the change in footing when I reached it still caused me to stumble and fall again. But once I was on the pavement, I knew the route by heart. I had run it many mornings in the opposite direction. I turned at the T and headed down the hill toward my apartment. Once I passed the water tower, there were a few street lights. After I passed the apartment complex where Bonnie lived, the lights increased in frequency, making it so I ran from light to shadow to light.

As my apartment came into view, I slowed and walked the last distance. When I reached the door of my apartment, I was still breathing hard, but even as my breathing was slowing, my shivering was increasing.

When I stepped inside, Joe was speaking into the phone. "Yes. No one has seen him for hours, and we have reason to feel something might have happened."

At that moment, Bryce, who was standing next to Joe, saw me, tapped Joe, and pointed in my direction. Joe turned and saw me and let out a sigh. He spoke into the phone. "He just walked in the door . . . Yes, thank you."

Joe hung up the phone and looked over at me. "Where the devil have you been? We've been worried about you all night."

"I just went for a run up the hill and across the farmland to the east."

"You just decided to go for a run in your Sunday clothes across the muddy roads and return at one o'clock in the morning?" Bryce said, exasperated. "Did you ever stop to consider that we might worry about you?"

"Especially with how mean Carol was," Joe said. "We were worried that you might have done something drastic or stupid."

"Or both," Bryce added.

I just shrugged. "I'm alright."

"Alright?" Bryce said. "Your pants and shirt are in tatters. You're covered in mud and blood. And you say you're alright?"

"It was dark when I started back, and I tripped," I replied.

"Tripped?" Bryce said. "You look like you've been through a meat grinder."

Just then, the door opened, and my other roommates came in.

"He's back," Joe called to them.

"Thank heaven," David replied. "We've been all over this town looking for . . ." He paused when he caught sight of me. "What happened to you? Did you get in a fight with a tyrannosaurus?"

All my roommates gathered around. "There's not too much to say," I told them. "I got a long way out, and it got dark, so I had to run home in the dark and couldn't see the road."

Some of my roommates rolled their eyes, and I could tell they felt I was holding back.

"I was on the phone with police when you came in," Joe said. "If you hadn't gotten home when you did, we might have had half the county looking for you."

"When Joe and David came home and told us what Carol said to you, we were worried," Bryce said. "Especially since they expected you to already be here."

"Then, as time went on, and you still never came home, we split up and went out searching for you," David added.

"I'm sorry," I replied. "I didn't mean to cause any problem. But I do appreciate you guys having my back."

"Have you had any dinner?" Joe asked.

I shook my head. "No. But I'm not really hungry."

"Maybe you should get cleaned up, and then you might feel

better," David said.

"Rochelle sent you some food," Joe added. "I need to call Rochelle and Shannon and let them know you're okay. You shower, and David and I will get the food warmed up."

David nodded. "Besides, we have some things to tell you."

After I had washed off all the blood and dirt and put on some sweats, I stepped out into the kitchen. As I ate, the others gathered around. I thought most of them would go to bed, but it seemed everyone wanted to hear what Joe and David had to say.

"When you walked Carol back to her apartment after church, she knew Mitch was coming," Joe said. "By the time David and I walked Shannon and Rochelle to their apartment, Mitch had already come."

"In fact," David added, "Carol had him hiding in the bedroom, totally against apartment rules. That's why she couldn't wait to get rid of us."

"Rochelle told us that Carol and Mitch sat on the sofa all afternoon planning what mean things she should say to get rid of you," Joe said. "Carol and Mitch would quit talking when Rochelle or Shannon would come into the room, but the two of them heard a lot. Still, neither Rochelle nor Shannon thought that Carol could be that mean and that it was just talk."

"But it wasn't," David said. "That's why she pushed the door open when she talked to you. Mitch was behind the door listening to her carry out their plan."

Joe nodded. "Apparently, they had this big idea that she would say all of those mean things to you, and when you got mad, as they were sure you would, Mitch would be the big hero and come to her rescue. But instead, you were kind, and a perfect gentleman, and it left them feeling stupid. It also left Carol feeling embarrassed."

David laughed. "You should have seen Carol's face when she came in with the plate of cookies."

"Once we understood their plan and told Mitch about you being an incredible collegiate wrestler, that was priceless, too," Joe added. "We let him know it was good he didn't go out there, or you might have hospitalized him."

"So, what's Mitch like?" I asked

"Well, you can understand a little bit what he's like when you think about him planning with Carol for the best way to humiliate you," David said.

"But does he treat Carol well? Is that why she likes him and wanted to get rid of me?"

Joe shook his head. "He orders her around like he owns her."

"So why does she put up with it? What does she see in him?"

"I asked Rochelle the same question," Joe replied. "She said it's the old adage that the good girls like the bad boys."

"With what she did today," David interjected, "I'm not sure she should be classified with the 'good girls.'"

Joe nodded and continued. "Rochelle said that the reason good girls like the bad boys is they feel they can save them or reform them. It's exciting to them."

"I've seen that," I replied. "And all that happens is that the bad boy ends up destroying the good girl. I've even seen some women in that situation who end up abused and battered."

"That's true," Bryce said. "But it doesn't sound like you're in any position to intercede in her behalf. If you try, you'll just be accused of being jealous and will probably make her mad."

I had to agree with him, and I knew the best thing I could do was keep my promise and never bother Carol again.

17

Horse Rides and a Good Friend

⁜

The next day, I felt kind of melancholy, and Ginny quickly noticed. I hadn't been in dance class long before Ginny asked me what was wrong.

"Why do you ask?" I replied.

"We've spent enough time together that I can tell."

"I just had a bit of a discouraging day yesterday," I said. "But I'm okay."

I did feel I was doing okay.

Ginny looked at me like she wasn't sure she believed me, but she seemed to sense I didn't want to talk about it. But when I reached out my arms to her for the first dance, and she saw the bandages on my hands, she gasped.

"What happened to you?"

"I just went for a run, and it turned dark, so I tripped and fell in some gravel."

"You went running after dark?"

I laughed. "It was light when I started. But I ran too far, and by the time I was on my way back, it was dark."

She sighed slightly, and I sensed she knew there was more to the story. "I have some nice aloe vera ointment that will help those cuts. I'll bring it to the dance studio this afternoon."

I worked hard in class, though I had danced better. My leg had healed, but it was still stiff from the long run. I was enjoying dancing more all the time. The better I became, the more I enjoyed it.

Sally, Linda, Brenda, and Danielle also noticed my bandages. They all came early to Performance Dance Team practice, and they gathered around as Ginny insisted on applying the ointment she brought. In fact, they all wanted to help. I was embarrassed and kept insisting that I was okay.

When I unwrapped my hands, Ginny gasped. "Your definition of okay isn't even close to Webster's."

The girls put ointment on my hands and arms and rebandaged them with the bandages Ginny brought.

When they finished, Ginny asked, "Do you have any other cuts?"

"That's mostly it," I replied.

"What about your legs?" Sally asked. "Surely, if you fell, you cut your leg, too."

"A little."

"Roll up your pants and let's see," Ginny said.

"Seriously. I'm okay."

Ginny looked annoyed. "Seriously, stop being macho and roll up your pants."

I did, and Ginny took a deep breath as if trying not to gag at the sight of the bloody bandages wrapped around my leg.

"You call that okay?"

She unwrapped the first bandage and looked like she was going to be sick. "You need to take better care of this, or you're going to get an infection."

Danielle unwrapped the bandage from the other leg, and the girls put on the ointment. I had to admit that it did feel good. They rebandaged my legs. As they did, Ginny said, "If I had known it would be this bad, I would have brought more bandages. You need to switch these as soon as you can."

Ginny said she would plan to bring new bandages every day for a while. I was grateful that the girls finished before most of the dance team was there. Jill always came early, and she stood across the room watching us. When Dr. Carlson started the class, Sally, Linda, Brenda, and Danielle left to join the others, and Ginny and I practiced.

On Tuesday, after the Performance Dance Team finished, Sally, Linda, Brenda, and Danielle came and joined Ginny and me. Dr. Carlson also came to talk to us instead of going into his office.

"I've never seen any group of people work as hard as you do," he said. "Would you like some more coaching?"

"You'd coach us more?" Linda asked.

"Actually, I think it would be good to have someone with a fresh perspective." He turned to me. "Tom, the others already know this, but you probably don't. My wife is an incredible dance teacher. She's the one who talked me into dancing when we were dating. She and I were International Ballroom champions ourselves, and it was mostly because of her."

"Yes. Ginny told me," I said.

"How would you like to have her come and coach you?" he asked.

"She'd be willing to do that?"

He nodded. "She'd love to. I just wanted to make sure that wouldn't offend you. Some students feel they're too good for coaching."

I laughed. "I don't. Sometimes I think I'm too bad for coaching."

It was his turn to laugh. "I might have thought so at one time, but you are becoming an incredible dancer. And part of the reason is your willingness to be taught. The other is your hard work and dedication. But just one word of warning—Maria is a perfectionist and can be demanding." He then turned to the girls. "Are you all okay with having her coach you, too?"

They all nodded, so he said he would talk to her.

After he left us to continue practicing, Sally said, "If we're going to have extra coaching, we should decide which dances we're going to compete in, shouldn't we?"

"What do you mean?" I asked.

"When we go to the competition, you can't dance every dance with all of us," she said. "So, we probably ought to decide which ones we will each do with you."

"That's true," Ginny said. "There are twelve competitive dance forms and the all-around."

"Ginny, you should compete with Tom in the all-around competition," Danielle said. "You were the one who brought us all together."

The others all agreed.

"But what about the other dances?" Brenda asked.

"We should try to split them up evenly," Ginny replied.

I looked around, noting there were five girls. "Five doesn't divide evenly into twelve," I said.

"Thank you, Mr. Calculus," Sally teased.

Linda turned to the other girls. "I think Ginny should dance the extras."

Ginny protested a little, but the other girls all agreed.

"You've worked the hardest with Tom," Brenda said.

"Besides," Danielle added, "you'll have the extra time while we're in Performance Dance to practice the additional dances."

They all insisted on it, and I think Ginny secretly wanted to, even if she wanted to be fair. That meant I would be dancing four dances with Ginny, along with the all-around. I would dance two dances with each of the other girls. To make the choice of dances fair, they decided to each choose one dance, starting with the oldest girl and moving down to the youngest.

Ginny was the oldest, and I realized that was also part of the reason all the other girls deferred to her. Ginny chose the waltz, then Brenda chose the quickstep. Linda chose the foxtrot, Danielle chose the samba, and Sally chose the tango. Sally wrote the choices on a piece of paper as each girl said them.

Ginny suggested they reverse the order of choice for the next round, so they did. Sally chose the cha-cha, Danielle chose the swing, Linda picked the rumba, and Brenda chose jive. That left three dances. Since one would be Ginny's choice and the other girls were going to give her the extras, that meant I would be dancing the Viennese waltz, the polka, and the Lindy hop with her.

From then on, when I practiced with each girl, I only practiced the dance styles with her that we would be competing in. Tuesday evening, I usually practiced with Linda and Brenda, but since the dances had been chosen, everyone stayed, and I practiced with each girl the specific forms we would be doing together.

The next day, as the Performance Dance Team practiced, I started feeling nervous about meeting Mrs. Carlson. Ginny realized what was wrong and told me not to be afraid. But I wondered if Mrs. Carlson would question whether it was worth spending extra time on me. I had progressed a lot and had gained more confidence, but the more I learned, the more I knew I still had to learn.

Wednesday would usually be one of the nights I spent practicing with Danielle and Sally after the Performance Dance class ended, but all five girls stayed since Mrs. Carlson was coming. She showed up shortly after class ended. Dr. Carlson brought her over to meet me, and she held out her hand.

"So, you're the young man that my husband said would like some extra coaching?"

I took her hand and shook it. "Yes. My name is Tom. And you must be Mrs. Carlson."

She laughed. "That sounds so formal. Call me Maria."

"That doesn't sound respectful," I said.

"Why?" she asked.

"Because my parents always taught me to address older people by a title."

She laughed. "So, you're saying I'm old?"

Everyone laughed, and I knew saying anything more would just stick my foot deeper into my mouth. She could tell I didn't plan to answer, and she laughed again.

"It's okay. I don't bite."

We started practice, but soon Maria stopped us. "Tom, you're very strong, aren't you?"

I figured it was my turn to tease back. "I suppose. But I did shower this morning, so I'm less strong smelling than I would be."

Maria laughed. "I think we're going to get along fine."

Sally answered Maria's real question. "Tom is very strong. He's on the college wrestling team."

"Was," I said. "Wrestling has ended for the year."

"A dancer and a wrestler, too," Maria said. "That's incredible. I can tell you're strong. I can see your muscles as you move."

I felt embarrassed, and the girls laughed.

"Tom," Danielle said, "you're blushing."

They all laughed again.

"We're going to make use of your strength," Maria said. "But let's start tonight on your form. I want you to walk on your toes for me." I did, and then she said, "Okay, that was pretty bad. Actually, it was really bad."

Dr. Carlson laughed, stopping when Maria looked at him.

He shrugged. "Tom, I told you that she would look for perfection."

She winked at him. "Don't you have work to do in your office?"

He laughed and took the hint. "I suppose I do."

He left, and she turned back to me. "Tom, dancing on your toes builds grace and smoothness. Have you ever seen ballet?" I shook my head, so she continued. "In dance, you don't stay on your toes, but should use the movement up and down, from toe to flat foot, to create a graceful form. Does that make sense?"

"Not yet. But I'll work at it."

"That's all I ask."

She then had all of us take steps, following her lead. I found it way out of my comfort zone, but the girls picked it up quickly. I took longer, but Maria indicated I was getting there. She then had me take Ginny in my arms, and we tried the waltz, stepping together on our toes. I couldn't seem to remember to step and get the rhythm with Ginny at the same time.

Mrs. Carlson stopped us. "Let's have the two of you just step forward and back."

That's pretty much what we did the rest of the two hours. I would switch partners and continue practicing. By the time we finished, I was feeling more comfortable with it. We ended with me dancing one dance form with each girl.

"Tom," Mrs. Carlson scolded me gently, "you keep slipping back into your old steps. Concentrate hard and try to do what we're practicing while you dance."

Thursday, as we started our morning dance class, Ginny asked, "With the big formal dance going on this weekend, are you still going home to work for your dad?"

"Yes," I replied. "In fact, my dad has a new horse that's only green broke that he wants me to ride."

Ginny could hardly contain her excitement. "You've got a new horse?"

"Well, my dad does," I replied.

"Does that mean you have two horses?" she asked.

"Yes. We have the older, gentler horse, and the new one."

Ginny could hardly breathe for excitement. "Do you think I could go riding with you?"

"You like to ride?" I asked.

She nodded enthusiastically. "On our ranch in Montana, I rode all the time."

"Why didn't you tell me? You could have ridden our horse any time you wanted."

"But I knew you only had one horse, and I wanted to go riding with you, not alone," she replied.

"I'll tell you what," I said. "With spring coming, my dad wants to put the cows in the upper pastures, so I need to check the fences. How about we fix up a picnic lunch, then we'll take the fencing tools and ride the fence lines? At the far edge of my dad's property, there's a nice pond, and we can have a picnic there. It's still chilly, so you'll need to dress for the cold."

She hugged me. "I'd love to ride and have a picnic." She paused and looked directly into my eyes. "So, what time will you have to be back for the dance?"

"I can be back any time," I said. "How about you?"

"I'm still not dating," she replied. "And you're not actually going to the dance, are you?"

I sighed and looked away. "No."

"Something happened this last weekend, didn't it?" she asked. I nodded, so she asked, "Is that also how you got so cut up?"

"Indirectly."

"But you had a date to the dance," she said. "What happened?"

"The military guy she was writing was released for drug use. She decided she would rather go with him. She told me I was a boring loser, and she didn't want anything to do with me anymore."

Ginny's face reddened in anger. "Tom, you're not boring, and you're definitely not a loser. You're the kindest, most interesting person I know."

"Thanks."

"Then how did you get so cut up?" Ginny asked.

"After what she said to me, I just needed to get away, so I ran up onto the farmland on the hill. It really did get dark, and I really did trip in the gravel on the way back."

"Well, we'll have fun horse riding, and it will be her loss," Ginny said. "A girl like that doesn't deserve a guy like you."

We didn't have any more time to talk since Dr. Carlson was starting class. But Ginny's words made me feel better, and I looked forward to horse riding on Saturday.

The practices went better for the next couple of days. Even Maria said so.

"Tom, you seem happier, and you're picking things up better," she said. "Keep it up."

Saturday morning, I pulled up in front of Ginny's at five-thirty, and she immediately came out. She climbed in my pickup and had a big grin on her face.

"This is going to be fun," she said. "I love horse riding."

As we drove the half-hour to my home, the moon hung over the highest peak on the mountain like a halo in a religious painting. It was a beautiful morning. Even though it was still March, it was relatively warm. We talked as we drove along. I thought about how lucky I was to have such a good friend.

When we arrived at home, Mom had breakfast ready for us. I ate quickly and headed off to work, telling Ginny I would be back just before noon to take her riding.

I hauled hay most of the morning, filling the barn with what the cows needed for the week. It was just after noon when I finished and saddled our gentle horse for Ginny. I went in to get her.

Ginny and Mom had already prepared us a lunch. Ginny could hardly contain her excitement. When we got to where I had the horses tied, I said, "Before you mount, let me take the new horse for a ride to see what he'll do."

"Aren't you going to saddle him?" Ginny asked.

"I've hardly ever ridden with a saddle, and I'm not used to them," I replied.

I climbed onto the back of the new horse, whose name was Dusty, and he immediately began jumping. I fought to keep his head up so he couldn't buck. He eventually stopped fighting me, but I was determined to not have any trouble with him.

"Ginny," I said, "I'm going to take him for a quick run through the sands to really tire him out and take some fight out of him. I'll be right back."

I kicked him into a run toward our north pasture, which was a deep, soft sand. He fought me all the way there, but once we hit the sand, he tired quickly. He was sinking up to the top of his hooves, and it was dragging on his feet. I continued to kick him into a run across it until he was stumbling from exhaustion. I then turned him back at a slow lope. By the time we came to a stop by Blacky, our other horse, Dusty, was willing to walk without fighting me.

I climbed off, and Ginny clapped. "We always rode with a saddle," she said. "I've never seen anyone ride bareback like that."

I packed some fencing supplies in a pack and hooked it onto the back of Ginny's saddle. I then gave Ginny a boost into Blacky's saddle. I packed the food into a backpack and slung it over my shoulders. I then climbed onto Dusty. He gave a little snort, but with a slight tug on his rein, he calmed right down.

We rode leisurely along toward the upper pastures, where I needed to fix the fence. The meadowlarks were singing their spring mating songs, and geese were flying overhead, arriving from their winter stay in the south. Ginny and I visited while we enjoyed the beauties of nature. When we got to the pond that was in the upper pasture, we stopped. I climbed off and then helped Ginny down.

While Ginny laid out the blanket for our picnic, I tethered the horses where they could eat some new spring grass. We had roast beef sandwiches and lemonade, with cupcakes for dessert. We took a minute to skip some rocks on the pond before I decided I needed to get busy fixing the fence.

I stretched a wire up tight and then Ginny went along pounding in the staples that were already there. I put in new staples on the spots where they were missing. We worked this way all afternoon, side by side.

I enjoyed her company. Ginny just glowed with a goodness that made her exceptionally beautiful. Usually, I worked alone, so it was nice to have someone like her to share the afternoon with.

As the sun started to drop toward the horizon, we packed up to head back. I helped Ginny into her saddle, and I had just climbed onto my horse when Ginny hollered, "Race you!"

She took off at full gallop across the pasture. Dusty had to snort and stomp briefly, so I was a fair distance behind when I got him moving in the right direction. Blacky loved to go home and was going full speed, but Dusty was taller, and we soon caught up. As I pulled up beside her, Blacky was huffing and puffing, and Ginny pulled her to a walk. We rode side by side, talking as we went.

We arrived back at the house about the time the sun was falling behind the western ridge, and the sunset was gorgeous. As the sun disappeared entirely behind the horizon, it shone on a cloud above the mountain rim, creating a multi-colored tiara on the highest peak.

Mom had lasagna and hot garlic bread for us to eat. Ginny and I ate with the family. Mom had made a large batch of homemade bread so Ginny and I could have some to take back to college.

As we drove back, Ginny happily told me more about her love for horses and her years growing up on her family's cattle ranch in Montana. The sun faded away, and the moon, full and bright, filled the night with silver streams.

After we stopped at her apartment, I walked Ginny to the door, carrying the loaves of bread Mom sent for her. When we stopped on the doorstep, she hugged me. "Thanks, Tom. That was an incredible day."

"Thank you, Ginny. It was so much better having you there."

"What are you going to do now?" she asked.

"I think I'll go to the computer center and type up some programs. It's usually empty on the nights of formal dances."

"I've never been to the computer center before," she said. "Where is it?"

"Do you know that hallway between the administration building and the library?" I asked. She nodded, so I continued. "The doorway to the north takes you into the computer center. There's a big sign there."

She hugged me one more time, and then I went on my way. When I arrived at my apartment, Joe, Rochelle, David, and Shannon were just finishing a fun formal dinner. Since Carol and I had planned to join them, it made the moment slightly awkward when I walked in.

"Hey, Tom," Joe said. "There's plenty of food; would you like some?"

"Thanks," I replied, "but I ate at home after I finished work."

They were about ready to leave for the dance, but I grabbed my books and was out of the apartment before they were. As I walked to the computer center, I watched couples streaming across campus, heading to the student activity center. The men were in nice suits, and the girls were wearing beautiful gowns. Though I liked seeing everyone all dressed up, all I could think of was how I had planned to be part of it. Then I thought of my day with Ginny and realized that I'd had a better time with her than I would have had at the dance.

When I arrived at the computer center, it was quiet. No one else was there, and both punch-card machines were turned off. I flipped the switch on the one closest to the door, pulled out the program I had written down, and started typing out the cards for it. I was concentrating hard on it, not hearing any sound except for the *tick-tick-tick-tick* of the machine punching holes, when suddenly my eyes were covered by two hands.

"Guess who."

I laughed. Even though she spoke in as deep of a voice as she could, I couldn't mistake Ginny's voice. I had felt those hands thousands of times as we danced, and I could pick out the perfume she wore across a crowded room.

"Hi, Ginny," I said.

She pulled her hands from my eyes as she spoke. "How did you know it was me?"

"You have a distinctive happiness to your voice even if you try to sound like a man."

She looked around the room. "So, this is where you spend so much time?"

I nodded. "Yes. I'm here so much I feel like they might start charging me rent."

She smiled and leaned her head over my shoulder so her face was right by mine. She looked at the card in the machine. "So, what are you doing?"

"Each card is a line of program code," I said. "As I type, it punches holes in the card at exactly the right place to indicate each letter. Then, when the program is run through the card reader, it knows what I typed."

"How many cards are there in a program?" she asked.

"I'm programming in FORTRAN," I replied. "This program will have around one hundred cards, but COBOL programs can be even bigger."

I looked into her eyes, and something told me she had a reason for coming, so I asked, "What brings you over here to our illustrious computer center?"

Ginny laughed. "The illustrious you. I wanted to see what this lab you talk about was like. And I also wanted to see if you would like to go up to the dance with me?"

I guess the shock must have shown on my face because she laughed.

"You don't have to look so shocked. I do like to dance."

"Yes, I know," I said, "but I thought you said you didn't want . . ."

"I'm not talking like it's a date," Ginny said, "but I love spending time with you, and why shouldn't we go to the dance?" She paused and then grinned. "That is, unless you would rather spend time with your typing machine."

"Not on your life," I said. "I'd rather go dancing with you. I have two more cards to do on this program. Let me punch them up, and we can go."

She pulled up a chair to watch me punch the cards. She watched me so intently that I messed up the first card twice and had to retype it. But finally, I was finished. I wrapped a rubber band around the set of cards and dropped them into the input box.

Ginny grabbed my hand and pulled me toward the door. "Come on. Let's hurry, and we can still catch most of the dance."

I walked with her to her apartment so she could change, and then I hurried to mine. My apartment was quiet. I hurried and showered so I wouldn't smell like horses. I put on my nicest suit, which was tired from years of use. I put on my best tie and the slightest hint of cologne. I then returned to Ginny's apartment.

She was waiting for me and stepped out and closed the door when I knocked. When I looked at her, her beauty took my breath away. She had a radiance about her that I was sure came from the goodness of her heart. That radiance, to me, made her far more beautiful than the most gorgeous model.

She took my arm, and we walked to the dance. The evening was slightly chilly, but for March it was quite warm. A few other couples were making their way there, but most of them were already inside. We could hear the music long before we arrived at the student center. Once inside, the music was much louder, mingled with the sound of many happy voices.

Ginny said she planned to pay the five-dollar entrance fee, but I insisted, and she let me. There were four big ballrooms. We found some room in one and danced. Ginny seemed a little tired and even trembled a little as we danced. I assumed it was from the long day riding horses and everything we had done, so we mostly just sat and visited.

I thought I might run into my roommates, but we didn't. We did see Bonnie and Kevin and spoke to them briefly.

After we separated, Ginny asked, "Isn't that the girl you were dating?"

"Yes," I replied.

"Who's her date?"

"His name is Kevin. He's a wrestler, too."

"How did they meet?" Ginny asked.

I sighed. "I introduced them at the wrestling banquet."

At first, I was afraid Ginny was smitten by him, too, but that wasn't the case. She said she was sure she knew him from somewhere.

As the night grew later, the ballroom was getting stuffy. We decided to step outside onto the balcony to cool off. When we did, we found it surprisingly empty. We quickly saw why. There was a couple out there making out so exuberantly that no one wanted to be around them. Ginny and I turned to go back inside when I realized the girl was Carol and assumed the guy must be Mitch.

As we returned to the ballroom, I stood for a moment and looked at Ginny.

She smiled a questioning smile. "Tom, what is it?"

"It's just that I'm glad to be here with a girl like you and not a girl like the one out on the balcony."

She laughed. "I'm glad you're you, too, and not like that guy out there."

I never did tell her that the girl out there was supposed to have been my date.

I ushered Ginny to a chair and went and got us some punch and cookies. Ginny seemed tired enough that we didn't dance the rest of the evening until the last dance. The last dance was announced, and the song was "Longer" by Dan Fogelberg.

"Come on," Ginny said. "You always have to dance the last dance with me."

We went out onto the dance floor, and I took her into my arms.

"What type is it?" she asked, as she had so many times in dance class.

"A waltz?" I asked as I listened to the first of the music.

127

She shook her head. "It sounds a lot like a waltz. But it's actually a slow rumba. It will be important to make sure you know those differences in the competition."

We danced a slow rumba, while many around us danced the waltz, and I could see the form made a lot of difference in how it flowed with the music.

As the song ended, I was thinking of the final words. "Longer than there've been stars up in the heavens I've been in love with you. I am in love with you."

Ginny leaned against me. "Tom, every couple ought to have a song that's theirs to share, one that can remind them of their good times together. I would vote this one for us. It doesn't need to be romantic or anything, but it can be the key to remind us of the good times we've shared and be our song."

She looked up into my eyes, and I nodded, unable to speak. When I did find my voice, I said, "I would like that."

She leaned against me for a while longer as everyone started to leave. After a while, we, too, headed on our way. As we walked, Ginny held my arm, and I could feel her trembling. I was concerned, but she said it was just from being tired after a long day. When we arrived at her door, she turned to me.

"Tom, would you like to come over tomorrow for dinner with my roommates and me?"

"Are you sure your roommates would be okay with that?"

Her eyes twinkled mischievously as she answered. "I think you'll be surprised how okay with it they are. But I must admit, I have an ulterior motive. After dinner, the four of us all go sing at the nursing home. We could use a male voice. Would you join us?"

"If you don't mind that I'm not always on pitch," I replied.

"I'm sure you'll do well. And the old people don't care. They're just glad to have someone come and visit."

"Then I'd love to."

When I arrived back at my apartment, Joe, Rochelle, David, and Shannon were there. They were surprised to see me walk in wearing a suit. When they asked where I'd been, I said, "A wonderful girl from my dance class and I decided to go up to the dance together."

18
Standing Up for Friends
✛

Church was at nine o'clock, and as I got up and showered, the wonderful memories of the previous night lingered with me. I was up, showered, and eating breakfast by the time any of my other roommates were awake. Not all of them got up in time to go to church. Joe and David were going with me, and Bryce joined us at the last minute. Rochelle and Shannon also went to our same congregation, and the six of us sat together.

Carol, being Rochelle and Shannon's roommate, also attended the same congregation. She and Mitch sat a couple of rows behind us in the chapel, and through the first meeting, they laughed and talked the whole hour, making it hard to concentrate on the sermon.

The second meeting was Sunday School. Our group of six sat about in the middle of the room, and Carol and Mitch sat in the back row. The lesson had barely started when Mitch and Carol began talking and laughing again. The teacher was flustered by it. But then something else happened. I was trying to ignore them and concentrate on the lesson when I felt something slimy hit the back of my neck. Immediately, Mitch and Carol burst into semi-stifled laughter.

I reached back and pulled a spit wad from my neck. Bryce was on one side of me, and Joe was on the other. They looked at what was in my hand, looked at me, and then looked at each other. Joe reached over and nudged David, pointing at what was in my hand. Rochelle and Shannon looked as well.

I could see the angry look on their faces, so I whispered to them to forget it. But almost immediately, another spit wad hit me in the back of the neck. When Carol and Mitch burst into laughter, I didn't even have to show it to those around me for them to know what had happened.

The rest of the hour went the same way. I felt angry, but mostly I felt sorry for the teacher, who had worked hard to prepare the lesson. As the class was ending, Bryce leaned across me and whispered to something to Joe that I didn't understand. Joe whispered something to the others.

When the prayer ended, instantly, Bryce got up and went one way, and David and Joe went the other. They moved quickly into position, standing on each side of Carol and Mitch. Mitch realized he was boxed in and tried to dart for the door.

Bryce pushed him back into his chair. "Where do you think you're going?"

Others in the room hurried out. Mitch looked frightened.

"Hey," he said, "I don't want any trouble."

"If you don't want any trouble, you don't chuck spit-wads at people," Joe replied. "Especially not at one of our roommates."

Carol said, "Mitch, I'll wait for you outside."

By this time, Rochelle and Shannon had joined the others in the back. When Carol stood, Shannon pushed her back into her chair.

"You're not going anywhere, either," Shannon said. "You were as much a part of it as he was."

I had taken my time joining them. But a few things were on my mind. The first was that we were in church. The second was that if my friends were to hurt Carol and Mitch, they would probably get into trouble. But most important were thoughts of the previous day's events with Ginny.

"Hey, everybody," I said. "Let's all calm down. We're in church."

"You're right," Bryce said, grabbing Mitch by the arm. "Let's take them outside and teach them some manners."

I grabbed Bryce's arm, making him let go of Mitch. "I think this is something I should deal with alone."

Bryce broke into a grin. "Yeah. I guess you could take care of this jerk plenty well alone."

"You two better get out of here before we change our minds," Joe said to Carol and Mitch.

The two of them stood, and everyone parted to let them through. As Mitch moved quickly to the door with Carol close behind, she turned and glanced at me, then turned her eyes away as she followed him.

"What are you going to do?" David asked.

I shrugged. "I don't know. But I think I should take some time so I can control my anger and think clearly."

Rochelle said, "I think you controlled your anger better than the rest of us."

When we left, Bryce and I went back to our apartment, but Joe and David went with Rochelle and Shannon to theirs. I considered eating lunch, but I didn't feel hungry. Eventually, I decided to leave.

"Are you going to have a little discussion with Mitch?" Bryce asked. I nodded, so he added, "Have fun."

I walked down the street and almost walked to Carol's apartment, but I could feel the anger swelling in me, so I turned and walked on down the street for a few blocks. I turned my thoughts to my wonderful experience the previous day with Ginny, and I felt my heart slow. When I thought I had my anger under control, I walked back. But once again, as I turned onto the sidewalk to Carol's apartment, I felt my anger surging.

Once more, I turned and walked a few blocks beyond and turned my thoughts to Ginny. This time I thought about what Ginny would do. I had never seen her get angry when someone was mean to her. The only time I had seen her upset was when Jill had talked unkindly about me. I wondered if I could ever be as good as Ginny was. As I considered it, I knew I didn't want to do something that would disappoint her. My anger subsided again, and I walked back. But once more, as I came to the sidewalk to Carol's apartment, my anger grew.

I turned and walked away again, turning my thoughts as before. I repeated this process three more times before I finally felt I would be able to control my anger. I turned onto the sidewalk to Carol's apartment and climbed the stairs. I took a few deep breaths to calm myself one last time; then, I knocked on the door.

Shannon opened it, and I smiled at her. "Is Mitch here?"

Shannon turned and said, "Mitch, it's for you."

When Mitch looked up and saw me standing there, his face went white. Carol started bawling and ran to her bedroom.

Mitch walked slowly out and joined me on the landing. Shannon shut the door behind him. I stood there for a moment and said nothing. Mitch glanced up at me, then turned his eyes to the ground and kept them there.

Finally, I said, "So, Mitch, why don't you tell me about yourself?"

Mitch still wouldn't look up, but told me about where he was born, about joining the Navy, and other things. I must admit that I enjoyed hearing the fear in his quivering voice. There were a few times that I felt the anger rising in me, once even doubling my hand into a fist so tight I could feel the blood pulsing through it. But each time, I was able to take some deep breaths, turn my thoughts to my previous day with Ginny and what she would think if I did anything out of anger, and I was able to calm down.

When Mitch finished, I said, "I'm sure you know that Carol meant a lot to me. But she has chosen you, and I will respect her decision. But I want you to always treat her well. Will you do that?"

Mitch looked up for the first time, realizing I didn't plan to harm him. "I will treat her well," he said.

"Promise?"

Mitch nodded. "I promise."

"Where I come from," I said, "a handshake is more binding than a written contract. Will you shake on that promise?"

I held out my hand.

He took it and said, "I will," as he shook my hand.

When I finished shaking his hand, I said, "Then that's all I ask."

I then turned and walked down the stairs. I walked back to my apartment. When I got there, Bryce was impatient to hear the news. Apparently, he had told our other roommates what had happened, and they quickly gathered around.

"Did you teach him a lesson?" Bryce asked.

I paused to think about it a moment and said, "I suppose. But maybe not in the way you think. I didn't lower myself to his level if that's what you mean. We had a good talk."

"That's it!?" Bryce said. "You had a talk!?"

I nodded. Then I turned to go to my room. "I'm really tired. I think I'll take a nap."

All of them stared at me as I walked to my room and closed the door. I slept for a time. But then I heard loud voices. I could tell that among them were Joe, Rochelle, David, and Shannon. Bryce's voice was the loudest.

"So, what happened?" Bryce asked. "Tom hardly told us anything."

I wandered out, and Joe turned to me. "What did you tell them?" he asked.

"I just said we had a talk."

Joe laughed. "Let me add to it. When you asked for Mitch, and Carol ran to her room bawling, David slid the window open, so we could hear the conversation. When Rochelle realized that you weren't going to beat Mitch up, she ran and told Carol to come listen. Your calmness, and you making Mitch promise to treat Carol well, really affected her."

"Especially because he acts like he owns her," David added.

"Then," Joe said, "after you left, Mitch walked in all arrogant like and said he scared you away."

"We all started laughing," Rochelle said. "Even Carol laughed."

Joe nodded. "When Mitch learned we had opened the window and heard how scared he was, he was embarrassed. So he turned to Carol and said, 'Let's go.'"

Shannon said, "I reminded him that he had promised to treat Carol well, and not boss her around. He got mad and told me it was none of my business."

"Then Mitch told Carol to come with him," Joe said, "and she told him to leave."

"Really?" I asked in surprise.

Joe nodded. "He did leave. But later, he came back, and she went with him."

Rochelle rolled her eyes. "She knows he's a jerk. But she has this idea that somehow she's going to save him. It's so stupid."

I looked at my watch and realized it was nearly time for me to be at Ginny's apartment. "Well, I have an appointment I need to head to," I said.

Bryce shook his head. "Tom, you're about the strangest guy I've ever known. You're the toughest, strongest one of all of us, and yet you didn't do anything to Mitch. Any one of the rest of us would have pounded him."

I shrugged. "As I said, I didn't want to lower myself to his level."

I left them talking about it and walked to Ginny's apartment. As I walked, I thought about how glad I was that I had stayed calm. I felt I could be comfortable knowing that Ginny would have been proud of me.

When I arrived at Ginny's apartment, I knocked. To my surprise, Sally opened the door. "Hi, Tom. Come in."

As I stepped in, Linda and Danielle were also there. I looked at them for a moment, and then I realized why Ginny said I would be surprised how much her roommates would be okay with me having dinner with them.

"Are you all roommates?" I asked.

They all laughed. "We just assumed you knew," Sally said.

Danielle took my arm and led me to the couch. "Ginny said she realized last night that you didn't know because you had never come into our apartment. She decided to surprise you."

"And Brenda?" I asked.

"She and most of the other girls on the dance team live in other apartments in this complex," Linda said.

Just then, Ginny came out of her bedroom. "So, Tom, I see you've met my roommates?"

She laughed, and we all laughed with her.

"I can't believe we haven't invited you over before this," Sally said.

"Probably because of all the time we spent together was dancing," Danielle added.

"And what time you weren't dancing, you were either working or studying," Linda said.

Ginny suggested we all move to the kitchen for dinner.

Ginny and Linda had cooked ham, potatoes, and corn. Danielle had made a Jell-O to go with the dinner, and Sally had made a cake for dessert. It was an excellent meal and a good time as we talked and laughed. Usually, I would have felt out of place being the only boy, but it didn't bother me. I really enjoyed their company. We all ate so much we decided we would wait on the cake until after we visited the nursing home. We had a little while to wait before the visiting hours started, so we moved to the living room.

"How about a game or two of UNO?" Sally asked.

"We play that all the time at my apartment, too," I replied.

We played for a while, and I lost every time. Linda said she thought Sally and Danielle had some teamwork going on because one or the other of them always won. It sounded just like what Bryce and David did, but even when they did work together, Sam still always beat them.

It was getting close to time to leave for the nursing home when I heard something that made me pause. The others apparently heard it, too, because everyone went silent. It was a male voice coming from outside, and he was loud and demanding.

"That's because you're stupid. If you'd do what I said, this wouldn't have happened."

A girl then replied, "Stop it, Taran!"

I was sure I knew the girl's voice, but I couldn't figure it out for sure.

"Who's going to make me?" the man said.

Everyone in the room stayed quiet and listened for some time. The sound of what was happening seemed to take the fun out of our party.

Danielle eventually turned to me and said, "Jill's boyfriend doesn't treat her very well."

That's who the girl was. It was Jill's voice I was hearing. I hadn't spoken to her in a long time, and that was why I recognized her voice but wasn't sure who it was. We listened to the man, who was apparently named Taran, swear at Jill.

Linda put the cards away. "What say we head to the nursing home?"

We all agreed. Ginny gathered up some music for us to sing while the voices outside continued. When we stepped outside the apartment, I could see that Taran was holding tightly to Jill's arm. She tried to pull away.

"Ow, Taran! Let go—you're hurting me!" Jill said.

I felt a battle inside my heart as we started to walk to the nursing home. I felt I should do something, and yet, at the same time, I knew Jill hated me. She would probably be upset if I interfered. I thought of Mitch bossing Carol around, and I finally stopped walking. The girls stopped and looked at me.

Ginny looked at me with raised eyebrows. "Tom?" she questioned.

"Why don't you ladies go on, and I'll catch up," I said. "Which way will you be walking?"

"We always walk up to Viking Drive and then down to the road the nursing home is on," Ginny replied.

"Go on ahead, and I'll be with you before you know it," I said. "I need to do something."

The girls glanced at each other, and then they started walking slowly away. I waited until they had gone around the corner of the apartment building, and then I turned back. I walked over to Jill and Taran. Taran had his back to me and still had an iron grip on Jill's arm. She was still pleading for him to let her go. I stopped just short of them.

"Excuse me," I said.

Taran turned toward me and snarled, "What do you want?"

"I think you're hurting Jill," I said.

"What's it to you?" he asked.

"You need to treat her better."

"What business is it of yours?" Taran said, somewhat threateningly.

"Jill is a wonderful lady. You should feel lucky to be able to spend time with her. There are plenty of young men who would feel honored to be with her."

"She would obviously rather be with me than a wimp like you," Taran said.

"True," I replied. "But you should be grateful for that and treat her better."

"Like I said, what business is it of yours?" he asked, still using his nasty tone of voice.

"Well, it's inappropriate for a man to treat any lady that way," I replied. "She's also my friend."

I said the last part before I even thought about it. I had no sooner said it than I immediately thought that Jill would say that wasn't true, and that I wasn't her friend, but she didn't say anything. Instead, someone spoke from behind me.

"She's our friend, too."

The voice was Sally's. I turned and there stood all four of the girls. They had not continued on to the nursing home, but had come back. I hadn't expected that. I didn't know what to do. I had hoped for a short visit with Taran—hoped he would let Jill go, and then I would quickly catch back up with the girls. I hadn't wanted it to be a big deal, and I especially hadn't wanted to talk to him in front of them.

"Oh," Taran said, letting go of Jill's arm. "And where did you all become friends?"

"In dance class," Danielle replied.

"Oh, you're all dancers," Taran said in a mocking voice. "How scary." He then looked directly at me. "Let me tell you something. I don't take orders from wimpy dancers. If you're smart, you'll mind your own business."

"We don't want any trouble," I replied. "We just want you to treat Jill better."

"Well, you're going to have trouble if you stick your nose in business that doesn't belong to you," Taran said.

Suddenly he took a swing at me. Without even thinking, my natural reflexes kicked in. With lightning speed, I grabbed his wrist with my hand as his fist was coming at my face. As I did, I turned with the flow of his movement. I rotated with my back to him, bringing my other arm under his body. Pulling his arm that I had grabbed and using his weight and momentum, I rolled him across my body and slammed him hard to the ground, knocking the air out of him. As he gasped for breath, I came down hard on him. It all happened so quickly that I didn't even have time to think about it.

I knelt on one knee and grabbed his collar with my left hand, pressing my left fist against his throat. I doubled up my right fist, ready to strike if he did anything.

"That was a really stupid thing to do," I said.

"Oh, did we forget to mention that Tom is a varsity wrestler?" Sally said. "How forgetful of us. We bad."

I jerked Taran to his feet and put him up against the wall with my left hand, my right fist still ready if he tried anything.

"I was trying to talk this out calmly," I said. "But if you want to start something, I will definitely finish it! Now, I think you owe somebody an apology."

Taran finally got his breath, and he apparently thought I was talking about me. He started to sputter in a trembling voice.

"I'm sorry. I shouldn't have taken a swing at you. I . . ."

"Not me!" I said, almost yelling. "I don't need your apology. But you owe one to Jill for how you treated her!"

I jerked him away from the wall, shoving him in Jill's direction. He stumbled, but recovered, coming to stand in front of her. He looked at her, then back at me. I could see the fear in his eyes. He then turned back to Jill.

"Jill, I'm sorry. I shouldn't have treated you that way."

As my anger started to melt away and I started to think more clearly, I thought Jill would tell him it didn't matter and tell me it was none of my business. But she didn't.

She looked right at Taran and said, "You're right. You shouldn't have treated me or anyone else that way. And I want you to leave and never come back."

Taran stood there for a moment, glanced at me, and then walked away. No one said anything for a while, and I felt uncomfortable. I turned and looked at the girls behind me. I couldn't distinguish the looks on their faces. Was it surprise, shock, or what? I just couldn't tell. I had never seen them with those expressions before. I was sure they were probably embarrassed that I would use force as I did. I had been taught by my father to never do so except as a last resort, and never in anger. I had been both angry and forceful in how I responded to Taran's attack.

I turned to look at Jill, and I could see she was about to cry. I realized I had probably just destroyed her relationship with Taran. That was not what I had meant to do. I wondered if maybe she thought I did it because I was jealous that she went out with him when she wouldn't go out with me. I looked down, unable to face her.

"I'm sorry, Jill. I didn't mean to ruin your relationship with him. I . . . I just couldn't stand to see him treat you that way, and I . . ."

I never finished.

Suddenly Jill started to sob and ran to me. She put her face against my chest. I was so confused I didn't know what to do. I looked back at the other girls, and Ginny signaled for me to put my arms around Jill. I slowly obliged, and when I did, Jill tucked her arms up inside mine, so she was entirely wrapped in my arms. She cried for quite some time, and when her tears started to subside, the other four came over and wrapped us in a big group hug.

After a time in the group hug, Jill looked up into my face and said, "Thanks, Tom."

"Then you aren't angry with me?"

Jill shook her head. "No. I've wanted to break away from him for so long, but I was afraid of him, and I needed someone to stand up for me.

Of all the people who had reasons not to help me, it was you. Yet you did."

"Well, if you ever have any more trouble with him, let me know," I said.

"That was a really brave thing to do, Tom," Danielle said.

I shrugged. "Guys like him are just ten-cent bullies. They try to boss people around that they think are weaker than themselves."

Jill laid her head back against me and wrapped her arms around me. I held her for a moment, though I felt quite awkward. I think Ginny might have sensed my feelings because she patted Jill on the shoulder.

"Hey, Jill. We're all heading to the nursing home to sing to the residents. Why don't you join us?"

Jill looked up at Ginny and smiled. "I would like that. It's been a long time since I was able to do anything with the rest of you."

We started walking to the nursing home. Jill stayed close beside me. Often, she walked so close that she was brushing against me. From what she said about her fear of Taran, I decided it must be because she felt more secure by me. Ginny held my arm on the other side. She seemed to be trembling like she had when we walked home from the dance the night before, and that concerned me.

When we got to the nursing home, the residents were in the living room area waiting for us. Ginny spread out the music among the residents and us. There weren't enough copies for everyone, so we all shared.

I enjoyed singing with them. Ginny told me she felt it sounded better having someone to sing bass, though I knew I wasn't that good. Afterward, we visited with the residents. One lady seemed to think I was her son. She thanked me for visiting her. Ginny told me the woman's son never came to visit and told me to just play along with it, so I did. The old lady hugged me before they wheeled her back to her room, and she seemed very happy.

As we walked back to the girls' apartment, Jill still stayed close as before, and Ginny walked beside me holding my arm. She was trembling even more. Everyone was much more talkative than on the way to the nursing home. When we got back, Sally invited Jill to join the rest of us for cake.

As everyone was entering the apartment, Ginny grabbed my arm and held me back. The others seemed to sense she wanted to talk to me alone, so they went in and shut the door. Ginny took my hand and smiled at me.

"Tom, thanks for what you did for Jill today."

"I didn't mean for it to happen the way it did. My father always taught me to avoid physical confrontation as much as possible. I really was trying to reason with him."

"You can't reason with a guy like Taran," Ginny said. "But the main thing is, the rest of us watched Jill being mistreated and should have done something earlier. She was friends with all of us, but that changed after what she did to you."

"I didn't want that to happen," I said.

"We didn't mean for it to, either," Ginny said. "It just happened. But we still should have stood up for her. I guess we justified our inaction by telling ourselves she chose it. But it was wrong of us. We weren't very kind watching what she was going through and doing nothing. Sometimes, kindness is loving someone more and treating them better than their actions deserve. Thank you for reminding us what was right."

"It feels strange being thanked for something like that, something I didn't want to do," I replied.

"When the right thing is hard to do," Ginny said, "it is a great man who does it anyway. You're a great man."

She squeezed my hand and smiled. I felt embarrassed because I didn't feel like I did any great thing. Ginny was about to open the door to the apartment when I touched her arm, stopping her.

"Ginny," I said, "you were trembling again tonight as we walked. Is everything all right?"

She just shrugged, brushing it off. "I guess I'm still just a little tired."

Then she opened the door to the apartment and pulled me in. We all ate cake and drank milk, and I felt happy knowing I had some wonderful friends.

19
Understanding Ginny and Jill
✦

ith my new understanding that most of the girls I danced with were Ginny's roommates, and the increased friendship I felt with all of them, I was even more excited for dance class. There was one nagging question, though. Should I ask Jill to dance? I was still not convinced that she thought of me as her friend, and I wasn't sure she wanted anyone at dance class to see us together. I wasn't sure, so I thought I would just dance with the girls I had been dancing with.

When I arrived at dance class, to my surprise, Jill was sitting with Ginny and the other girls. Sally saw me walk in and ran to me, grabbing my arm and pulling me to where they were all sitting. She spoke excitedly as we walked.

"Dr. Carlson told us that from now on, we're going to only dance with our competition partners."

"But we've been doing that ever since you girls decided which dances we would compete in together."

She nodded. "That's true. But now it's official."

I realized that took care of my dilemma. Since my partners were already determined for all the competitive dance forms, I wouldn't be asking Jill. It was a relief to have that question answered for me.

When we reached the other girls, Jill smiled at me, and I smiled back. We all chatted together until Dr. Carlson started class.

"I know a lot of you have already heard the news, so let me make it official. For this last month, you will be dancing exclusively with your competition partners for each form. If you boys have not determined partners for the different forms, you need to do that immediately. Some days you will dance only with your all-around partner, but most days you will dance with the girls that you will compete with for the individual forms. As the music starts, it will be your responsibility to determine which dance form it is and find the girl you will compete with in that form. And you cannot dance more than four forms with the same girl."

I thought it was good the girls had split up the dancing the way they had. Sally had provided me with a copy of the list, and I memorized it so I would remember. I felt confident I would recognize each dance form as the music began. Ginny had taught me, having me say it each time a new song played.

Dr. Carlson turned on the music for the first song. I immediately knew it was a polka. I went to Ginny and bowed slightly. She curtsied and took my arm as we moved onto the dance floor. The music was lively, and we were doing well, but Ginny seemed to be stumbling a little. I finally stopped and pulled her into my arms.

"Ginny, are you all right?"

She nodded, and we continued dancing, but I still felt something was wrong. When the song ended, I put my arm around her as we walked off the floor because she didn't seem too steady. The next song was a swing, and I thought that Danielle and I danced it flawlessly.

The third song was a waltz. I went to Ginny, bowed, and put out my hand. She smiled and took my hand. But as we walked to the dance floor, there was no doubt that she was quivering.

"Ginny, are you sure you're all right?" I asked.

Again, she nodded, and we started to dance. But the more we danced, the more she trembled, and the more concern I felt. Suddenly, she began to slide from my arms, and I realized she was passing out. I tightened my arm around her and called for Dr. Carlson. I gently laid her on the floor.

Dr. Carlson was immediately by my side. Everyone else crowded around. Dr. Carlson felt for Ginny's pulse then turned to me.

"Let's get her to the hospital. Tom, can you carry her to my car?"

I nodded and picked Ginny up into my arms.

"Brenda," Dr. Carlson said, turning to her, "will you please run the music for the class while I take Ginny to the hospital?"

Brenda nodded.

I followed Dr. Carlson to the parking lot. He unlocked his car and opened the back door. I carefully set Ginny on the back seat.

I turned to Dr. Carlson. "Can I please go with you?"

"Of course."

I slipped into the other side in the back. Ginny woke briefly and said, "Tom?"

"I'm here," I replied.

I put my arm around her to steady her. She leaned against me and passed out again.

When we arrived at the hospital, Dr. Carlson pulled right up to the emergency room door. He ran in to get help while I lifted Ginny out of the car. Soon nurses came out with a gurney, and I laid Ginny gently on it.

The nurses strapped her to it and took her into the hospital. As they wheeled her to a hospital room, I tried to follow but was told I couldn't.

"Just wait here in the waiting room," the nurse said.

Dr. Carlson had to leave to fill out paperwork. He also said he needed to call the school medical office to let them know what happened and have them inform Ginny's family. As I sat alone in the waiting room, I didn't know what was wrong with Ginny, and I was scared for her. All I wanted was for her to be okay. I prayed, and I could feel tears coming. I felt I was just about to lose control of my emotions when Sally, Danielle, Linda, and Jill came.

"How's she doing?" Sally asked.

"I don't know. They wouldn't let me stay with her."

My emotions must have been showing because Danielle patted my arm and said, "She'll be okay."

The way she said it made me realize that she didn't just hope it. She seemed to know.

"Do you know what's wrong with her?" I asked.

Danielle exchanged glances with the other girls, and I realized they all knew. I was the only one who didn't. Danielle slowly nodded.

"What?" I asked.

"We can't tell you," Linda said. "Ginny made us promise not to."

"But she'll be okay," Sally added.

I felt confused. What would make Ginny pass out, and why couldn't I know? But the others' confidence that she would be okay helped me feel better.

I suddenly realized that Dr. Carlson also hadn't seemed overly concerned about what was happening.

"Does Dr. Carlson know what's wrong, too?" I asked.

Danielle nodded.

"And no one can tell me?" I asked.

"She thought she could get through the school year without this happening," Linda said. "She'll have to be the one to tell you."

I felt better, but I was still concerned. What if they were wrong and it was something different from what they thought?

It seemed like we were there forever. Eventually, Brenda joined us. We all sat in the waiting room, saying very little. I had other classes to go to, but I didn't care. My only concern was for Ginny.

Finally, Dr. Carlson came back. "I've had the department secretary cancel the rest of my classes for today. I'll stay here and wait to see if Ginny needs anything," he said. "You can all go back to school."

"I'd rather stay," I replied. The others said the same.

After a short time, the doctor came and told us that Ginny was awake and doing better.

"Can we see her?" I asked.

"She would like to see everyone," he said, "but I don't want too many at a time. Maybe Dr. Carlson and her roommates can go first, then the rest of you."

Dr. Carlson, Linda, Danielle, and Sally went to see Ginny. Brenda, Jill, and I stayed in the waiting room. A while later, they returned. A nurse came with them. She said that Ginny wanted to see Brenda and Jill.

"What about me?" I asked.

"She wants to see you last—alone," Dr. Carlson said.

Dr. Carlson decided there wasn't much more he could do, so he left to go back to work.

"Would you like us to stay with you?" Danielle asked.

"I'll be okay as long as I get to see Ginny."

Brenda and Jill went to see Ginny, and the others left, leaving me in the waiting room alone. The clock claimed it was just over a half-hour until they returned, though its hand seemed to have slowed to a near stop. But finally, it was my turn.

A nurse showed me where Ginny's room was. I stopped at the door and knocked. Ginny's voice was weak as she called for me to come in. She looked pale and tired. But she smiled when she saw me.

"How are you doing?" I asked.

"Fine. How are you?"

"Worried," I replied.

"Tom, I'm sorry. I haven't been fair to you. I should have told you about this. But I hoped you'd never need to know."

"Tell me about what, Ginny?"

"Tom, I have a degenerative muscle disease in the lower part of my body. When I overexert myself, it tends to exacerbate it."

"So, the horse riding and dancing on Saturday was the cause?"

She smiled weakly. "That may have been part of it, but I wouldn't have given it up for anything."

"What does this mean for you moving forward?"

"Eventually, I'll be confined to a wheelchair. For now, I've been able to take medicines that have reduced the effect, but they can't hold it off forever."

"But if you can't walk, you won't be able to dance anymore."

At the thought of Ginny not being able to do what she loved so much, I could feel my emotions ready to break loose.

"No," she said, "but I will still have a good, long life, and there are other things I love that I can still do."

"Like what?" I asked.

"When I get out of here, I'll show you."

We sat quietly for a moment, and then another thought came to me. "Ginny, was that why you said this was your last chance to win an International Ballroom Championship?"

She nodded. "Alex and I knew it would be my last chance, and we were planning for it. When he died, I not only lost my best friend, but I lost a dream. I became severely depressed and prayed for help. My mother encouraged me to find someone else to take the Competitive Dance class with. I prayed that if God wanted me to try again, that He would help me find someone. To be honest, when I saw your struggles on that first day of class, the thought of finding someone to compete with actually left me because all I could think about was how you needed help."

"That's an understatement," I replied.

She laughed. "Tom, you discount yourself too much."

"But if you wanted someone to compete with, hoping to win, why did you keep helping me?"

"At first, all I could think about was that you needed me. But then I realized you were helping me."

"Me helping you? How?"

"You made me consider what I would feel like if I was the one struggling in the class, and my discouragement and concern for my own troubles started to fade away. But then, within a couple of days, I began to feel you had more ability than anyone knew, especially you. I also began to feel like God was telling me that he sent you as the answer to my prayers—all of them."

"Because you thought I could win?"

"I think you can," she replied. "But I felt like God was teaching me that, as wonderful as dance is, there are more important things in life. I have realized that no matter how wonderful honors like dance championships are, they're not nearly as important as people. I'd questioned why God let this happen to me. I'd wondered if I'd done something wrong. But as I've watched all the challenges you've been through so far this semester, I began to understand that hard things happen to good people. Maybe even more so. That's part of what makes them good. But above all, I have realized your friendship is more valuable to me than any dance championship ever could be."

Suddenly, I could hardly keep my emotions in check. As I fought to hold them back, I felt my heart was going to choke the air out of my lungs, and I struggled to breathe.

"You know, Ginny," I said, "I think you have been the answer to my prayers, too, even though I didn't pray them. I think God must have known I needed you, too."

Ginny smiled, took my hand, and pulled me closer. "The doctors are adjusting my medicine, and I should regain some strength and be able to compete. But, Tom, there's a favor I have to ask."

"Sure, Ginny. Anything."

"Don't say anything until you know," she said with a slight laugh. Then she became more serious. "I think I can dance the waltz and the Viennese waltz with you, but I probably better forgo the polka and the Lindy, so I can save my energy for the all-around. I'm hoping you might consider dancing them with Jill."

"Are you sure she would even want to dance with me?"

Ginny nodded. "Last night after you left, she stayed and talked with all of us. There's more to why she treated you the way she did then any of us knew. I'm not excusing her actions, and I'm not trying to take the decision away from you. After the way she treated you, I will still understand if you choose not to dance with her. But I would like you to at least talk to her so she can explain."

"I think it will be awkward for both of us."

"I knew it might," Ginny said. "So I told her I'd ask you to meet her a half-hour before the Performance Dance Team practice at the studio so you two can talk alone. Will you do that?"

I nodded.

Ginny smiled at me again. "Thanks, Tom."

I paused a moment, and then asked one last question. "Ginny, does your not wanting to date have something to do with this, too?"

She nodded. "I had hoped you would never have to know about this or see me in a wheelchair."

"I hope you know that wouldn't bother me."

"I know that," she said, "but I felt if I were to become involved in a romantic relationship, it would be easier to do it after I was in a wheelchair so the man would know what my life would be like from the moment he met me. Also, I never really dated Alex. Our relationship was the purest of friendships, without the entanglement of romance. I haven't dated anyone since he died, but I suppose that especially with you, in some ways, I hoped to recreate the same type of relationship I had with Alex. Does that make sense?"

I paused a moment and then shook my head.

Ginny laughed and said, "Well, at least you're honest. Sometimes it doesn't make sense to me, either. But all that aside, you're only eighteen, and you may not realize that I'm almost ten years older than you. I've been all over the world with dance troupes. I've seen Europe, Asia, the Middle East, Africa, and most of North and South America. I want you to have the opportunity to live and enjoy life, not be bound to someone in a wheelchair."

We talked for a while longer, then the nurse came in and said Ginny needed some rest. I could see Ginny was tired, so I prepared to leave.

"Can I come back this evening?" I asked.

Ginny said she'd like that, and the nurse said it would be okay.

I left and went to my last class of the day. I had missed all the others in between. After class, I found a quiet place to study for a half-hour before going to the dance studio to meet Jill. I felt apprehensive, but I had promised.

As I approached the glass doors leading into the studio, I could see Jill sitting on the bench waiting for me. I paused for a moment, then went in. Jill looked up at me, stood, and smiled. I smiled back, but I felt an uncomfortable wrenching inside of me.

"Ginny asked me to come visit with you," I said.

Jill nodded. "I wondered if you would come. I wouldn't blame you if you didn't." She paused for a moment, then said, "Tom, I'm so sorry for how I treated you. After it happened, I felt horrible. I wanted to apologize. I waited by the doors here before Performance Dance, hoping to talk to you, and I tried to approach you in our Competitive Dance class, but you seemed to be avoiding me. I don't blame you for that. I would have avoided me, too, if I were you."

Her voice quivered, and she was so sincere. I couldn't help but feel some of the hurt I felt leave, being replaced with empathy for what she was feeling. I motioned to the bench.

"Would you like to sit down?"

She nodded.

We sat down, and she appeared ready to cry. Finally, she seemed to regain control of her emotions so she could speak.

"Why I turned you down had nothing to do with you. Something had happened in my life, and I took it out on you. I was engaged to be married last fall. At Christmas time, my fiancé and I went to our different homes for Christmas, and we called each other every day. But when we came back to school, he immediately broke off the engagement. He didn't

146

give me any reason why—he just did. Then, only a couple of weeks later, I learned he was engaged to another girl."

This time Jill did cry, and I didn't know what to do. I felt awkward but felt I should do something. I reached over and put my hand on her arm. She put her other hand on top of mine as if she needed to feel I was there. After a while, her tears subsided, and she spoke again.

"I went through all sorts of emotions. I went through hurt, anger, and discouragement. As the Winter Formal approached, I wanted revenge, so I announced at Performance Dance class that I was looking for a date to the dance. I guess I wanted to show him that I could find someone else, too. That's why Ginny suggested you ask me. But there was one problem with you asking me."

She paused for a moment and looked at me, then looked away as she continued. "I felt anger and hatred toward you because . . ."

She stopped speaking, so I tried to fill in. "Because I was such a bad dancer."

She shook her head. "No. That wasn't it at all. I hated you because I knew you were a wrestler, and so was he."

I gasped at the realization. "Kevin!"

She turned quickly to me. "You know him?"

I nodded. "Of course. We were on the same team."

"What I mean," she said, "was how did you know I was talking about him?"

"There's no other guy on the team that treats girls as trophies like he does," I replied.

We sat there, saying nothing for a brief time, then Jill finally spoke. "I'm sorry, Tom. Because you were a wrestler, I struck out at you unfairly. It was like I could get back at Kevin by taking out my anger on you."

"It's okay," I said. "I understand more than you realize."

"The thing that hurt most," Jill said, "was that he hardly knew the other girl. She was just drop-dead gorgeous with beautiful blond hair. The fact that he dumped me for a girl he didn't even know made me feel like I wasn't pretty. It made me despise her."

"First off, you are pretty," I said. "And second off, you might want to know that he's not engaged to that girl anymore, either."

Jill suddenly sat upright and stared at me. "How do you know he's not?"

"It's a long story," I said.

She looked at me and pleaded. "Please tell me. I need to know."

"Sometime after I asked you, a girl named Bonnie asked me to preference. We dated for a while. When wrestling season ended, she went with me to the athletic banquet. Bonnie is beautiful, and Kevin saw her and immediately came over to meet her."

"Don't tell me," Jill said. "He dumped his fiancée and started dating the girl you had been going out with."

I nodded. "You know, Jill, I think you're better off without a guy like that."

"I realize that now. But after being dumped like that, and after what I did to you, I struggled to feel I was worth anything. I was willing to take anybody that came along, and that's how I got into the relationship with Taran. He was obnoxious and mean, but I needed someone to want me. But it just made things worse, and I couldn't get rid of him. You'll never know what it did for me when you stood up for me. And when you told Taran I was your friend, and that he needed to treat me better, I felt like I might have some redeeming value after all."

"I was actually afraid it would bother you that I told him you were my friend."

She turned more to face me. "Oh, Tom, I'm proud to think of you as a friend. I'm ashamed I ever said anything to the contrary."

"Ginny told me you're one of the nicest girls she knows. I'm sorry I haven't a chance to know you better."

"That's my fault," Jill said. "But I hope there's still time."

We both sat there, saying nothing for a while. Finally, I remembered the other part of what Ginny had asked.

"Jill," I said, "Ginny asked me to dance the polka and the Lindy with you."

She looked away. "I know. She mentioned it to me, too. I understand if you don't want to."

"Ginny said she won't have the strength, and I think it would be fun to dance with you."

She turned and stared at me with a look of total disbelief.

"I mean, that is, if you want to," I said.

Suddenly, unexpectedly, she threw her arms around me and hugged me. Then she pulled back and seemed embarrassed at her impulsiveness.

She smiled and said, "Sorry about that."

"Is that a yes, then?" I asked.

She nodded. "Tom, there's nothing I would like more."

"Well, then, as Ginny said to me when I decided to compete, 'Let the training begin." I paused and then said, "By that, I mean you training me."

She laughed. "I'm not sure who will be training who."

We continued to talk. We were still talking when Dr. Carlson came. He saw us together and came over.

"It's good to see you two talking."

"Ginny asked us to," I replied.

He nodded. "Ginny explained a lot to me." He paused a moment, and then he said, "Tom, what are you planning to do tonight for practice?"

"I thought I'd do some homework. Ginny asked me to continue practicing with the other girls. I think she felt I needed it, partly so I wouldn't be thinking about her being in the hospital. But Monday is one of the nights I practice with her after Performance Dance."

"I could practice with you, Tom," Jill said.

"There was also something else Ginny and I talked about," Dr. Carlson said. "She feels she won't have the energy to practice for long times on the evenings that it's her turn to practice with you, especially after practicing while the performance team is in class. I suggested that my wife come and dance with you on the evenings you usually spend with Ginny. Maybe she and Jill could spend that time with you. Would you be okay with that, or would you feel awkward?"

"It might feel a bit strange to dance with Mrs. Carlson, especially as good as she is. But wouldn't it feel strange for you having her dance with me?"

He laughed. "My wife is a professional. She teaches classes and dances with all sorts of men. And we'd both love to see you and all the girls you dance with win some medals in the competition. If there's anyone who can help you win, it's Maria."

"When will we start?" I asked.

"How about tonight? Ginny mentioned, as you did, that her own dance night practices with you were on Mondays and Thursdays. Since Jill volunteered to practice with you, perhaps those nights could become Jill and Maria's nights. Maria said she'd be willing to also dance with you on the nights when you practice with the other girls if the age difference doesn't make you uncomfortable. And then when you dance with the others, she could watch and coach you."

"That would be great. But I do have a question for you, Dr. Carlson. Is Ginny's condition the reason she isn't on the Performance Dance Team?"

He nodded. "But it wasn't my choice. She was afraid she would be in the middle of a performance and not be able to finish. Also, Alex was her main partner. After he was gone, the memories made it difficult for her."

We talked for a few more minutes, and then the other class members started coming in. Linda, Brenda, Danielle, and Sally came over, and we visited about Ginny. I told them I was going back in the evening to visit, and they thought they would, too.

While the class practiced, I worked on my homework. Not long after they finished, Maria came. She and Jill practiced with me. Dancing with Maria was a whole new experience. The slightest movement I made she would respond to, whether it was right or wrong. If it were wrong, she would let me know. My signals for movements to her gradually improved.

I would dance with Jill, then dance with Maria to the same music, and she critiqued and helped me. Then I would try it again with Jill, and I did far better. What it showed me was how far I still had to go. I could also see how Maria would be able to help me perfect my dancing, but I wondered if there was enough time before the competition. I expressed that sentiment to her.

Maria laughed. "For you to realize that you have a long way to go is the hardest part of the battle. Too many people I work with feel they have arrived when they aren't even in the same country as their destination. If we keep working hard, I think we'll get there."

20

A Portrait of Ginny

$\dashv$

After dance practice, I called the hospital to see if Ginny was awake and ready for visitors. I was able to talk to her, and she said she was not only awake, but some of the dancers and her roommates had come over after Performance Dance to visit. She said they were just leaving.

"Have you eaten?" I asked.

"No," she replied. "Hospital food isn't that good, so it's hard to have an appetite for it."

"What if I brought over some pizza and pop, and we had dinner together?"

"That would be wonderful. Let me check with the nurse and see if it's okay."

The nurse said Ginny had no special dietary restrictions, so it would be fine. I purchased a pizza and some pop and went to the hospital. When I arrived at Ginny's room, the nurse was just finishing a check of her vital signs, and the doctor was there. He said Ginny was doing better, but he wanted to keep her at least one more day.

After the doctor and nurse left, Ginny and I shared the pizza. She was not as pale and looked like she was feeling better.

"My mother called today," Ginny said. "She was going to make a trip to come see me. But I told her I was getting better and to save it for the dance competition because you and I were going to be in it."

"I appreciate your confidence in me," I said.

We also talked about the visit I had with Jill.

"Jill called and wants to come visit," Ginny said. "But she's going to let us have some time alone first. I'm sure she won't want you here when she comes, anyway, because she'll want to talk about you."

"That makes me nervous," I replied.

Ginny laughed. "As it should."

We talked for a long time. In fact, Jill came, sure we'd be done. When she came, I left so they could talk alone. I went to the library and worked hard on my homework so I could get it done and have more time to visit Ginny.

The next morning at dance class, Dr. Carlson announced that Ginny was okay and would be out of the hospital later that day. When the dancing started, I missed Ginny, especially when the music was a waltz or a Viennese waltz, the ones I was supposed to dance with her. Instead, I chose one of the other five girls in my group. Jill seemed so happy when I danced with her that I was glad we had worked it out.

After my classes, I worked on homework until about the time the Performance Dance team practice would be ending. I then went to the dance studio. I hadn't been there long when Maria came. It was practice night with Sally and Danielle. We worked the same way I had with Jill the night before. I would dance with Sally or Danielle, dance the same song a few times with Maria while she tutored me, and then dance again with the same girl.

As we were finishing, and I was preparing to go to the hospital to see Ginny, Maria stopped me.

"Tom," she asked, "how many hours per week are you putting into dance practice?"

I took a minute to total an average week. "Five in dance class and Dr. Carlson's Friday open hour, five during Performance Dance class, ten on evenings after Performance Dance class, and three each of the four nights when there are evening dances. That makes thirty-two."

When I said it, the number staggered me. I hadn't realized how many it was. It wasn't much different than what I had put in for wrestling, including running and everything, but I just hadn't added them up.

Maria must have seen by the look on my face that I hadn't thought about it before because she laughed.

"That's an incredible amount," she said. "I thought it had to be something like that, and the progress you're making suggests it's a lot. You have worked the equivalent amount of hours in one semester that some would have done in years."

As I left and went to the hospital, I thought about that. It was a lot of hours, but if I was going to make up for what I lacked, I needed all I could get.

When I got to Ginny's room, she informed me that the doctor said she could go home, as long as someone came to drive her. I had brought my pickup, hoping that would be the case.

"Have you eaten?" I asked.

She shook her head. "I was hoping to eat with you again."

"Would you like to go for a hamburger?" I asked.

"I would love that," she replied.

The nurses insisted on wheeling Ginny out, so I went and pulled my little pickup up to the curb by the door. I opened the door and helped Ginny in.

We went to a hamburger place, and I bought us some hamburgers, fries, and milkshakes. I told her about how I was practicing dance with Maria. She thought that was a great idea. We took our time eating so we could visit longer. When we finally left, and I took her to her apartment, I felt better knowing she was okay.

We had barely pulled up to her apartment complex when word got out that Ginny was there. Suddenly, there were lots of people there to welcome her back. Most of them were girls from the Performance Dance Team that lived in the same complex. Ginny's roommates were among them.

I told those gathered that Ginny needed rest, so they said their greetings quickly and then went on their way. Ginny held my arm as we walked to her door.

"See you tomorrow at dance class," she said as I was saying goodbye.

"It will be good to have you back," I replied.

The next morning at dance class, Ginny was already there when I came. She was much better and only trembled slightly when she danced with me. She didn't dance too much, either. The rest of the day seemed mostly back to normal.

After the two-hour practice following the Performance Dance Team's practice, Ginny said she wanted to show me something.

As we walked, Ginny said, "Tom, I never did thank you for taking Jill into our group for the dance competition. She's a good person, and it's good to have her back as a friend."

"After we talked," I said, "I understood why she had done what she had. Kevin, the guy who was her fiancée and my teammate, caused problems for both of us. I couldn't blame her for feeling animosity toward me when she knew I was a wrestler."

"After Jill told us about it on Sunday night," Ginny said, "I realized why I had recognized Kevin at the dance on Saturday. He had always been hanging around the apartment complex with Jill last semester when they were engaged. Knowing he was dating the girl you had been dating was part of the reason I wanted you two to talk."

We walked to the art and communication building, and she took me to a classroom. The walls of the room were sectioned off, and it appeared that each section was the artwork of a different student.

"Why don't you walk around and look at them and see what you like the most," she said.

I walked around the room and stopped at one display. The artwork was phenomenal. There were landscapes and drawings of people. They were as good as photographs. In fact, they were better, since the artist could remove anything that was undesirable. I was drawn in as if traveling into another time and place.

"This one is incredible," I said.

Ginny laughed. "I would hope so. That's the teacher's artwork. What do you like next best?"

I continued around the room and looked at the others. There was one that drew me back a second time. The scenes were tranquil vistas with grand open skies. There were horses. There were also other pictures of children, musical performances, and people dancing. There were married couples, young and old. One painting I especially liked showed an elderly couple on a bench with a heart carved into the back of the bench. The couple had their backs to the person looking at it, and, hand-in-hand, they were watching a sunset as the old woman leaned against the old man. As I looked at these paintings, it was as if I was experiencing life, not just visually, but deeply in my emotions.

"These are incredible, too," I said.

"Why don't you look at the name of the artist," she replied.

I glanced at the signed name on the pictures, but couldn't quite make out the signature, so I looked at the name listed above the section of the wall.

"Genevieve Broadhurst," I read out loud. I turned to Ginny, and she was smiling. "Do you know her?" I asked.

She didn't answer, but started to giggle, and she raised her eyebrows slightly. Suddenly I realized what she was telling me.

"Ginny—Genevieve. That's you, isn't it?"

Ginny nodded.

I laughed. "I've never known you by anything but Ginny."

"Ginny is just my nickname. It came from my little brother who couldn't say, Genevieve."

"Ginny, your artwork is incredible."

She chuckled slightly. "You don't have to act so surprised. I do have other talents besides dancing."

I felt embarrassed. I stammered my response. "It's just that I've never personally met an artist who was so good. I could never do artwork like this."

Ginny frowned slightly. "You always sell yourself short, Tom. You could if you worked at it and had training. With what I have seen from you and the way you work, I feel you could do anything if you had time."

"Maybe, but I don't plan to live past ninety."

Ginny laughed slightly and rolled her eyes. "I'm sure it wouldn't take you that long."

"I don't know. I was still trying to learn to color within the lines when I graduated from high school."

She laughed again, then kindly reached out and took my hand. She pulled me close to her.

"Tom, remember how in the hospital I told you that even if I couldn't walk, I would still have a good life and be able to do things I love?"

I nodded.

"This is something I also enjoy," Ginny said. "And I love children. When I finish my college education, I will not only have a degree in art, but I will have my certification for teaching. I won't have to walk to paint and to teach children to paint."

I nodded. I knew Ginny would always be positive and happy. I could imagine how much she would touch the lives of the children she would teach. I was happy Ginny would have things in her life that she enjoyed. But my heart still ached at thinking of Ginny unable to walk or dance.

To try to ease my feelings, I attempted humor.

"So someday, when I hear people call you Genevieve Rembrandt as they admire your masterpieces, I will be able to tell them I knew you. Of course, they probably won't believe me."

Ginny smiled slightly. "I'm sure it will be me amazing people when I tell them I knew you. Besides, I have a long way to go to create a masterpiece."

"What do you think it will be?" I asked.

Ginny was quiet for a moment, but when she spoke, she spoke in a serious tone. "I once had an art teacher who said that the painting an artist is currently working on is his masterpiece, no matter what he or she has done before. But the one I'm working on right now is going to be one, at least to me."

"Can I see it?" I asked.

She shook her head. "I'm an artist who doesn't like to show her work before it's finished. Besides, it's more in what it represents and the story it tells than in the artwork. And right now, I'm still painting the story. Or the story is still painting itself and coloring my life."

As we turned to walk from the art classroom, she didn't relinquish her hold on my hand. As I walked with her to her apartment, we never said a word. The feelings I felt couldn't be put into words. Apparently, Ginny felt the same way about hers.

21
Preparing for Competition
✦

During the last month before the dance competition, Maria became more exacting in her expectations. I worked hard, but I knew I was still falling short. Sometimes she became exasperated with me, but she would always come back with encouragement. I hoped for a day when she wouldn't find anything that needed correcting.

One evening, after finishing a hard practice with Ginny and Jill that went well beyond the two hours, I was preparing to leave. Maria had been exceptionally demanding and somewhat critical, and she stopped me before I could go.

"Tom, I know that sometimes I'm hard on you. I'm sure Richard is probably hard on you, too. But I want you to know it's because we believe in you, and we believe you can win."

"Thanks," I replied. "I really need that, because I don't always feel I can."

"We believe in you, too, Tom," Ginny said.

Jill smiled and nodded.

"There's another reason I sometimes expect a lot," Maria said. "You may not know that Richard is retiring this year. He's having a retirement party right after the International Ballroom Championships. It's been his biggest dream that, before he retires, he will help coach an International Ballroom Championship couple and possibly have a team that places in the top three. He believes you and the girls you are dancing with are an important part of the best and last chance he has. I would love to see all of you accomplish that for him. Well, to be honest, I would like to see you accomplish it for me, too—and for you—all of you. I admire your tenacity and the diligence you and the six girls in this group are putting in."

"But Dr. Carlson has so many wonderful dancers on the Performance Dance Team that will also compete," I said.

"Yes," she replied, "but no one besides this group will perfect themselves. Too many of them feel they're already good enough. Richard has invited them to come after Performance Dance to have me train them, but none of them come except for you and the girls you dance with.

"That's true," Jill said. "He has invited everyone in the class."

"I know you're an athlete," Maria said. "Have you ever run track?"

"I did in high school," I replied.

"Do you know what the usual time difference is between the first and second place runners?"

"Usually it's seconds or microseconds," I replied.

She nodded. "And the same is true in dance. It's the tiniest items that make the difference between first and second, or even between first and no medal at all. What I'm trying to do with you is to make that difference, and I hope you'll never dislike me for it."

"I could never do that," I replied. "And in fact, I have a related question that I wanted to ask. Dr. Carlson said you professionally train people to dance. If I had to pay you for all of the time you have spent and will spend helping me, what would that kind of training cost?"

She laughed. "Thousands of dollars."

"That's what I thought," I replied. "So how could I be upset when I am getting the help for free?"

She laughed again. "You're an interesting man, Tom."

*****

The days went by quickly. Ginny still went home with me when I went to work on Saturdays. We didn't feel she should go riding anymore, so she usually sat in a chair looking out the window as she painted. I was usually out working and didn't see her much during the day except for lunch. But I looked forward to that time and even more so to the time traveling back and forth when it was only her and me. When I went to the evening dances, I usually danced with the other girls in our group and Ginny rested, watched, and coached. But we always saved the last dance for each other.

One evening, Ginny asked all the girls in the group to come over after the Performance Dance Team practice to where we were. When Maria came, Ginny asked her if she would give us some direction on what would be the best dress.

"I was beginning to think about that myself," Maria said. "Much of it depends on the dance form. In some dances, the man would look best in slacks and a fancy polo shirt, while in another, he will often wear a tuxedo. But since you are all dancing with Tom, if you qualify in multiple dance forms, which I expect you will, he won't have time to change."

"So, what do you suggest?" Ginny asked.

"I would suggest that Tom has a nice suit. When it's a formal dance, he can put on the coat and tie. When it's more of a casual dance, he can take off the coat and tie and unbutton his collar."

"What about us girls?" Sally asked.

"You all might have time to change to match the dance form, depending on the dance order. Richard should have received the order list from the competition officials by now, so we can check it out. But we will want to match each of you to Tom so you don't overdress or underdress in comparison to what he's wearing."

The girls expressed their agreement, but I sat there quietly, so Ginny turned to me.

"Tom, does that all sound okay?"

"Ginny, you know what my suit looks like. It's old and worn."

"We can all pitch in and buy you a new one," Jill said.

"Yeah," Ginny said. "We know you've given up a lot of opportunities to earn money to spend time practicing with us."

The girls and Maria all nodded in agreement.

"No," I said. "That's not it. I'm fine buying my own suit, and I insist on it. But if I go to a suit store, I'm not sure what I should buy."

"Well, then," Maria said, "maybe I'll need to come with you."

"Can I come, too?" Sally asked.

"I want to be there," Danielle said.

The rest of the girls responded similarly.

"Why don't we all do that and then go to my house for pizza?" Maria said. "What do you say, Tom?"

"It might be a little embarrassing having everyone see me modeling clothes," I replied.

Maria laughed. "What about when tens of thousands of people are watching you dance?"

I hadn't thought about that, and suddenly the idea scared me to death. The girls and Maria seemed so excited about the prospect of a new suit for me that I finally, reluctantly, agreed to us all going together.

"So what night do we do it?" Linda asked.

"How about tonight?" Jill replied. "Right now."

All the girls liked the idea, but I was hoping for some time to get used to it.

"There's one problem with that," Maria said. "I think for the best effect, we should have Tom wear a black suit. But his tie should match whatever dress you girls are wearing as much as possible. We will need to determine your dresses first."

The girls agreed with that, so I found myself with a small reprieve. They decided they would all bring their dresses the next night, and Maria would help them decide what to wear. This night was my night to practice with Brenda and Linda, so they stayed, and the other girls left to look through their closets.

The next night, the girls brought their dresses and hung them up on the rack that was meant for the Performance Dance Team when they were performing. After the class, once Maria came, the girls and Maria gathered and started going through the dresses to determine what would be best. The seven of them seemed like children in a candy shop. They couldn't seem to decide on anything but were enjoying making the decision. I stood a short distance away, watching.

Dr. Carlson came up and put his hand on my shoulder. "Feeling a little awkward?"

I nodded.

"This was always one of the parts of dance that made me feel the same way," he said.

There were dressing rooms connected to the dance studio, so the girls tried on the dresses and modeled them. Maria made suggestions and even pinned a few that she wanted to adjust. For the twelve dance forms, they decided on dresses for nine of them. But Maria wasn't satisfied with any for the tango, the rumba, or the Lindy. She also wanted a special dress for Ginny for the All-Around. She suggested Sally, Linda, Jill, and Ginny come over to her house and see what she had. The other girls wanted to come, too, so she invited them all.

"What about you, Tom?" Sally asked. "Don't you want to come?"

"Um, I'm good," I said. "I think I'll just take the night off from dancing and do some homework."

Dr. Carlson chuckled, and Maria gave him a look that I assumed meant to tell him not to make a big deal of it.

Maria and the girls left, taking all the dresses with them. I headed to the library to study.

The next day, the girls brought the dresses they would be wearing—all but two. Maria was not happy with anything they had found for the rumba, so she was going to make one for Linda. And Maria decided she and Ginny were going to make a special one for the all-around competition. Maria had already purchased the two different fabrics and patterns. I wouldn't wear a tie for the rumba, but Maria had a piece of the fabric for Ginny's dress in the all-around so she could match it to a tie. I was grateful that Maria and all the girls insisted on modest dresses. I knew I would feel more comfortable. I mentioned that to them.

160

"But be aware, Tom," Maria said. "Not all of the dance teams will feel the same way. You'll probably see more skin than you're used to here at our little religious college, unless you like to frequent bikini beaches."

"With all the time and money you're spending, what if we don't qualify even to compete?" I asked.

Maria didn't even pause to consider it. She just said, "You're good enough. You will. Besides, the college is allowing some budget for it."

I had hoped for a few more days to get used to the idea of them all being there when I bought a suit and had hoped they might change their minds. But Maria felt it would be best for them to wear their dresses to match my clothes. They also decided we should walk to town since it was only four blocks from the college to the town center. So I found myself walking with an entourage of six beautiful young women and one beautiful older woman, all of them carrying dresses to try on to compare to my suit. I hoped no one would see me. Then I thought about it more and considered that maybe I wanted everyone to see me.

When we got to the suit store, the suits were nice but high priced. The clerk measured me, and Maria picked out the style she wanted me to wear. The problem was, with my athletic build, the clothes fit more like tents. That's how all my suits fit.

"Don't you have anything that tapers more?" Maria asked.

"His coat size is forty-eight, and his waist is twenty-eight," the clerk said in frustration. "There's no way you're going to find a suit that tapers like that anywhere."

"Can you have one tailored?" Maria asked.

The clerk nodded. "We can, but it will cost quite a bit more."

"How much?" I asked.

Before the clerk could answer, Maria did. "It doesn't matter, because I'm paying for it."

I objected, but she insisted. We found a black suit that was the closest fit possible, and Maria had me put it on. The clerk put in the markings for the tailoring. Then I just had to stand there while the girls put on their dresses and picked out matching ties.

"We want to pay for the matching ties," Jill said.

I tried to tell them I would, but they insisted on it. I was grateful. I didn't realize how much a small piece of cloth could cost. I put on each tie Maria chose, and the girls took turns standing next to me in their dresses. Sometimes Maria didn't like the match, and we tried another tie. She never found one she liked sufficiently well to match Ginny's dress for the all-around, so she decided she would make me a tie from extra fabric from Ginny's dress.

This all took longer than I expected. I realized that what Dr. Carlson said about Maria was true—she was a perfectionist.

There are very few things I hate more than trying on clothes, and this process seemed to go on forever. But finally, everything was decided. I paid for the suit, the girls paid for the ties, and Maria put some money down on the tailoring. The girls were excited about the clothes, and I was just as excited to have it over with. But the pizza at Maria's house was delicious and almost made the shopping worth it.

Over the next week, practice went as usual. Then one day, the girls all came with their dresses to Performance Dance Team practice.

"Maria called us and said your suit tailoring is done," Sally told me. "She's bringing it so we can practice dancing with you in the different dresses."

Ginny and I practiced in our school clothes during the class, but shortly after it was over, Maria walked in with my suit and the two dresses she had sewn. She had gotten the list of dances and the order they would be in from Dr. Carlson, and she wanted us to practice them in that order in our proper dress. I went to the dressing room and put on my suit pants and shirt. When I came out, Maria handed me the tie to match Ginny's dress for the waltz. I had just put it on and slipped my suit coat on when the girls started coming out in the dresses they would wear for their first dances.

"Wow, Tom!" Danielle said. "You look incredible in that suit."

"Uh, thanks," I said, feeling my face growing warm.

"Tom, you're blushing," Brenda said.

"Woo! Woo!" Sally called out in kind of a cat-call.

"So, will you marry me?" Linda teased.

"No way," Jill replied. "He's mine."

Ginny laughed and said, "Maybe that isn't the best way to build confidence, but it ought to."

"But I don't feel I'm anything compared to you beautiful ladies, especially when you're dressed in your dance dresses," I said.

I felt embarrassed and wanted to get started. But something was troubling me. Dressed like this, I began to think about what Maria said about performing in front of thousands of people. The last time I remembered doing that was the church dance festival when I was in high school, and parts of that hadn't gone so well.

Maria speaking to me brought me back. "Tom, you're very handsome, and you're an incredible dancer. So it's fun for the girls to

162

dance with you on multiple accounts. But we need to lose the old church shoes."

"I didn't know we were going to have our dress clothes today," I said. "My nicer church shoes are also getting old, but I thought I might go buy me a new pair of shoes for dancing."

"Not on your life," Maria replied. "It would be hard to get them broken in before the competition. Just polish up what you have and bring them."

Finally, it was time to dance. As I reached out my hand to Ginny, Maria had some coaching.

"Tom, hold your hand out with the palm almost flat, but with your thumb up just slightly so she can put her hand gently on it."

I didn't get it just right, so she took my hand and turned it until I had it how she wanted. Ginny put her hand on mine, and Maria had Ginny pull her hand back so her fingers were barely over the side of my hand.

As we started to walk to the dance floor, Maria stopped us. "Tom, keep your hand up. You're guiding her out gracefully as if leading her, not like you're dragging her out to an athletic event."

The girls giggled slightly, and I raised my hand higher. Maria had me practice with Ginny a couple times before she felt I had it right. Finally, Maria started the music, and Ginny and I began to dance. But dressed as we were, all I could think about was thousands of people staring at us, and I made simple mistakes. Finally, Maria stopped the music.

"Tom, what in heaven's name is wrong?"

"It's . . . It's just that dressed like this, and where you said thousands of people would be watching. Well, I'm just . . ."

Maria turned red with frustration. "Tom, you just need to . . ."

Ginny cut her off. "Maria, may I take this, please?"

Maria nodded and spoke with frustration, moving a short distance away. "Be my guest."

Ginny looked kindly at me and spoke in a near whisper. "Tom, I don't think Maria understands what you've been through. But it doesn't matter if you're in front of thousands, or it's just us. Just look at me, concentrate on me, and think only of us together. Okay?"

I nodded, and Ginny asked Maria to start the music again. The music began to play, and I looked at Ginny, and she smiled. I suddenly felt incredibly grateful to be with her, and nothing else mattered. We danced, and it seemed as natural as if we were one person gliding around the dance floor, and no one else was there. When we finished, I realized that I hadn't heard a single comment from Maria.

Maria looked somewhat confused at the difference, but she smiled and said, "See? You can do it." She then looked at her paper and called "Tango."

Sally stepped forward, and I switched my tie to match her dress. Maria adjusted my tie.

She looked at the two of us side by side and said, "Let's lose the coat."

I took off my coat and led Sally to the dance floor, as I had Ginny. Maria stopped us.

"Tom, that might have been the way to lead someone out for the waltz, but it isn't right for the tango. This one is more like a . . ." She paused, and then grinned as she continued. "Like an athletic event. You can lose the contest just by how you lead the girl to the floor. Each style has a few things that are different."

She showed me how she wanted me to lead Sally to the floor for the tango, and we practiced it a few times. Then Maria turned on the music. I concentrated on Sally, not paying any attention to anything else. I looked at her light red hair cascading around her shoulders and looked into her green eyes. She smiled at me as we went back and forth across the floor, and that encouraged me. When we finished, Maria only had two comments.

"Exaggerate some of the body movement a little more. And for heaven sakes smile, Tom. You look like you're concentrating on a calculus problem." She then called out, "Foxtrot."

Linda stepped forward, and I switched my tie and put my coat back on. Maria showed me how she wanted me to lead Linda out for the foxtrot. I began to wonder if I was going to be able to remember everything. Once we had practiced walking to the dance floor until Maria was satisfied, she turned on the music. Once again, I ignored everything around me and concentrated on Linda, looking into her blue eyes and watching her blond hair swirling around us. I let my subconscious take control of my movements without even realizing it. It felt natural.

When we finished, Maria said, "Both of you keep your arms up a little more."

Next was Brenda with the quickstep, then back to Ginny on the Viennese waltz. Jill followed with the Lindy. Maria had a hard time finding Lindy music on the tape player. I was visiting with Jill as we waited, and Maria stopped everything.

"Tom, Jill, what should you be doing as you wait if the music isn't playing?"

I shrugged. "I don't know."

"Let say you're in a theatre performance and the curtains open, but the lights don't come on. What would you do?"

"I've never been in a theatre performance," I replied.

Maria let out an exasperated sigh. "You would stand still, in position, ready to perform. The same is true with dance. The minute you step onto the ballroom floor, you're on stage. You stay in position and don't move until the music starts."

She had us go off and walk back onto the dance floor. I held Jill in position for the Lindy, and we stood there as still as possible. When Maria felt satisfied, she turned on the music.

Maria waited the music every time from then on to make us all practice holding our position. That was how we practiced all night, with me switching ties and my coat and the girls changing dresses. Other than training us to stand in position, Maria kept the dance music moving, and by the time the two hours were up, I was sweating profusely. Even some of the girls were perspiring.

The next day, by the time Maria came, I was already in my suit, and the girls were in their first dresses. Maria looked at me and scowled.

"Did you shine your shoes at all, Tom?"

I nodded. "I even did two coats of shoe polish."

I thought they looked good, but Maria obviously thought otherwise.

"They may be old, but I think they can look better than that. You leave them with me when we finish."

"But I didn't bring any other shoes to wear," I said.

I must admit that I hoped to take them home and try again so Maria would feel I could do something right. But she wasn't going to let me get away with that.

"I'm sure Richard has something in the dance costume closet."

We practiced the two hours, and when we were done, she motioned me over to the costume closet. Maria rummaged through the shoes, but the only thing she could find that I could wear on my feet were some kind of slippers, and they were so tight they cut off my circulation.

"But these aren't really shoes," I complained.

"And what you did to yours wasn't really a shine," Maria retorted.

When I walked back to my apartment to get my tennis shoes, I tried to avoid anyone I knew. And the minute I entered my apartment, I took the slippers off and walked in my socks. The next day when I went to the studio, I wore my older shoes and carried the slippers. I dressed and waited in my socks for Maria to come.

When she came, she handed me my shoes. But I hardly recognized them as mine. They shined like new, and many of the scratches and blemishes were somehow buffed away. I was stunned.

"How did you get them to look so nice?" I asked.

"I took them to a shoe repair shop and had them professionally done."

"I should pay you for . . ."

Maria didn't even let me finish. "You should get in and dance," she said.

*****

For the next week, we practiced through the rotation of dance forms each night. Dr. Carlson started having us do the same thing in class and Friday open time. All six girls stayed every night and came to the open time, too. On some nights, Maria had me practice every dance form with Ginny to prepare for the all-around competition. When we did that practice, both Maria and Ginny insisted that I call out the dance form after only seconds of hearing the music. I missed very few, and as time went on, I didn't miss any, even when Maria tried to throw in something unusual.

When we reached the two-week point before the competition, Maria insisted that we send all the dresses and my suit to the dry cleaner.

"The Performance Dance Team will need the costume space in preparation for their performance next week, anyway," she said. "And no offense, but you are all beginning to smell."

The girls all nodded, and I knew I was the worst, having to go from dance to dance.

"That's not a bad thing, though," Ginny said. "It means we've been working hard."

The next Saturday would be the qualifying competition. I learned that the college could only bring five competitors in each dance form, and Maria let us know that she expected us to qualify in every one of them.

"In all of the years that Richard has worked here, we have only had two couples qualify in every dance," Maria said, "And in both cases, there were just the two of them with no other girls or guys in the mix."

Then Maria said something I hadn't realized before.

"Anyone who qualifies in any dance form will automatically qualify to compete in the all-around competition."

A problem with that suddenly dawned on me. Jill must have seen the concerned look on my face.

"What's wrong, Tom?" she asked.

"If I were to qualify with every one of you, that would mean you were all eligible for the all-around competition. But I can only dance with Ginny. That's so unfair to the rest of you. All of you should have a chance to compete in the all-around."

"Well, Mr. Logic," Sally said, "for your information, none of us would have had partners for dancing at all if it wasn't for you."

"That's right," Danielle said. "Most boys will end up competing with only one girl for every dance, and that girl is their girlfriend. None of us have boyfriends except for Brenda."

"And he's not a dancer," Brenda said.

"I can't understand why every one of you doesn't have a boyfriend. You're all beautiful, wonderful ladies."

"That's nice," Linda replied, "but the fact remains that we don't."

"Maybe it's because we spend all of our time here and don't have time for anything else," Danielle said.

"Or maybe it's because the other boys see us with you and are intimidated by your muscles," Sally said.

"I don't think so," I replied.

"I know for me, I've had enough of other boys for a while," Jill said. "I'd rather spend time here with all of you."

"But what about not getting to dance in the all-around competition?" I asked.

"I don't think I'm speaking just for myself when I say that none of us would prefer to dance with anyone else," Linda said.

"There's another big advantage of having multiple girls dancing with you," Maria added. "The girls will have time to be in the dresses appropriate for their particular dance forms, and that will give you an added advantage. The costume plays a part in the judging, whether it is supposed to or not. You will need every advantage you can get, because the competition will be tough."

"And don't feel bad about us not getting to compete in the all-around," Jill said, "because we want you and Ginny to win it, and we want to be on the side cheering you on."

Ginny took my hand and looked into my eyes. "The girls and I have already talked about this, Tom. They'll cheer us on, and hopefully, we can feel any win would be for all of us."

Maria smiled and sounded like she was about to cry. "I don't think I have ever seen a group that is as unified as the seven of you are. That alone makes you a winning team."

As the week progressed, there was something else that began to concern me. Ginny was starting to tremble again. When I asked her about it, she brushed it off. But this time I knew the reason, so I privately visited with Maria about it. She had already noticed it, and she took Ginny and me to conference privately in Dr. Carlson's office.

Ginny was concerned she would have to give up her dream of winning the all-around competition and had a hard time admitting she was feeling weak again. But she finally realized she had to face it.

"Then we're going to adjust things a little bit," Maria said. "Tom is strong enough to carry you if he needs to. We're going to bring you in even closer to him, at least in the slow dances, so he can put his arm further around you, and you can rest against him."

As Maria adjusted our dances, the other girls understood what was happening without even being told. It wasn't a big change, and it didn't take much to get used to it. By the end of the week, Ginny and I were dancing as if we had always done it that way. She leaned heavily on my arm, and I found myself tiring more, but I was in good enough shape that my muscles would rejuvenate between dances.

Maria, for her part, just smiled. "It looks even more like Ginny is just gliding around the floor on her tiptoes."

There was one other thing we did. Ginny asked me to take her to the hospital for a blood test, and the doctors checked the levels of the different medicines in her blood. They adjusted them a little, and within a day, Ginny said she felt somewhat better, even if she still trembled.

On Thursday that week, the Performance Dance Team was performing for the university on the stage in the large, main gym. On Wednesday, in Competitive Dance, Dr. Carlson announced that he was retiring and that the Performance Dance Team's presentation would be the last he directed at the college. They would be going on tour after the semester, and then he would pass the direction of the team to someone else.

"I'm having a big retirement party in the evening after the International Ballroom Championships," he said. "I want it to be a Performance Dance Team reunion. All team members past and present are welcome. So if you are in contact with any members from previous years, please invite them."

I looked forward to the team's performance, and I had purchased tickets the minute they became available so Ginny and I could have seats near the stage. Because Ginny and I practiced each night during the time the Performance Dance Team practiced, I knew everyone on the team.

Ginny and I cheered for all of them as they performed, but we especially cheered when there were dances that Sally, Danielle, Linda, Brenda, or Jill were in. It was an outstanding performance.

We had one more day before the Saturday qualifyings. Jill had been joining the rest of us at the Friday open hour since she had become part of the group again, and the five of us were there practicing. A few extra people showed up that day and asked Dr. Carlson to show them a few things, but he mostly spent his time with us. The Performance Dance Team had the day off from class since they had performed the previous night, so the seven of us met to practice for the four hours. Maria also came to coach us and brought the freshly cleaned clothes. She didn't want us to wear them until the next day, and she insisted on taking my shoes to have them "shined professionally and properly."

"But I didn't bring my other shoes," I complained.

"Well, you know what we're going to do about that," Maria replied, pointing to the costume closet.

When we finished that night, we all agreed to meet at the dance studio at six-thirty the next morning. The qualifyings didn't start until eight o'clock, but we didn't want to feel rushed.

22
Qualifying

✢

The next morning, I got up, showered, and walked to the dance studio. I was right on time, but Maria and the girls were already there. A few other couples were there, too, warming up. Each of the girls had their hair done in a different style. They were all beautiful.

I dressed in my newly dry-cleaned suit. Maria hadn't let us wear our dance clothes since she'd had them dry cleaned. She handed me my shoes. I thanked her and put them on. The girls each put on their first dresses and carried the others as we walked across campus to the student activity building. The competition would be there in one of the ballrooms.

The judges were going to be some dance teachers from local dance studios, along with others from the college. Dr. Carlson and Maria were not allowed to judge since Dr. Carlson ran the Competitive Dance class and coached the Performance Dance Team. As it grew closer to eight o'clock, the room started to fill up. On one end, rows of chairs had been set up for spectators and for dancers who were not currently dancing. I learned that some couples planned to only compete in a few forms—some only one. None of these were on the Performance Dance Team. Everyone from that team who was competing was participating in every form. They made up the majority of the dancers.

Before the first dance started, Maria looked us over. She almost looked like she would cry.

"You're quite a group," she said. "I don't think I have anything to say. Well, yes, one thing. Don't forget to smile, Tom. And just let your reflexes work for you."

"That's two," I said.

She laughed. Her laughter helped, but I was still so frightened I could hardly breathe.

When they made the first call for the waltz, Ginny took my hand and looked at me. Suddenly she seemed very anxious.

"Tom, I can feel your pulse in your hand."

I nodded. "I'm scared to death."

"Don't be. It's no different than in the studio. Take some deep breaths and just concentrate on me."

"I don't even know exactly how this works," I said. "Dr. Carlson talked about tap out, but I don't even know what that means."

Ginny laughed. "I can't believe we've never explained it to you. The judges walk around, and if they see someone make a mistake, they tap the man on the shoulder, and the couple is out."

"So just keep away from the judges so they can't tap you?"

Ginny laughed again. "That's not quite how it works, but it's not a bad idea."

As I concentrated on Ginny while we talked, I could feel my heart slowing.

The second call for the waltz came, and I took Ginny by the hand and led her to the dance floor just as Maria had shown us. There were probably a hundred or more couples on the floor. Ginny and I held our position until the music began to play. We started out rough, but as the music played, and I looked into Ginny's eyes, my heart slowed further, and my reflexes took over. At one point, Ginny smiled emphatically and raised her eyebrows, and I realized I was concentrating again and not smiling. I smiled, and gradually everyone else in the room left my consciousness, and the dancing felt natural.

They paused only seconds between songs. Ginny and I held our positions, and I didn't look around. I was afraid it would throw me off. Eventually, the music stopped and didn't start again. I was still concentrating on Ginny when a voice came over the sound system.

"Will the final five contestants please report to the judge's table?"

I looked around, and we were one of only five couples still on the floor. As the crowd cheered, I pulled back from Ginny, holding her by one hand, and I bowed as she curtsied as Maria taught us. We then went to the judge's table to have our names recorded. The judges also had the couple that had been tapped out last come over, and their names were recorded as an alternate in case someone couldn't perform at the competition the next week.

We walked over to where our group was. Maria was only half smiling.

"You were lucky no judges were near you when you started. If they had been, you might not have qualified. As it was, I think you barely made the top five."

I switched my tie and took off my coat as Ginny slipped away to change into her second dress. Almost immediately, the first call was made for the tango. Maria looked into my eyes.

"Just relax, Tom, and let your reflexes do the work. Your body knows what it needs to do. Let it do it. And don't forget to smile."

I reached out my hand to Sally, and she took it. We waited until the second call came, and then I escorted her to the floor. I kept my concentration on Sally. She had a pretty smile, though it almost seemed mischievous. Her smile helped me remember to keep my own.

Though Sally was the youngest of the girls, what she might have lacked in experience, she made up for in enthusiasm. Her energy always rubbed off on me, and soon I had forgotten anything but dancing and was enjoying myself. I was surprised when the music stopped and didn't start again. I could hardly believe the tango competition was done. Once more the announcer called for the last five contestants to come to the judge's table.

Everything seemed to be going well. Linda and I qualified in the foxtrot, and Brenda and I were doing well in the quickstep when the strap on her shoe broke. She hardly missed a beat. In an instant, she pushed on the back of her other shoe with her stocking foot, pulling that shoe off as well. She danced the rest of the dance in her nylons. A judge picked up the shoes, and I wondered if she would tap us out, but she didn't. Once more, we qualified.

When we came back to the group, Maria was excited.

"Incredible job, you two!"

"It wasn't me," I said. "Brenda just kept going, and I stayed with her. I actually thought we would have to stop."

Maria gathered us all around. "That needs to be a lesson to all of you. If some part of your clothing fails, just keep going. It's unlikely you would be disqualified for a clothing malfunction."

"What if we're totally naked?" Sally asked with a smirk.

"That might be the exception," Maria said. "But where you girls are all wearing bloomers, it's unlikely. I've seen girls' skirts stepped on and ripped off more than once."

The rest of the dances went similarly, except there were no more mishaps. We qualified in each one. Maria let us know how she felt we did compared to the other four qualifying couples by merely saying, "That was great!" or "We still need some work."

If she said, "That was great!" I knew she felt we were the best couple out there. If she said, "We still need some work," I knew she felt others were better.

Each form was allotted half an hour. Some took less, but the schedule was set, so there were a few times that we had a welcome break. Some couples dancing in only one form would come at the scheduled time for their dance and then leave. When the competition ended at around two o'clock, I felt exhausted—as tired as after a long day at a wrestling tournament. But it was a different tired. It was more mentally exhausting.

As we walked back to the studio, Maria said, "One competition down, one to go." She then turned to me. "Tom, you're only the third person since we've been here to qualify in every form, and the only person to qualify with multiple partners. Make sure you're ready, because it will take longer to whittle down the competitors at the International Ballroom Championship, and they will only give about ten to twenty minutes between forms. Less if they start to fall behind schedule."

When we got to the studio, we changed back into our regular clothes. When I came out of the dressing room, Maria was waiting for me.

"Tom, I need your suit."

"What for?"

"To dry clean it, of course."

I started to say something about her having just done it, but a wrinkle of her nose, and I stopped and retrieved it.

When I carried it out, Sally held her nose. "Good call, Mrs. C."

The other girls and Maria laughed.

"Just remember," Maria said, "he had to dance six times as much as any one of you and only had one outfit."

"So, what are you all going to do now?" Danielle asked everyone. "Would you like to go have some pizza to celebrate?"

"I would love to," I said. "But where it's spring, my father could use all the help on the farm he can get."

"Then how about tonight after it's too dark to work?" Linda asked.

We all agreed that would work.

"Can I go home with you, Tom?" Ginny asked.

"Sure. I'd love to have you along."

It was nearly four by the time Ginny and I made it to my home. My mother had some food ready. We didn't eat a lot, and I told her we wouldn't be eating dinner later because we were meeting the others for pizza.

I worked hard getting the main things done my father needed, and soon it was too dark to work. I showered, and then Ginny and I headed back. We went directly to the pizza parlor. The other girls were already there, and so were Maria and Dr. Carlson.

Dr. Carlson shook my hand. "That was quite the performance today, Tom."

Maria patted her husband's arm. "Don't go giving him a big head. It isn't anything compared to what he'll face next week."

As we all ate, laughed, and had a good time, I tried to forget about the next week and just have fun.

23

The International Ballroom Dance Competition

⟊

here was no dance class the next week. Instead, it was
replaced with time for the qualifying couples to practice. Dr. Carlson said
that with some people qualifying in two or more dances, there was a total
of ninety-six different dancers who would be representing the college,
including the alternates. He hoped to win a team trophy and asked all
qualifying couples to come for coaching.

I was amazed to see that only thirty-five people showed up. Our
group of seven was among them. We practiced hard. Dr. Carlson and
Maria both went around the room making suggestions. When class
finished, Dr. Carlson invited anyone who wanted extra help to come to the
dance studio from one o'clock until five o'clock.

When I arrived at the dance studio at one, Maria and Dr. Carlson
were there, and so was Sally. The other girls soon arrived. I assumed
some of the other couples would come, too, but none of them did.

As we practiced, both Dr. Carlson and Maria would give us
pointers. If there was anything they differed on, Dr. Carlson always
deferred to Maria's opinion.

The rest of the week went much the same way, except the number
of couples coming to dance class for coaching faded away. Soon there was
our group and just a couple of others. Maria got my suit back on
Wednesday, but we just hung it up to wait for Saturday. The girls also
dressed in their school clothes. On Friday, Maria wanted to take my shoes
to have them polished again. I had started wearing my tennis shoes and
carrying my dance shoes just in case. I didn't want to wear slippers again.
Though I had tried not to let anyone see me, the last time I had worn them,
some of my roommates saw me before I could take them off. I thought I
would never hear the end of it.

Our group gathered around to talk about plans for the next day.
Our college had never hosted an International Ballroom Championship
before, so it was considered a big deal.

"Does anyone have any questions before we talk about the
agenda?" Maria asked.

"I have a lot," I said.

"Ask away," she said.

"So, if they stop with the last five people, how do they know who placed first, second, third, and so on?"

Maria laughed. "You never have competed in one of these, have you? Didn't Richard talk about it in class?"

"Not really. Everyone else had been to one before. So last Saturday was my first experience."

"Well," Maria said, "this is slightly different. Since they are looking for placings and not just qualifiers, they will go until only one couple is left. When they get down to the last ones—and it's ten, not five—they will record the ordering of elimination to determine placing."

"How will they know our names?"

Maria laughed. "It's funny that those of us who have done it take it for granted and don't even think about it. But what happens, Tom, is that you're assigned a number. So as you exit the floor, they just write down the number that is pinned to your back and then correlate it to your name."

"Will the girls' and the boys' numbers be like in football, where the number you wear has something to do with your position?"

Maria laughed again. "Well, I just learned something. I didn't even know the numbers meant anything in football."

"Sure, they do. For example, linemen and backs have different numbers from each other so the refs know if somebody is somewhere they shouldn't be."

"It's not like that in a dance competition," Maria replied. "First off, only the boy wears a number, and his partner is correlated to him and his number on each dance. And secondly, there is no difference in position for different couples in dance."

She laughed and then continued. "You really have been into athletics, haven't you? How did you get into dance?"

"It's a long story," I said.

"Do you have any more questions?" she asked.

"Just one. Are there going to be teams from schools all over the world? We have almost a hundred competitors from our school alone, so how are we all going to fit in the gym with the spectators? It only holds about ten thousand."

"I should have expected that from someone in math. But first, you need to understand, Tom, that even though it's called an International Ballroom Championship, it isn't quite like sports, where you compete at different levels moving up. It's one overarching international ballroom organization, and they sponsor different championships all over the world, each called an International Ballroom Championship. If a country is small, it might have one. If a country is big, like the U.S., it might have a few. This is the one for this region of the United States."

"I get it," I said. "It's like our regional wrestling tournament but with a fancier name."

Maria laughed. "Yes, something like that. But don't be fooled. It will be packed and will be a big event. Not only is it schools, but dance academies will also be there. Winning one of these is still an incredible feat for anyone." She paused and looked at me and asked, "Do you have any more questions?

"Not right now," I replied.

"We have a few complimentary tickets the college has paid for," Dr. Carlson said. "Do any of you have family, friends, or roommates coming?"

All the girls raised their hands, and Dr. Carlson started giving them tickets.

"Don't you have anyone coming?" Maria asked me.

"It's kind of hard for my family to get away from the farm in the spring," I replied. "And I didn't tell my roommates, because I don't think they would believe I qualified in dance, anyway."

"Oh, I'm sure that's not true," Maria said.

All the girls had family members coming.

"It will be fun to meet them," I said.

"We want them to meet you, too," Ginny replied.

"Absolutely," Jill added.

The others added their agreement, too.

"My dad said he'd pay for dinner for all of us tonight," Sally said. "Maybe your families could all join us, but it would be Dutch for them."

The girls all liked that idea. Sally told us it would be a restaurant called The Golden Corral. We decided on six-thirty so we could all get home and get changed first.

"The competition starts at nine," Maria said. "It will take some time to get checked in, so let's meet here at seven tomorrow morning for that."

Everyone agreed to that, too. No one had any more questions, so we went to our apartments. Just before six-thirty, I went to the restaurant. Some cars were arriving ahead of me, and I wondered if any of them were the girls' families. When I climbed from my pickup, Sally came running, pulling a lady behind her. I had to smile. The lady looked like a mirror image of Sally, only older. She had the same light red hair, the same mischievous grin—everything.

"Tom," Sally said. "This is my mom."

I laughed. "I would have guessed either that or a sister."

She laughed the same laugh Sally did. "You and I are going to be good friends."

The other families started arriving. Brenda came with Brett, her parents, and two brothers. Danielle came with her parents, one brother, and three miniature models of herself. Linda's family were all blond like she was. Jill's family came next. She brought her mother, father, two sisters, and two brothers. When Jill introduced her father, he reached out his hand.

I took it, and he didn't just shake my hand but held on. "I want to thank you for what you did for Jill. She had told us a little bit about Taran, but I didn't know how bad he was until he was no longer in her life. She's extremely grateful for you, and so are we."

Ginny's family came last. There was her mother, two older sisters, and one younger brother. As we moved into the restaurant, Ginny's mother talked about when Ginny's father had died in a ranch accident when Ginny was about sixteen. That was when Ginny's mother had to sell the ranch. I had learned a lot from Ginny as we traveled to and from my parents' home each Saturday, but her mother shared details Ginny hadn't.

"Ginny told us all about going horse riding with you," Ginny's mother said. "She hasn't done that since we sold the ranch."

Ginny's mother also talked about how, after Ginny graduated from high school, that Ginny would work fall and winter and use the money to travel with a dance team to different parts of the world in the summers. But eventually, she decided she needed to go to college.

As we moved into the restaurant, all the families said they were fine paying for their own daughters, so Sally's dad didn't have to.

"Well, at least let me pay for you, Tom," he said.

"I can pay," I replied.

He shook his head. "Sally has told me how you're paying your own way through college, and you gave up working extra hours to practice dance. The least I can do is pay for your dinner."

"Thank you, sir," I replied.

As her father was paying for us to go in, Sally grabbed my hand and pulled me inside.

"Have you ever eaten here before?"

I shook my head. "I don't eat out much."

"You're going to love it," she said. "It a buffet. All you can eat for one price."

Sally's dad had reserved a big conference room in the back for all of us. There were a couple of long tables. Sally claimed a seat on one side of me, and Ginny sat on the other. I ate more than I should have, and I realized I better stop, or I would be in no shape to dance the next morning.

We all talked more than we ate, and it was about eight-thirty when Dr. Carlson suggested we ought to get some sleep so we would be ready to compete.

I drove to my apartment and went right to bed. But between the food, my noisy roommates, and my apprehension about the next day, it was a long night. My dreams were interspersed with strange things, too. I dreamed I was dancing in competition, but then I realized I was dancing the wrong dance form for the music. I next dreamed that I got the wrong day and missed the dance competition altogether. My last dream was the strangest. I came into a ballroom, and the six girls were all waiting for me in their beautiful dresses. Then I realized I was dressed in my wrestling singlet. But the strangest part was nobody seemed to notice, and I was the only one concerned about it.

I was glad when I woke up. I got up at six o'clock, showered, dressed, and then ate breakfast. When I left to go to the dance studio, my roommates were all still asleep. I was right on time, but when I walked in, Maria, Dr. Carlson, and all of the girls were there. Each girl again had her hair done beautifully, even more so than the week before. I wondered what time they had to get up to do that. When I asked about it, Danielle answered my question, but not directly.

"We all met at our apartment, and our mothers came and helped us get ready," she said.

I dressed in my suit and the girls dressed in their first dresses. Maria had my shoes ready for me. When we gathered together, I looked around the circle, and I thought that these were the most beautiful, wonderful girls and friends a person could have. And as I realized that our time together was nearly over, and after finals and graduation the next week, I might not see any of them again, it was all I could do to hold in my emotions.

Maria didn't hold back hers. "You seven are the most wonderful . . ." She paused, unable to speak, as the tears rolled down her face. Finally, she was able to speak again. "You are the most wonderful seven young people I have ever met. And today, I want you to know that win or lose, I'm proud of you and the work you have put in to get here."

Maria checked everyone's clothes, especially making sure my tie was straight and my hair was smoothed down. The others who had qualified were to meet there at seven-thirty, and they soon started coming in. Maria was checking their dress as well. She insisted on modesty since the college was a religious school.

Dr. Carlson and Maria gave us a pep talk, and then we all walked as a team to the main university gym. It was barely eight o'clock, time for check-in to start, but the lines were already long. There were multiple tables with different letters of the alphabet indicating which school the competitor was representing. All of us boys got in the line for Q to S. When Dr. Carlson told the check-in person our school, she turned to the right page. Each boy stated his name, then the person at the table called out the boy's number, and an assistant looked through the stack of numbers and retrieved it.

"Tom Johnson," I said when it was my turn.

The woman scanned through the names. "Tom Johnson," she repeated. "Number 876."

The girl with the stack of numbers found mine and handed it to me.

The girls were taking the numbers and pinning them on the boys' backs.

Ginny took mine. "May I have the honor, Tom?"

There was a little box of pins on the table. Ginny got one and pinned the number onto my suit coat.

"Don't forget that when Tom switches in or out of his suit coat, he will need to switch the number," Maria said to all the group. "You girls can help remind him."

It wasn't long before the gym started to fill. I looked up in the seats behind where our team was and could see all the girls' family members. Some of them waved, and we waved back.

A man swaggered over to Dr. Carlson.

"How do you think your little school is going to do this year?" he asked in an arrogant tone.

"I suppose we'll see," Dr. Carlson answered, somewhat coolly.

"Maybe if your school was a four-year school instead of a two-year college, so you had longer to train them, you might do better," the man said with a bit of a laugh.

After the man returned to his own team, Dr. Carlson turned to Maria. "I have always said I've never met a man I don't like, but I'm willing to make an exception for Dr. Traverson."

Maria smiled, and when Dr. Carlson realized we had all watched the exchange, he spoke to us.

"Dr. Traverson's team has won first and has had the overall champions for the last four years in a row. But he's not against using tricks to get there, and he can be quite mean to his students. We have never placed in the top three and won a trophy. But we have come close. The fact that we are much smaller school and have still nearly won gets his goat."

When the announcement came for everyone to clear the basketball court where the competition would be, Ginny took my hand.

"Tom," she said, "I can feel your heartbeat through your hand again."

"When I said I was frightened last week, it was nothing compared to now," I replied.

She took my other hand, too. "Just look at me," she said, "and take some deep breaths."

I took some deep breaths and looked into her eyes. I could feel my heart slowing.

"Don't you get scared when you wrestle in front of a crowd?" she asked.

I shook my head. "Wrestling isn't scary."

My heart was beginning to calm by the time they made the first call for the waltz, and then I felt it start to race again. Once more, she had me take deep breaths.

The second call came for the waltz, and I took her hand and led her to the dance floor. We stepped into position and held, waiting for the music. A few seconds passed as the judges moved into their positions on the floor. Finally, the music started.

Once the music started to play, the rest of the dancers faded out of my consciousness, and I was able to dance. I did have to watch for other dancers to avoid crashing, but Maria had had us practice this, placing the girls that weren't dancing on the floor around us. Without thinking about it, I would see other dancers out of the corner of my eye and avoid them.

The floor was filled with hundreds of dancers, and we went through many dances. Finally, I felt a tap on my shoulder and turned into the smiling face of a judge, and I knew I was out. I turned to see that there was only one other couple on the floor.

"The waltz champions," the announcer said, "is couple 231."

"We took second!" Ginny said.

I thought of a sign that Coach had hanging in the wrestling room. It said, "Second place is nothing more than a first-place loser." But the way Ginny said it, it sounded like she didn't think we had lost.

"Is second good?" I asked.

"It's wonderful!" she replied.

"Will the following couples report to the floor for their medals, and please line up in order." the announcer said. "Teams 231, 876, 542 . . ."

As we received our medals, a lady in a beautiful gown placed one over my head, while a man in a tuxedo placed one around Ginny's neck.

As we were making our way back to our team, we passed the section where Dr. Traverson was sitting. I heard him say to his assistant, "We need to keep an eye on 876."

I started looking around, and when we got to our team, Maria asked what I was looking for.

"When we passed Dr. Traverson's team, he told them they needed to keep an eye on 876. I'm trying to see whose number that is."

Maria grabbed me and turned me so my back was facing her. Then she laughed.

"It's yours."

"Oh yeah," I said, somewhat embarrassed. "No wonder I couldn't see it."

The tango was next, so Sally unpinned my number from my suit coat. I took off my medal and handed it to Maria, and then I took off my jacket and switched my tie as Sally pinned the number to my shirt. We had just finished when the first call came.

Sally took my hand. "Remember, just concentrate on me."

I knew that Ginny had talked to all of the girls. They were all encouraging me in this way to help me not to be nervous. When the second call came, I took Sally by the hand and led her to the floor. Her family cheered, and the other families joined in. We stood in position, still as statues until the music started. We danced through a few different songs, and everything was going well. But then there was a disaster.

Sally had a skirt that came to her knees in the front, but it came down near to her ankles in a v in the back. It was fascinating to watch it as I swooped down with her, and it swept across the floor. One couple kept moving closer to us, and to avoid them, I had to keep backing away. But then I did one low swoop with Sally, and in the instant when Sally's dress swept across the floor, the girl from that couple stepped away from her partner and stepped on Sally's dress.

I saw it coming, but I couldn't slow our momentum. Sally's skirt ripped away, leaving Sally in her bloomers. There was slight twittering laughter from the crowd, but Sally didn't miss a beat.

In a dance step, she stepped away from her skirt, saying, "Keep dancing!"

We did keep dancing, and Sally acted as if nothing had happened at all. She was still vibrant and tenacious in her form. But I could see the fire in her eyes that matched the amber color of her hair, and I knew that she knew, as I did, that the girl had done it on purpose.

A judge must have thought so, too, because she immediately tapped the couple out. The songs came and went, and Sally didn't act embarrassed at all in her bloomers, dancing as if she were still in her elegant dress. But eventually, the tap came on my shoulder. I looked, and there were two other couples still on the floor.

I turned to find Sally's skirt, and the judge who had tapped out the other couple smiled and handed it to me. As I led Sally from the floor, the smile on her face was unflinching. But the instant we stepped off the floor by our team, everything changed.

The smile disappeared from Sally's face, and she said, "I'm going to go kick somebody's butt!"

She turned toward Dr. Traverson's dance team, but Dr. Carlson grabbed her arm. "No, Sally. That's what they want you to do. They would love nothing more than to have you confront that girl and find yourself disqualified from the competition."

"Besides," Maria said with a slight smile, "they're going to call the medalists to the floor soon, and you might look a little better if you were wearing your skirt."

Sally took a deep breath and let Maria pin the skirt on her. Maria had just finished when the announcer started calling the medalist numbers.

Before we stepped onto the floor, Maria grabbed Sally and hugged her.

"I'm very proud of you," Maria said. "You just kept going. I'm sure the crowd feels the same way."

Sally smiled, and that seemed to calm her anger more than anything else anyone said. And just as Maria predicted, when Sally received her medal, the crowd rose to a standing ovation, giving her far more applause than the couples who placed ahead of us. When the crowd kept cheering, Sally hugged me, and I looked to see Dr. Traverson scowling while Dr. Carlson gave us a thumbs-up sign.

Before the next dance, Dr. Carlson pulled me aside.

"Tom, what happened out there with you and Sally was no accident. I think Dr. Traverson's team is trying to sabotage your dancing. Try to stay as far away from his team members as possible. They're easy to distinguish. Every one of them is wearing teal and black."

"Teal?" I asked.

"Greenish-blue," he replied. "They may have different styles of clothes to match the different dances, but the colors are all the same."

I did watch for them, and I tried to keep my distance. Sally's courage seemed to invigorate our team. Linda and I placed first in the foxtrot, and another couple on our team placed fifth.

Brenda and I didn't place in the quickstep, but when we were tapped out, a fast count told me we were in the top fifteen. It was Ginny and me again in the Viennese waltz. I had learned from Ginny that she had chosen the first waltz because it was slow, and she was trying to save her energy for the all-around. She was also happy she got the Viennese one, too. I was also glad they were early on so she would have time to rest before the all-around.

The dancing was going well, and I was concentrating on Ginny when I saw the teal color on both sides of us. We were on the edge of the floor with little room to maneuver. I'm sure they were hoping to force me to back away and possibly stumble into the crowd. Instead, I stepped up toward them as they approached. They were coming toward us from different directions, but I realized one was just one step back from the other. Ginny and I danced in place for a split second. I hoped my timing would be right.

Just as the two couples took a dance step toward us, I swung Ginny in an arc, and we moved outside the couple that was farthest back. Without saying a word, Ginny responded to my directions perfectly. The other couples turned to block us, but instead ran into each other. Almost instantly, the judge who had handed me Sally's skirt was there and tapped both couples out.

I felt like the judges, at least the one, could see what was happening and was watching for it. As Ginny and I continued to dance, the two couples who had been tapped out walked to their team. When they reached the side, Dr. Traverson started screaming at them. I couldn't hear what he was saying as I concentrated on the music, but I felt sorry for them.

Ginny and I continued to dance, and no tap came. Finally, the music stopped, and I looked around. We were the only couple on the floor.

"Winning the Viennese waltz is couple 876," the announcer said.

Ginny and I turned to the audience, she curtsied as I bowed, and the audience erupted into applause, led by Ginny's mother, sisters, and brother.

When we came off after getting our medals, Dr. Carlson laughed slightly. "Nice maneuver, Tom."

Maria took my arm. "How are you doing, Tom?"

"I'm fine, why?"

"Each dance form is taking forty minutes or more. It's longer than the organizers planned for, and they sent word to all the teams that they have canceled the lunch break. One judge will sit out to rest on each round, and that judge will eat then. They said that dancers need to eat whenever they can grab something because they don't plan to have any breaks. The problem is, you're in every dance."

"I'll be okay," I replied. "Remember that wrestlers are used to losing weight."

She laughed, and I didn't tell her that I never dropped weight.

"There's one other challenge, Tom," Dr. Carlson said. "All seven of the next dances are full-energy."

"Don't worry," I said. "As long as the girls can stand to be around me when I sweat, we'll be okay."

He smiled and slapped me on the shoulder as the first call for the Lindy came over the speaker system.

Maria and Dr. Carlson tried to coach and help all five members of our team each time we headed out to the floor, but they were most concerned about the ones who had multiple dances in a row. I was the only one who had qualified in all twelve forms, so they seemed most concerned about me and getting me ready and back out.

Jill and I were doing well on the Lindy. But right at the end, I missed a move and was tapped out. We would have fifth. Jill seemed happy with that, but I felt bad for my mistake. As we came to the edge of the dance floor, I turned Jill to face me.

"I'm sorry I messed up."

She smiled and said, "Tom, you were wonderful!"

When it was time for the medals, another teammate received second, so I felt better knowing we did okay in the team standing.

Danielle and I went to the floor for the samba next. When I had first started dancing the samba I had asked Ginny about it.

"This is a strange dance," I said.

"You ought to see it done in South America. There it is often done as singles and not as couples."

As Danielle and I waited to move to the floor, I realized what Maria meant about some of the costumes not having much to them.

I joked to Danielle. "The amount of cloth in your costume could have made ten of some of these."

She smiled. We danced it well, but unfortunately, we didn't place.

When Sally and I stepped to the floor for the cha-cha, the crowd recognized her and cheered and clapped before the dance even started. Of course, her enthusiastic family helped fan the flames of recognition, but with her distinctive red hair, it wasn't too hard for people to know who she was.

I felt we performed flawlessly, and I never saw any teal dance costumes come near us. I think they figured that, especially with Sally, they were being watched. Once again, we ended with no tap out. When the announcer said, "The winning team for the cha-cha is couple 876," the crowd again rose to their feet cheering. Sally's performance through the loss of her skirt in the tango had made her the darling of the day.

Sally stayed stoic through the reception of the medals. But the minute we stepped off the side by our team, she started squealing and hugged me.

The call for the rumba was so quick I barely had time to get my tie in place. Maria adjusted it, and Linda and I went to the floor. But toward the end, we were tapped out without placing. I wasn't sure what we had done wrong, but apparently, the judge had seen something I missed.

I had a slight breather and had my tie in place before the first call came for the jive. I love the music and movement for the jive, and I enjoyed dancing with Brenda. Brett was cheering loudly for her, and it made her smile. We placed sixth. I was hoping we would do better, but I was beginning to learn that getting any medal at all was good. It was so different from wrestling.

Again, I was barely able to get my tie in place before the swing was called. Danielle and I went to the floor. The dancing was going well. I tried to stay away from edges after what happened to Ginny and me. The swing takes lots of space, and I saw some teal-dressed dancers tightening in on us. I pulled Danielle in close and rolled us in between two teal-dressed couples. But then, instead of spinning her out where there could have been a collision, I rolled under her arm, pulled her out to me, and we were outside the other dancers. One of those couples was immediately tapped out, and we never had trouble with them again. When I felt the tap on my shoulder, I looked to see only one other couple on the floor.

After Danielle and I received our medals, we went to the side, and Maria handed me a towel. I wiped the sweat from my face and hands. The whole inside of my shirt was wet, and I wished I could have done something about that.

"Only one more dance form," Dr. Carlson said. "Give it all you've got."

The call for the polka came quickly. Maria must have known it would. She had my tie tied. I just slipped it over my head and pulled it tight. Maria straightened it, and Jill and I stepped to the dance floor.

The polka was one of my favorite dances, and despite how tired I was, Jill's energy was contagious, and we ended up with a third-place win. I kept an eye out for anyone in a teal and black dance costume, but I didn't see any.

As Jill and I came off the floor from receiving our medals, I looked at the clock. It was almost six. I hadn't had any food since breakfast and had only had what water I could quickly grab between dances. I was beginning to feel the toll. But there wasn't time for anything, because the all-around competition was about to begin. Dr. Carlson pulled our team together.

"Right now, the team point standing is just a sliver apart for the top five teams. Winning the all-around would put any one of the five into first place, unless some other team wins multiple places. We're currently in third. In second is a dance team from Arizona, and in first is . . ." He paused and sighed, somewhat resigned before he continued. "In first is Dr. Traverson's team. I hate to say it, but I would rather beat him than win a trophy. However, I'd prefer to do both. But all of you who will be competing in the all-around need to keep your eyes open, because his team is not against making questionable moves, as we have already seen a couple of times today."

We had thirty-eight couples competing. I was glad to know all of us would be out there together.

The announcer came on the sound system. "Will all dancers who are planning on competing in the all-around please move to one of the three designated sections."

Dr. Carlson pulled me aside. "Tom, I know you're exhausted, and I hate to tell you this, but I have had Ginny go reserve seats for the two of you to make sure you'll be in the first section for the all-around."

"What does that mean?" I asked.

"There are so many dancers they can't fit them all on the floor. For everyone to dance, they're dividing the dancers into three groups. Each round will narrow that group to about one-third of the dancers in it. Once all three groups have been reduced, the remaining dancers will come together for the final round. I wish you could have some time to rest, but I felt that if Ginny could be in the first round, that would give her two rounds to rest before the final. That would be almost an hour."

"I'm glad you did that," I said, "and I appreciate your confidence that we'll make it to the final round."

"I'm sure you will," he replied. "There's one other thing," he said. "I've realized something as I have watched the performances. There is one judge who is especially vigilant in watching for Dr. Traverson's team trying to get you. She's the one who handed you Sally's skirt. Dr.

Traverson seems to be aware of it as well because when she's on the floor, none of his team tries anything. I'm sure that's why no one bothered you and Jill. But if she's not on the floor, be especially mindful of those around you."

"Thanks for the warning," I replied.

I gulped down what water I could, slipped the tie Maria had waiting for me over my head and pulled it tight. She straightened it, hugged me, and said, "Win it!"

I nodded and left to find Ginny. It took me some time to find the section she was in. I got the seating backward and was looking in the third section. One of my teammates eventually saw me and came to my rescue.

I slid into my seat by Ginny just as the announcer started explaining the process for the all-around.

"Tom," Ginny said, "you look exhausted."

"I am a bit," I replied. "I just hope you can stand to dance with me, as sweaty as I am, and won't be embarrassed to stand by me when we win."

She smiled. "I'm glad you're feeling more confident. The fear seems to have left you."

"I have some dances under my belt, and I'm too tired to be scared."

"Are you going to be okay?" she asked.

"I'll be fine," I replied. "You worry about you, let's hang on to each other, and let's win this."

The announcer finished, and all of us in section one moved to the floor. I looked around, saw the judge who had given me Sally's dress, and breathed a sigh of relief. Ginny and I held our position, and finally, the music began to play.

We danced, and I held tightly to Ginny. She trembled some, but she was doing well. We danced a mixture of dances. When we finished a swing dance, I could feel her trembling more. By the time we reached the last dance in that set, she was trembling so much that I wondered if we would make it through. But it was a slow dance, and I held her close. I was grateful when the directors decided the numbers had been reduced enough.

Those of our group not yet eliminated moved back to our section, and the second group went to the floor. When a couple from Dr. Traverson's team was tapped out, I figured that was one less couple that would cause us problems. But when one of our team couples was tapped out, I would feel some loss at not having them in the last round with us. I had not had much chance to watch anyone else dance all day. During the short time I had been off of the floor I had been switching ties, drinking water, and preparing to go back on.

I had been watching the dancers for quite a while when I turned and looked at Ginny. She was sitting there very still, her eyes closed. I thought she was probably resting. But she was so still, and after a while, I grew concerned. I reached over and took her hand.

To my relief, she opened her eyes, but when she looked at me, an expression of shock showed on her face. That expression quickly gave way to one of excitement and joy.

"Alex!" she exclaimed.

I was so taken aback by this that I said nothing for a moment. When I could finally speak, I simply said, "Ginny?"

I didn't know what else to say. Was Ginny so sick she was delusional? I just stared into her eyes, trying to understand what was happening. She looked at me, smiling for most of a minute and said nothing. Eventually, her smile changed from one of ecstatic joy to her normal one. Then she said, "Tom?"

"Ginny, are you all right?" I asked.

She started to cry. "Oh, Tom. I was praying for help, and when I opened my eyes, you looked like Alex. It was like he was you—or you were him—or something. It seemed you not only looked like him, but you appeared to be dressed in the clothes he used to wear and everything. I felt like I heard his voice, and he said he was here with me—with us—that he was proud of us and would help us."

She paused, and I handed her a handkerchief to dry her eyes. Then she looked back at me and forced a smile.

"You probably think I'm crazy."

I shook my head. "No. I believe that sometimes those we love who have passed away are closer than we realize."

"It was strange," she said. "After I thought he spoke to me, everything changed back to normal."

"What I think is that when we return to the floor, let's believe the help is there, and it probably will be."

Ginny nodded and laid her head against me. "Thank you for not doubting me."

As we continued to watch the other dancers, I prayed for help, too. It had been a long day, and the break while watching the other groups was helping me recover. But I wasn't sure whether Ginny and I would have the strength to perform at our top level.

It was far too soon that the third group finished. The directors decided to make it as fair as possible by giving them a fifteen-minute break. Still, we were soon moving out to the dance floor. As we did, I looked for those from our team and those from Dr. Traverson's team. It was hard to pick out our team members because we all dressed in different colors. But Dr. Traverson's team members were all dressed the same, and there was still a sea of them to contend with. I looked to see if the judge who kept Dr. Traverson's team in line was on the floor. She was, and I again breathed a sigh of relief.

When we started our first dance, Ginny seemed to have a new level of energy, which surprised me. We did well. But after a few dances, especially once we had danced a swing, a jive, and a Lindy all in a row, I could see her energy fading. The number of dancers was reduced a lot, but I could still see quite a few dressed in teal and black.

As I held Ginny in position, waiting for the next music to start, she was really trembling. I also noticed that the judges were rotating in and out on each song, not staying in for the whole round. That's when I saw the judge who kept a check on Dr. Traverson's team step off the floor. Feeling Ginny tremble and knowing we lost the judge we needed, I prayed that we would at least have a waltz or something slower where I could hold on to Ginny. When the music started, I immediately knew it was a samba, a lively one, and my worst dance. I thought to myself, if Alex is here to help us, he's not doing a very good job.

As we danced, I could see Ginny's energy fading quickly. But then I saw something else that concerned me. I saw three couples dressed in teal and black moving in tandem toward us. There was no way I could move around them, and they kept coming. There was little I could do besides back us away. But like a blockade, they kept pushing us back farther and farther until we were forced to a corner of the gym floor.

I could do nothing but keep Ginny close and use smaller and smaller movements. It was destroying our dance form. I saw a judge coming toward us, and I was sure she would step through them and tap us out. I'm sure that's what the three couples expected because they left just enough room between them for a judge to step through, but not enough for a couple dancing the samba to make it without crashing into them.

When the judge reached us, she stepped between two of the couples, but instead of tapping us, she tapped the couple on either side of her. They looked stunned. The third couple immediately started trying to dance away, but the judge took a couple of quick steps toward them and tapped them out, too.

I immediately heard Dr. Traverson's voice as he swore and started yelling. The judge seemed unfazed by it. I thought the couples would quickly leave the floor like they were supposed to, and then Ginny and I could move out to where we would have some more room, but the couples hardly did more than act like they were moving to the side. Ginny and I were still blocked in. After about ten seconds, which seemed like forever when dancing in a small space, the judge spoke, which I had never heard a judge do on the floor before.

She said to the three couples, "If you don't vacate this floor in about a half a second, I'm going to start deducting team points."

The couples immediately moved off the floor. And then the judge did something else unexpected. She looked at us, smiled, did a little nod of her head, and walked toward the middle of the floor. Apparently, there was more than one judge who was watching Dr. Traverson's team.

Ginny and I had barely taken a few samba steps out into the more open floor when the song ended. Ginny and I stepped into our pre-dance position with me holding her with one arm, and our other arms extended. With the other girls, our hold position would be side by side holding one hand with the other hand out, but Maria had changed that for Ginny and me so I could hold her and she could rest on me. My arms were tiring from holding Ginny, and I was beginning to feel them quiver.

As we stood in position, I considered what had happened. I realized that if Ginny and I had danced the samba in open space, with the full movements and the energy of it, she might not have made it. Without realizing it, Dr. Traverson's team members might have saved us by forcing us to dance in a small space. Maybe Alex was helping us after all.

I looked around and counted. There were about three dozen couples left. A fair amount were dressed in teal and black. The judge that had previously stopped Dr. Traverson's team members from their attempts to interfere with our dancing returned to the floor.

As Ginny continued trembling, I prayed for a slow dance, and when the music for a waltz started, I said a prayer of gratitude in my heart. I held Ginny close, and she rested against me as she seemed to float around the room.

The two judges that helped us appeared to keep a close watch on Dr. Traverson's team members. I think some of the other judges did, as well. They must have watched for any small mistake and tapped them out for it, because when that dance finished, only about a dozen dancers were still on the floor, and there was not a teal and black costume among them.

Ginny was still trembling a lot, though her smile was constant, and I could sense her determination. I hoped again for a slow song, and Viennese waltz music started to play. Ginny and I danced it almost flawlessly, and I was amazed at her. When we ended, three couples remained, and the crowd was cheering. I felt wonderful knowing we would at least get third. But when I looked at Ginny and saw her teeth clenched in a smile, I realized that this was one time when even second wasn't good enough.

The music started again, and I immediately knew it was a swing. Ginny danced with energy beyond what I knew she had. When we ended, we were both perspiring. I held Ginny close, and she continued trembling, but she was doing all she could to hide it. The judges consulted, and one couple was removed. It wasn't us.

I hoped and prayed for a slow song, but when the music started, I realized it was a polka. However, it wasn't a fast polka, and I was grateful for that. Polka was also one of my best. Once again, Ginny performed beyond what energy I felt she had.

When we finished, and both couples came to a hold position, the crowd was so loud it was deafening. After the judges consulted, the announcer could not even be heard over the sound system. Finally, the crowd quieted down enough that we could hear.

"The judges have not been able to come to a consensus, so we are going to have the two couples dance one more dance."

The crowd started screaming so loudly I doubted I would be able to hear the music when it began. I was again praying for something slow. I didn't feel Ginny could do one more high-energy song. I knew she was afraid of passing out and was fighting to hold on with sure determination.

Finally, the crowd quieted. As the music started and the lyrics came, I recognized the song:

> Longer than there've been fishes in the ocean
> Higher than any bird ever flew
> Longer than there've been stars up in the heavens
> I've been in love with you.

It was the song by Dan Fogelberg that Ginny said we would make our song. I remembered that when Ginny asked me what it was, I said "waltz," but she said it was a slow rumba.

I pulled Ginny into rumba form, and we started dancing. Even as slow as we were going, she stumbled a little, and I reached out and held her. It was barely noticeable, but I was sure the judges would see it. Still, we did very well, and finally, the music ended.

I pulled Ginny beside me, and we stood in the hold position. I think Ginny might have said something to me, but if she did, I couldn't hear it for the cheering of the crowd. The judges consulted, and then the announcer spoke. But no one could hear him, and he had to ask for quiet.

Finally, the crowd quieted down, and he spoke again.

"The judges determined that both couples made some small mistakes. Couple 472 started out in waltz form when the dance is actually a slow rumba, but they quickly adjusted. Couple 876 had a couple of small stumbles in the middle. So, the judges have decided that the International Ballroom Champions will be . . ."

He paused for a moment for effect, and everyone was silent. Then he said, "Both couples!" Immediately, the crowd roared their approval as the announcer tried to shout over the noise. "Couples 472 and 876 will be Co-International Ballroom Champions. We don't have four medals, so we will give each couple one and try to get a second one to their schools."

I barely heard all he said. As he was shouting over the sound system trying to be heard, people were flowing onto the floor from every direction. I was sure that a lot of them were our teammates, but they were coming from all points of the gym. But as they came, others followed, until the whole floor was full of people.

In that instant, I could sense Ginny starting to fall, and I pulled her entirely into my arms and held onto her as if I was hugging her. And indeed, I did hug her, and she hugged me back. But it gave me a chance to hold her and let her rest in my arms. We were quickly enveloped in a circle of our teammates, all hugging us and speaking excitedly. In the center of it was Sally, Linda, Danielle, Brenda, and Jill.

The announcer kept yelling over the sound system. "Ladies and gentlemen, will you please take your seats. Ladies and gentlemen, will you please return to your seats. We still need to give the final medals and trophies. Ladies and gentlemen . . ."

Eventually, everyone returned to their seats, or at least off the dance floor. Ginny was able to stand again, but I still held tightly to her. The announcer then said, "It's customary that the winning couple, or in this case, couples, have a victory dance. But with the length of the competition, we will say the last dance was sufficient. Will the following couples please report to the dance floor to receive their medals? Couples 472 and 876. Couples 954, 173 . . ."

When all the couples were there, they started giving the medals, starting at tenth place. As each medal was presented, the crowd cheered, led by the team the couple was from. As they continued down the line, Ginny was resting heavily on my arm, and my arm was aching.

When they got to us and the other winning couple, the crowd again cheered so loudly the announcer could hardly be heard. Both couples would be given their medals at the same time.

As the women in the beautiful gowns approached, I asked Ginny, "Can you stand on your own for a moment?"

She nodded. As the woman stepped in front of us, she paused, as if unsure which one of us to put it on.

Ginny pointed to me. "Give it to Tom." She then smiled at me. "Tom, you've worked so hard that this should be yours."

"No, Ginny," I said. I turned to the lady and put out my hand. "May I?"

The lady smiled and handed it to me. I held it open, Ginny dipped her head, and I slipped it around her neck. "It's yours, Ginny."

She smiled as I continued. "What I received was greater than any medal. I've had the friendship of someone who cared enough to help me believe in myself. That's the greatest reward I could ever have."

Ginny started to cry and threw her arms around my neck.

The crowd continued to cheer as we moved to our seats. As I helped Ginny to her chair, she slumped down with exhaustion.

Maria was standing there, and I said, "I'm actually glad we didn't have a victory dance. I'm not sure Ginny could have made it through one more."

Maria smiled. "Richard thought as much. Dancers aren't supposed to run onto the floor like everyone did, but he figured that if they did, the victory dance would be ignored. He sent team members to all different parts of the room to lead the charge, thinking that other teams would follow their lead. And it worked. He was worried about Ginny, and he's not above doing something to help her. He knew it might have cost some team points, but he was willing to lose them for her."

"I thought it was our teammates coming from all directions," I said.

Maria smiled. "There are advantages to everyone wearing their own dance costumes and not being all dressing alike."

The announcer once again called for quiet, and finally, everyone settled down. He began to announce the placings.

"In third place, from California, Elegance Ballroom Academy."

The crowd cheered as a couple stepped to the floor.

"In second place, our sponsoring school, Ricks College from Rexburg, Idaho."

Our team started to scream with happiness, but another team did as well.

As I looked at them, wondering why they would cheer for us, Maria said, "They must realize they won first."

Dr. Carlson looked in our direction. "Tom, Ginny, do you feel up to getting the trophy?"

Ginny nodded, and I pulled her into my arms. With my arm tightly around her, we made our way to the floor.

"And in first place," the announcer said, "the winning International Ballroom Dance team, from Arizona, Dance Right Dance Academy."

The crowd went crazy, especially the winning team. They were the ones who cheered when our team was announced for second. Everyone was cheering. That is, everyone except Dr. Traverson's team. They stood quiet and stone-faced. Without any medalists in the all-around, they had moved out of the trophy standings.

Ginny saw me looking at them and said, "One team is going to have a long ride home."

The couple that joined us on the floor to accept the first-place trophy was the other all-around first-place couple.

As each trophy was given to the team representatives, the crowd cheered again. When the lady held out the second-place trophy to us, I nodded toward Ginny, and the lady handed it to her. I was holding Ginny tightly with one arm, and she had one arm around me as well. She took the trophy in the other hand and held it up as our team cheered.

I looked at our team, and though Dr. Carlson and Maria were both smiling, tears were streaming down their faces.

24
Part of the Team
✦

When the awards were over, I helped Ginny back to a seat on the side. Immediately, there was a rush of people congratulating us. But mostly, people just wanted to congratulate Ginny because she was the one they knew. I moved aside as people bent down to hug her.

More and more came, and gradually I stepped farther and farther away from Ginny. Though people would stop and shake my hand, they quickly turned and joined the line to Ginny. Soon I was standing outside a reasonably large crowd, and though people were still shaking my hand, I desperately wanted to see Ginny. I wanted to see people congratulating her, see the joy showing on her face as they did, but I knew there was no way I would get back through the crowd.

Then I thought of an idea. If I climbed the stairs to the main floor landing, I would have a good view. As I moved to the stairs, a few people shook my hand and congratulated me, but by the time I hit the stairs, it stopped. Away from the group, no one recognized me as Ginny's partner. I was okay without the attention because I felt awkward anyway.

I climbed the stairs and then went around the auditorium to a point where I could see Ginny's face. I didn't want to be straight across because I felt that might be awkward, but I was at an angle where I had a good view.

As people hugged her, they talked excitedly. Ginny, though exhausted, was also very animated. I stood there for some time, leaning on the railing and enjoying Ginny's happiness. But I suddenly had a strange feeling that someone was watching me. I turned, and there stood Maria.

"Oh, hi, Maria," I said.

"Tom, why are you up here?"

"So many people wanted to congratulate Ginny that I was outside the crowd, and I couldn't see her. I wanted to watch as people congratulated her." I turned back to look at Ginny. "She seems really happy."

Maria walked up beside me and leaned on the railing, also watching Ginny. "But Tom, you won, too. You ought to be down there."

I shrugged. "It's okay. This is Ginny's moment, and I'd rather watch her."

Maria turned and just stared at me for some time. When she finally spoke, there was a new realization in her voice.

"You didn't do this for you, did you?"

I shook my head.

"You're a strange person, Tom. I've never seen anyone who would do all of this work for someone else."

I turned and looked at her. "It's not that I didn't gain something from this, Maria. But what I've gained means more to me than any of the medals."

"So, what have you gained?"

"I've gained friends who believed in me in a way I didn't believe in myself. Friends like Ginny, Jill, Danielle, Sally, Brenda, Linda, and you and Dr. Carlson. I never believed I could dance, but you all made me feel like I could do anything if I tried hard enough."

She laughed. "It's hard for me to believe that you felt you couldn't dance."

"Well, it's true."

The auditorium had grown quite empty, except for groups excitedly talking here and there, one being our team. As the congratulations to Ginny and others on the team started to slow down, I breathed a deep breath.

"Well, I'm no longer needed here," I said. "I suppose I ought to go see if I can get some homework done. You'll make sure Ginny gets home okay after the celebration party, won't you?"

"What do you mean you're not needed here? Of course you are. And you're going to come to the pizza party at the student activities ballroom, aren't you? You do remember that Richard is paying for pizza for all former and current team members as part of his retirement gathering, don't you?"

"I'm not on the dance team, and I never have been."

Maria's smile turned to a look of surprise. "But you practice with the girls who are, and Ginny was on the team."

"That's because I met them in Competitive Dance."

Maria laughed and spoke like she thought I was teasing. "Right. Richard said everyone in Competitive Dance was on the Performance Team except for one clumsy athlete who accidentally got into the class, and . . ."

Suddenly she stopped and stared at me.

"And crashed and burned on the first day?" I asked.

"That's not quite what I was going to say."

"Well, it's true. I not only crashed, but I took others with me."

"But partway through the semester, Richard told me he was going to allow that athlete to drop the class because the girls were so mean to him."

"I chose not to drop. I figured if Ginny and the other girls in our group believed in me, maybe I should stay."

"But Richard never talked about that athlete again."

"Did he talk about Tom after that? That's when he started calling me by my first name."

Maria spoke quietly when she answered. "I suppose that is when he started talking about you by name. I never realized the two were the same. I thought the athlete he had been talking about dropped, and Richard's concern became more for another dancer named Tom to win at the ballroom championship."

"Well, we are definitely the same person," I said.

"So why were you always there when I came at the end of the Performance Dance Team practice?"

"Ginny and I practiced in the adjoining room while the team practiced. When I counted that time as practice time, I didn't mean with the team."

"I must admit that I didn't see you in the Performance Team show last week, even though I looked for you. I just assumed you were on the stage somewhere."

I laughed. "I was at the performance. But I wasn't on the stage. I was with Ginny in the audience. We did go backstage after."

She nodded. "I saw you then, and that's part of the reason I thought you were on the team."

Neither of us said anything for a moment, and I turned to leave, but she grabbed my arm.

"Tom, I owe you an apology. When you said you were frightened about performing, and I got mad at you, I didn't realize what you had been through. Richard told me about some of what he had learned about your early experiences, but I hadn't put it together that it was you."

"I suppose that's good," I said. "That means by the time we met, I had improved."

I meant it to be funny, but she didn't even smile.

"I was so hard on you," Maria said, "because I not only didn't understand what you had been through, but I felt you had far more experience than you really did."

I laughed. "You know what? I'm glad you were hard on me. I

don't think I could have done what I have if you hadn't been."

"Tom, I'm sure Richard didn't mean to exclude you when he invited the Performance Dance Team members. I'm sure he would want you to come."

"It's okay," I said. "With all the practice we've been doing, I'm behind on my homework and need to get it done. Besides, I think I would feel awkward around all of the team members because they're so professional, and I'm not really part of them."

Maria raised her eyebrows. "Do I need to tell you how stupid that sounds coming from someone who has just won the International Ballroom Championship? You're just as professional."

I laughed. "You know, that just seems weird to think about, especially considering where I started."

"Is there no way I can convince you to come to the party?" Maria asked.

I shook my head. "It's a party for those on the Performance Dance Team who have worked, traveled, and performed together. I just don't think I'd belong."

"Where do you belong, Tom?" she asked. "According to Richard, you're an incredible athlete, you're strong in academics, and to top it off, you're now an incredible dancer. Most people in one of those areas don't cross over into the others."

I thought about how my athlete friends teased me about being smart, and how some of the students in calculus didn't want to check answers with me because they thought I was a dumb athlete. I thought about my roommates' comments about how bad I danced.

"I don't know, Maria," I said. "Sometimes I don't know where I belong."

As I turned to leave, she pulled me into a big hug. When she pulled back, she was crying.

"Tom, one place you'll always belong in is in a very soft spot in my heart."

"And you in mine," I replied.

I turned and walked slowly down the hall. I kept pondering what Maria had said. Where did I belong? For the first time in my life, Maria, Dr. Carlson, Ginny, and the other girls made me feel like I did belong with them; like I was in their circle and part of something important. But I wasn't part of Performance Dance, and I was sure I would never step onto a dance floor in competition again.

When I reached the trophy cabinet, I stopped. There were some new wrestling trophies, some I had helped win. There was also a new plaque which read "Academic All-Americans" and at the top was my name. Again, I asked myself, "Where do I belong?" I didn't really know. I felt like I was part of multiple worlds but did not fully fit in any of them.

I turned to leave the building when I heard someone call my name. I turned to see Jill hurrying toward me. She called out again, this time saying, "Tom, wait!"

As I waited, she ran to me. She grabbed my arm and looked right into my eyes. "Tom, please come to the pizza party."

"But I'm not part of the Performance Dance Team," I said.

"But you're part of us, all of us. Especially those of us you danced with."

"But most of the girls on that team that were in our class seemed embarrassed to know me, and I'm not sure they want to have anything to do with me."

Jill bit her lip for a minute, and when she spoke, she cried. "There's not a girl on that team who treated you poorly who doesn't wish they hadn't. I know no girl treated you worse than I did, and there's nothing I regret more. But I would never turn you down again. I feel it's an honor to be with you. We all want you there. When everyone was congratulating Ginny, she suddenly stopped and asked where you were. When Maria told us that you left because you weren't part of the team and didn't want to interfere with the party, Ginny started crying. Tom, please. We all want you there. Ginny said she didn't want to go if you weren't there."

"But I think I would feel out of place. You're all such good dancers, and I'm . . ."

I stopped. Just like Maria said, it did sound funny after the events of the day. Why were those old feelings of inadequacy still nagging so strongly at my heart?

"Tom, you're an International Ballroom Dance Champion. You're just as good, or maybe even better, than anyone."

"You know, Jill, when I think back about this semester, starting with the disaster at the beginning to the conclusion of today, the whole experience seems surreal. It's like a fantasy dream from which I will hear the clock strike midnight and awake to find myself a peasant in ragged clothes."

Jill smiled slightly. "It's not going to happen, because it is real. Besides, we all want you there, and I know you haven't had anything to eat all day."

"I must admit, pizza does sound good," I said.

She grabbed my hand. "Come on. Ginny and the other girls are waiting and won't go to the party without you. I told them I wouldn't come back until I had you with me."

I squeezed her hand. "Thanks, Jill."

She smiled and pulled me toward the gym. "Come on."

When we arrived back at our team, it felt a little awkward, everyone telling me they were glad to have me back. I wasn't trying to make a big deal of it. I just didn't want to push my way into something when I didn't feel I was part of it.

Ginny took my hand. "Tom, we want you with us. All of us."

The girls I danced with all nodded vehemently, but so did the others on the team.

Dr. Carlson put his hand on my shoulder. "Tom, I didn't mean to exclude you when I said it was a party for the Performance Dance Team." He then laughed. "We all feel you are part of our team. Besides, you were probably involved in winning over half our points today."

"And we know you've got to be hungry," Sally said.

"Wrestlers can eat lots of pizza," I warned.

Dr. Carlson laughed. "I think I can handle it."

As we prepared to go to the ballroom for the party, Ginny tried to stand but collapsed back into her chair.

"Tom," Dr. Carlson said, "why don't you carry Ginny to my car, and we'll drive to the ballroom?" He then turned to the others. "We'll meet you there."

I lifted Ginny into my arms. She leaned against me as I carried her. Dr. Carlson opened the back door of his car, and I set Ginny in. I went around and climbed in the other side, and Dr. Carlson and Maria climbed in the front.

When we arrived at the party, I carried Ginny in. Sally and Jill retrieved a big plush chair from the foyer for her to sit in. They pulled around other chairs so the seven of us could sit in a circle. We were still in our nice dance clothes, so we had to be careful eating the pizza.

As we ate and visited, Ginny's energy revived somewhat. The girls were animated and happy.

At one point, Maria whispered to me, "Did you think these girls were going to let you get away with not coming here? Of course, I was going to tell them you left."

There was dance music, and some people danced, but I felt danced out. The girls in our group didn't seem inclined to do anything but sit and talk. As I looked at the medals around their necks, I smiled. They were all such wonderful ladies.

Ginny asked if I would get her a little pop, and I was happy to oblige. When I came back, the other girls said they were going to get some more pizza and left us alone.

Ginny thanked me for the pop and asked, "Tom, are you going to the graduation dance on Wednesday?"

I shook my head. "My father needs some extra help with spring planting and everything, so I thought I'd head home after graduation."

"So, you don't know who to ask, huh?"

I didn't answer. Ginny knew me too well for me to deny it.

"Tom, there's not a single one of those girls that wouldn't love to spend the evening with you."

"Right, Ginny. I love to spend time with all of them. But which one do I ask? Which one do I say is the most important while the others aren't? Every one of them is an incredible young lady and a good friend."

She nodded. "I never considered that dilemma." She paused for a moment, and then said, "My pizza is a little cold. Would you mind getting me a warm piece?"

"I'd be happy to," I said.

I went to get the pizza, and when I turned back, I saw that the girls were gathered around Ginny, and they appeared deep in discussion. When I came back, Ginny smiled, thanked me for the pizza, and then set it aside.

"Tom, how would you like to go with us—uh, me—to the Graduation Dance? I'm sure it will be the last dance I can dance at."

The other girls were all grinning mischievously.

"I'd love to," I said.

"I want to plan it, but I'll probably have some of the girls come to get you when I'm ready because I don't know how strong I'll be feeling," Ginny said.

"Okay," I replied.

The party went quite late. It was after midnight when it ended. Dr. Carlson and Maria drove Ginny and me to her apartment. I carried Ginny in. Her roommates had walked down to the studio and picked up our clothes, then met us at the apartment. They handed me mine.

"See you tomorrow for dinner?" Sally asked.

"I'd love that," I replied.

As I was walking home, I thought about my roommates. I pulled the medals from around my neck and slipped them into my suit pocket. When I walked in, about half my roommates were still up playing Uno.

"How did you do?" Joe asked.

"Okay," I said, as I headed to bed.

It all seemed to strange to talk about.

25

The Last Dance

✦

I was quite sore when I woke the next morning. I was concerned about Ginny. When I called and talked to Danielle, she said Ginny was doing better, but she could use some help getting to church. I dressed in my older suit since my new one smelled sweaty, and I drove to the girls' apartment. Ginny was up and dressed, but still quite weak. I held onto her and helped her into my pickup.

"Can we ride in the back?" Sally asked.

"In your church dresses?" I asked.

Sally nodded, and the other girls laughed.

"Sure, why not?" Danielle said.

"Okay," I replied.

Jill came, too, and I'm sure we were quite a sight driving down the road with four girls in the back of my pickup, dressed in their Sunday best.

When we got to church, I held on to Ginny all the way to our seats. Though I didn't usually attend their congregation, that day I did. Afterward, I made sure Ginny got home safely.

I took a nap in the afternoon and felt much more rested by evening. At dinner time, I made my way to the girls' apartment. Jill was there, and so were Brenda and Brett. Since the first time Ginny had invited me to dinner, the girls had invited me every Sunday, and Jill, Brenda, and Brett started coming, too.

I had insisted on helping with the food, and the girls seemed surprised that I could cook as well as I did. But this Sunday they said they had it covered. We had a delicious meal and enjoyed visiting. I liked Brett, and having another guy there made it so the girls, especially Sally, teased me less.

When it came time to sing at the nursing home, I prepared to drive Ginny over in my pickup. And sure enough, the girls all rode in the back. Brett and Brenda joined us, but they rode together in his car.

We had a good time singing together, and then I took the girls to their apartment.

Monday and Tuesday were finals. When I arrived at calculus on Monday, I waited for Bonnie. She came into class, late as usual because of her final hug and kiss for Kevin.

"Bonnie," I said, "I heard you're engaged."

She nodded.

"Well, I got the two of you a wedding present. It isn't much, but I thought you would like it. It's a gift certificate to the Golden Corral restaurant. I thought that after you were married, when life was really busy, it might be nice."

She hugged me. "Thanks, Tom."

The next day, I waited outside a classroom door where I knew Carol had class. When she came out, I stopped her.

"Hi, Carol," I said.

"Hi, Tom. It's nice to run into you. I've missed having you visit. Why don't you walk with me to my apartment?"

"No," I said. "Rochelle told me that you were engaged."

"That's kind of up in the air, and Mitch is gone right now, anyway. So why don't you come?"

"Thanks, but I really feel it would be inappropriate. And I didn't just happen to run into you; I was waiting for you. I know I won't be able to make it to the reception or anything, so I wanted to get you a present."

I handed her the envelope, and she asked, "What is it?"

"It's not much," I said. "And it's not very creative. It's just some coupons for dinner to the Golden Corral restaurant. I thought that after you were married, a night out might be nice."

"Thanks, Tom. You sure you won't come visit?"

I shook my head. "Thanks, but no."

I finished up my tests, and all the Competitive Dance class students had a scheduled time to visit with Dr. Carlson. We had to justify to him what we felt our grade should be. As I waited for my turn in his office, I filled out the form he had for us. It asked us how we felt we had done and what we felt our grade should be. I put a C. I had never had lower than an A in a class since I started high school, but I felt that in this case, it was a fair average for the whole semester.

When I stepped into his office, Dr. Carlson shook my hand, and then I handed him my paper. He had me take a seat, and then he looked at it.

"What?! A 'C'?!" he said in surprise.

"I figured if I averaged how well I did in the beginning and how well I did in the end, it would average out. I did pass, didn't I?"

He covered his eyes for a moment and sighed, then looked at me. "Tom, I don't even know why we're having this conversation. Only a math person would think in terms of average. But the grade is not based on an average of how you did, but on participation and improvement. In both of those, you far exceeded any student I have ever had. But there's nothing higher than an A, so I'll have to stick with that."

"The improvement grade is only good because I started out so bad."

He laughed. "But it's more because you ended up so good."

As I left his office, I thought about how good it felt to get an A in a class I was sure at the first of the semester that I would fail. It also felt strange not going to dance practice, anymore. It did give me more study time, and I had done well on my finals.

On Wednesday morning, I walked up to graduation with my roommates. But when I got there, Sally and Danielle were waiting for me.

"Come on, Tom," Sally said. "Come sit with us."

My roommates looked surprised as the two beautiful young ladies each took me by an arm to show me to the seat they had saved for me. When we got there, I found we were in the middle of Ginny's, Jill's, Linda's, and Brenda's families. Brett was also there.

My roommates Bryce, Joe, Sam, and David graduated, as did Bonnie. I clapped for all of them when they went through. But watching Ginny, Linda, Jill, and Brenda touched my heart. All four of them went up together. Jill and Linda were each on a side of Ginny, helping her. Brenda went ahead of them and handed the reader their cards.

He read, "Miss Brenda Barnes, Miss Jill Sanderson, Miss Genevieve Broadhurst, and Miss Linda Manning."

They walked through together, and our section cheered. I had never had friends like that. A lot of my life I worked alone out on the ranch with cattle and horses, and though I had some friends, I was never part of a group that watched out and helped each other as these girls did.

When it was over, we took pictures of them in their caps and gowns. The girls wanted some pictures of all of us. I thought they would want one as roommates, but instead, they wanted all seven of us, and added Brett, too.

We had previously all pooled our money, and Brenda's mother had purchased everything for hoagies. We went to a park and had a fun lunch together.

The others left, but Ginny said she wanted to visit for a minute. She just wanted to tell me that I should be ready for the dance any time after five o'clock. She didn't know exactly when she would be ready, but it would be after that. She talked to me for some time about a few trivial things, and I wondered if there was a reason for the visit that I wasn't catching. Then her mother and sisters took her back to her apartment.

Because Ginny asked me to the dance, on Monday I had taken my suit to the dry cleaner. I picked it up on the way back to my apartment. When I walked in, Bryce pointed at a large manila envelope lying on the table. "Some girls just brought that and left it for you. They said it was from their roommate."

It was from Ginny, and I realized that at the park, she had been delaying me so her roommates could deliver it. Inside was a note in Ginny's handwriting.

"Does the artist make the masterpiece, or does the masterpiece make the artist? The story is now told. Our time together is the story."

In between two pieces of cardboard was a painting of me. And yet it wasn't me. The way she had done my expression, especially my eyes, gave a depth to me that was not quite describable.

Bryce looked over my shoulder at it, looked at me, and then looked back at the painting. All he said was, "Wow!"

Others came in and wanted to see it.

"It makes you look like someone incredible, like Abraham Lincoln or something," Joe said.

A few of my roommates were heading home, but most of them had evening activities and were then going to the dance.

"Did you ever ask anyone to the dance?" Joe asked.

"A girl actually asked me," I replied.

"The same one who drew the painting?"

I nodded.

He said, "She must really like you."

They left, and I waited. Ginny told me to dress in casual clothes and bring my suit. At about five-thirty, there was a knock at the door. There stood Danielle and Sally. They had on dark glasses, and they had their fingers pointed like guns.

"We'se ere to kidnap you," Sally said in a terrible Italian accent. "Grab yo' suit and come wit' us."

I smiled, picked up my suit, and walked with them. But we didn't go to their apartment, as I expected. Instead, we went to the dance studio. All the girls were there, and so was Brett. The girls had decorated one corner like it was Hawaii, and we were having a Hawaiian Luau. They had Hawaiian music and interesting, good food. We played Twister, and since Ginny didn't feel up to playing, she ran the spinner.

We had a lot of fun, and it seemed like no time at all before it was close to nine o'clock and time to go to the dance. All the girls dressed in their dresses, and Brett and I put on our suits. That's the first time I realized that all the girls, except for Brenda, were going to be my dates.

"I hope you're okay with five dates at the same time," Sally said.

"Being with five beautiful women at a dance?" I replied. "I can handle it. But I bet I make all of the other guys jealous."

We started walking to the ballroom, but Ginny was having a hard time.

I stepped in front of her, bowed, and said, "Allow me, my lady."

Before she could say anything, I swept her into my arms. She laughed and held onto my neck, and I carried her all the way to the ballroom. She wanted to walk in, so I set her gently on her feet once we were there.

Brenda and Brett had gone ahead, so I was there alone with the five girls. I reached for my wallet to pay, and Sally said, "No, you don't. This is on us."

But suddenly, Dr. Carlson was there. "No," he said, "This one is on me."

The girl taking the money said, "I'm not quite sure what to charge. Everyone else is in couples. How do one guy and five girls count?"

Dr. Carlson told us to go in, and he stayed to figure out what to pay. When we got inside, Brenda and Brett had already taken in a soft chair for Ginny. I realized that was why Dr. Carlson knew we were there. As I walked across the ballroom with the five girls, me holding tightly to Ginny, we were a sight that was hard to miss. My roommates stared, as did Bonnie and Kevin, and Carol and Mitch. Occasionally, they would dance close to where we were to stare at us.

Brenda danced with Brett, and Ginny didn't feel she could dance, so the other four girls took turns dancing with me in whatever style came up on their turn. I found myself smiling at how strange it felt to dance a style with one of the girls that was different from the one I usually danced with her.

When the night was half over, Dr. Carlson, who was running the music, came on the sound system.

"Tonight, we would like to let you know that the team representing our college at the International Ballroom Championships did something we have never done before. We brought home a trophy. We took second place."

Everyone broke into applause.

"Tonight," Dr. Carlson said, "we would also like to announce the medal winners from our team and have them start us off in the style of the dances they won. We will have them dance in the center of the floor. You are welcome to join in after they begin. Starting us off, with second place in the waltz, we have Miss Genevieve Broadhurst and Mr. Tom Johnson."

He had me step out, and he had Ginny wave.

"Ginny is not feeling well tonight," Dr. Carlson said, "so she has asked Miss Danielle Peterson to take her place."

I escorted Danielle to the center of the room, as my roommates and others who knew me stared. Dr. Carlson started some waltz music. We began to dance, and everyone watched us for a short time. The crowd all started to clap, and then others joined in the dancing.

As we danced, I said, "I didn't know he was going to do this."

Danielle laughed. "That was part of the reason we needed you here. We also just wanted to spend the evening with you, dancing for fun and not in competition."

When the song ended, I escorted Danielle back, and the crowd clapped again.

"Winning third in the tango, we have Miss Sally Smith and Mr. Tom Johnson."

I escorted Sally to the floor to the clapping of those gathered.

This went on through all twelve dance forms. The others from our team who had won were announced, too, and started the dances. Ginny had Linda dance the Viennese waltz with me. Soon all the dances for which our team had someone place had been announced, and everyone went back to dancing as usual. I thought Dr. Carlson might mention the all-around, but he didn't, and I assumed it was because Ginny was not up to dancing.

The night went on, and I danced much of it. I did take time to sit and visit with Ginny and the girls. But when Dr. Carlson announced the last dance, I thought for sure Ginny would want to dance it—at least attempt to. I went to her and asked if she would like to dance it with me.

She patted the chair by her. "Tom, come sit by me."

My heart felt heavy as I sat down. Ginny had never passed up the chance to dance the last dance with me, and now that she was, I knew she must not be doing well. Would we never even be able to have one last dance together?

She leaned her head against me. "Tom, do you remember how for a brief moment at the competition, you were Alex to me?"

"Yes, I remember."

"Well, I hope you don't feel like I would rather be with him than you, because I wouldn't."

"It wouldn't have bothered me, anyway," I said. "From what you said, the two of you had been friends for over twenty years."

"I want you to know that I'm grateful for you more than you'll ever know."

"I think I know," I replied, "because I'm grateful for you, too."

"You're my best friend," she said.

"And you're mine," I replied.

She continued to lean against me until the song ended. Then Dr. Carlson did something I didn't expect.

Dr. Carlson spoke over the sound system. "Ladies and gentlemen, before you leave tonight, we have one last announcement. At the International Ballroom Championships, we had another first for our small college. One of our couples won the all-around championship, the highest award a couple can win in International Ballroom. Usually, the winning couple is allowed a solo victory dance, but that didn't happen that night. So tonight, as a final dance, we would like to welcome to the floor International Ballroom Champions, Miss Genevieve Broadhurst and Mr. Tom Johnson."

The whole ballroom burst into applause. Some of my roommates were close enough that I could see the astonished look on their faces. I also saw Sherry, the girl who talked me into signing into the class at the first of the semester, and the look on her face was priceless.

Just before we stood, Ginny whispered to me. I smiled and nodded. I then stood and pulled Ginny into my arms. But instead of making our way to the floor, we stood there, and Ginny reached out to Dr. Carlson, indicating she wanted the microphone. He handed it to her.

"Tonight," Ginny said, "is Dr. Carlson's last night here. He will be taking the Performance Dance Team on tour, and then he's retiring. He has taught here for almost forty years. He and his wonderful wife, Maria, have been our dance coaches and our friends. Years ago, Dr. Carlson and Maria were also International Ballroom Champions. Tom and I would like to ask Dr. Carlson and Maria to join us tonight for this victory dance."

I looked over at Dr. Carlson and Maria, and with tears pouring down their faces, they nodded.

Dr. Carlson turned to Brenda and asked, "Brenda, will you turn on the music? It's all set to the right place."

Brenda nodded, "Sure, Dr. Carlson."

I escorted Ginny to the dance floor, holding her carefully, and Dr. Carlson escorted Maria to the floor. Brenda turned on the music.

The familiar words began to play.

Longer than there've been fishes in the ocean

Higher than any bird ever flew
Longer than there've been stars up in the heavens
I've been in love with you.

I smiled at Ginny. "It's not a waltz, it's a slow rumba."

She smiled at the memory.

"You and Dr. Carlson planned this, didn't you?" I asked.

Ginny nodded. "But he didn't know I planned to invite him and Maria to dance with us."

"It's as it should be," I replied.

The clapping continued for some time as we danced, but gradually it faded. Then people moved out the doors until the ballroom was quite empty. The beautiful ladies of our group positioned themselves at equal intervals in a circle around us, like five points on a star. As Ginny and I swirled around between them, and I looked into their smiling faces knowing this unusual, but wonderful experience of my life was coming to an end, I could not keep my tears from coming. As I saw each one, I would say her name in my mind. "Sally, Danielle, Linda, Brenda, Jill."

Just as all good things come to an end, the song eventually finished. Ginny leaned against me, her tears also flowing freely. I put my arms around her and held her close.

When I could finally speak, I said, "Thank you, Ginny, for believing in me."

She smiled and said, "Thanks, Tom, for dancing my last dance with me."

About *Under Open Sky* Books

People often ask me if my stories are true. The *Under Open Sky* series, of which this book is a part, is loosely based on events from my own life. However, these books are still fiction. Even on the events that did happen, I openly admit that I take plenty of literary license. The story I want my readers to experience becomes the most important driving factor in my writing. Also, many of the events occurred years ago, so minor details have long been forgotten.

Though many of the characters in these stories match people I have known in my life, few are solely a single individual. Often, each person in the book has characteristics of multiple individuals that I have had the privilege of knowing.

Daris Howard

If you enjoyed this book, please a review on Amazon at:

https://www.amazon.com/dp/1629860204

Would you like to see the *Life's Outtakes* column running in your local paper or magazine? Suggest it to the editor. If an editor runs the *Life's Outtakes* column due to your suggestion, we will send you a free autographed book by Daris Howard. Find out more at:

http://www.darishoward.com

Read stories, purchase books, or subscribe to our short story list by going to:

http://www.publishinginspiration.com

Daris Howard's Amazon page:

http://amzn.com/e/B004H76UGK

For inspiring plays and books, as well as discounts for booksellers, go to

http://www.publishinginspiration.com

About the Author

Daris Howard, an award winning author and playwright, grew up on an Idaho farm. He was a state champion athlete, competed in college athletics, and lived for a time in New York.

Daris has worked as a cowboy, a mechanic, in farming, and in the timber industry. He is now a college professor. He has also been a scoutmaster, having up to eighteen boys in his scout troop at a time. In his wide range of experience, he has associated with many colorful characters who form a basis for his writing. Daris has had plays translated into German and French, and his plays have been performed in many countries around the world. For many years, Daris has written the popular column *Life's Outtakes*, which consists of weekly short stories and is published in various newspapers and magazines in the US and Canada.

www.ingramcontent.com/pod-product-compliance
Lightning Source LLC
Chambersburg PA
CBHW061149170626
46809CB00003B/1037